HER JOURNEY WITHIN

Viraj Kulkarni

Her Journey Within

Copyright © 2017 Viraj Kulkarni

ISBN 978-93-5268-698-8

www.virajkulkarni.org

To my mother, who taught me the importance of thought and reason; and to my wife, who showed me a world beyond them.

Acknowledgements

It took me over four years to turn this book from an idle dream into a reality. For making it possible, I would like to thank:

Aravind Tavase for the invaluable conversations that led to the genesis of key ideas presented in the book;

Shruti Mahadkar, Swati Nahar, Shantanu Vaichal, Priyanka Kulkarni, Christian Franz, Sahil Deo, Niramayee Sarpotdar, and Nikhil Warrier for their feedback and suggestions;

Laxman Kulkarni, my father, for his support without which this book would not be possible;

Tanvi Kulkarni, my wife, for being my first reader, a patient critic, and a constant companion through every step of this journey;

Ramana Maharishi, Swami Vivekananda, Ayn Rand, Lucius Annaeus Seneca, and Friedrich Nietzsche for influencing this book across time and space and lending to it their teachings, words, and wisdom;

And many others I have not named here for their encouragement and involvement.

TABLE OF CONTENTS

Chapter 1: The Wadi

ASMI SMILED LOOKING IN THE mirror. Twenty-three years old, of average height, with fair skin and long hair skirting her slender waist, the girl in the mirror smiled back weakly. She was beautiful, but Asmi did not know that yet.

"Let's do it!" Asmi said excitedly.

"Are you sure?" the girl in the mirror asked nervously.

"We discussed it! This is the only way!"

The girl did not reply and just stood there staring at her. Asmi rolled her eyes and looked away. She had made up her mind. She had taken the most important decision of her life and had to wait patiently for the day to run its course. She never took even the smallest of decisions without thinking once, thinking twice, and then thinking again. Yet, for the first time, when taking the most important decision of her life, she had abandoned the cold comfort of reason and decided to follow her heart instead! Her husband, Sunil, was getting ready to go for an outing with his friends and would be back in the evening; she would cook his favourite breakfast today. Like most married women in her town, she lived with her husband and his parents. Sunil's parents were going to visit their relatives in a neighbouring town; they, too, would be gone for the day. Asmi did not usually leave the house when Sunil was at home. She stayed back to keep him company and to make him his evening tea. But today, she had the whole day to herself. She would visit her elder sister Neha in the morning. After that, she would visit her parents for lunch.

Sunil's parents had breakfast and left. Sunil left fifteen minutes later. Asmi stood at the door to say goodbye but he left in a hurry without looking back. As she saw the car disappear around the bend, she closed her eyes and took a deep breath. She went to her room, pulled out a suitcase from under the bed, opened the cupboard, picked out some clothes she would carry with her, and dumped them in. She slipped in a file of documents and a small pouch of personal belongings and closed the suitcase. She picked up her mobile phone from the table and dialled Shweta.

"Hey, I'm ready!" she said.

"Great!" Shweta replied. There was a pause. "Asmi, are you sure you want to do this?"

"Yes, I'm sure! Will you please come to my parents' house for tea? We can leave from there together." Asmi wanted Shweta to be there for support. Leaving her family would be the most difficult thing she had ever done.

"Of course, I will! Keep your luggage at home. We'll pick it up on the way to the bus stand."

Asmi and Shweta had grown up together in the small town they called the Wadi. For centuries, the Wadi had been a quiet uneventful village in Konkan - the narrow strip of land between the mountains and the sea on the western coast of India. The two of them were inseparable during their childhood. Every afternoon, as soon as the bell rang, they would rush out of the school gate running carelessly along the road holding hands. Their school was at the far end of the town, and they never took the direct route back home. Instead, they would return running, jumping, and skipping along the edge of the Wadi, along the edge of the river, talking incessantly till somebody pulled them apart. They studied together, ate together, played together, and laughed and cried together. Their thick companionship ended abruptly

2

when Shweta left for the city to study engineering, and Asmi enrolled at a local college in a nearby town to study arts.

"Baba, I also want to go to the city and study engineering like Shweta!" Asmi had pleaded to her father.

"What will you do becoming an engineer?" he had asked incredulously.

"Aai, please tell Baba how desperately I want to go!" she had implored her mother.

Her mother had continued silently wiping the table without looking up.

Asmi reached Neha's house. Her elder sister, like Asmi, lived with her husband's family. She had been waiting for Asmi all morning and was delighted to see her. Five years elder, she had been the first one to get married. Her son, Saurabh, would turn two in a few weeks. Asmi loved playing with her nephew; he made her forget all her worries.

"Neha, why don't you come with me for lunch? We'll have our mother's food!" Asmi said.

"No, Asmi, I cannot! I must cook and Saurabh still needs to be bathed. Today, being a Sunday, I have to clean up the kitchen too!"

Asmi felt bad for Neha; she was so inextricably caught up in day-to-day affairs, always occupied with some or the other household chore, that she never found time for herself. She was a talented classical singer. Her music group often performed in the neighbouring towns and sometimes even in the cities of Mumbai and Pune. It was her dream to perform with them, but her husband refused to let her travel. Every time she got an opportunity, there was always some work waiting for her: there was a house to be taken care of, food to be cooked, servants to be watched, or guests to be attended to. Neha held her boy in her lap and poured out her frustration over a new domestic squabble.

Asmi listened patiently. She felt her sister's pain. She wanted to reach out, hold her hand, and tell her to leave all this behind and come with her, but she knew it would be in vain. With a sigh, she got up to say goodbye. She hugged her and kissed her nephew. It was time to leave.

Asmi walked slowly towards her parents' house. She needed time to compose herself. She had really wanted to study engineering. She had wanted to escape from the narrowness of both the streets of the Wadi and the minds of its inhabitants and pursue her dreams in the city.

"Baba please let me go! I have scored better grades than Shweta. I'm sure I'll get admission!" Asmi had begged her father.

"Asmi, you are a girl! What will you do becoming an engineer?" he had asked again.

"I will work! I'll do what other engineers do!"

"But you will soon get married, and your husband's family will not let you work! The college fees and the costs of living in the city are exorbitant. We don't have money to squander on such useless quests!"

"Shweta says her parents will let her work in the city before she gets married!"

"Asmi, you are a girl! You will not become an engineer!" Baba had yelled at her with finality in his voice.

Asmi stepped into the house she had grown up in. Built eighty years ago by her great-grandfather, it was two storeys high and had spacious rooms with plenty of open spaces. There was a courtyard in the front and an empty piece of land in the back, which used to be a vegetable garden. At the time it was built, it had been the largest house in the Wadi. Now, most of the upper floor was in disuse, and instead of fresh leafy vegetables, only thorny shrubs and dry grass grew in the back.

4

Asmi's family had lived in the Wadi for generations. Her great-grandfather was one of the prominent personalities of the small village that the Wadi was in his days. His son, Asmi's grandfather whom she called Abba, was the first lawyer from the Wadi. Abba studied in Mumbai and worked for a few years at a reputed law firm there. He got married to Asmi's grandmother, and they had a baby boy. Abba's fledgling career came to a standstill when he left the city and returned to the Wadi to take care of his ailing parents. His parents did not live long, and the responsibility of his two sisters fell on him. They were considerably younger to him, and he almost treated them as his own daughters. His wife never got along with them. After they got married in nearby towns, the sisters visited the Wadi lesser and lesser until the only correspondence they had with Abba was through infrequent letters.

Asmi's father, their single child, was the only straw that kept Abba and his wife together. They had a troubled marriage. There was little money in the house. The meagre income he earned by doing paltry legal work that came his way in the Wadi was barely sufficient to keep the house running. His wife severely resented the fact that he had spent all their savings on his sisters - their college fees, their dowry, their weddings!

"Those witches ate up everything we had, and now they don't even come to see your face!" she would relish reminding him. He had, despite her tantrums, insisted on sending them to college! "What good did education do for them? Now they are married and just sit at home! If you had not forced them to college, we would have money in the house, and we wouldn't be raising our only son in such poverty!" was her high-pitched rebuttal to any reconciliation he attempted.

They fought every day. Mostly, she screamed, and he listened. Their adolescent son was terrified of these fights. He did not understand them, but his young mind picked up like a sponge his

5

mother's judgment that if his father had not spent money on educating women, their family would have been happier, and there would be money in the house.

In spite of the parental problems, Asmi's father turned out to be a bright student and topped his class. His graduation was marked by the opening of the first bank in the Wadi. He applied for a job and was selected from over a hundred applicants. People said he had a bright career ahead. A noteworthy position with the only bank in the Wadi made him famous and earned him respect. Good fortune lasted for a few years, but the winds of change soon started blowing. The Government declared the area outside the Wadi as an industrial zone. New manufacturing units sprung up. There was a large influx of industrial workers, and the Wadi transformed from a small, quiet village into a bustling town almost overnight. The migrants lived in large settlements outside the Wadi and kept to themselves. There was a time when he knew every shopkeeper in the market by name. He had grown up with them, and they were always nice and courteous to him. Now, most of those shops had been bought out by migrant traders, who spoke a different language and were hostile and rude. The Wadi that had been a peaceful family sharing bonds for generations slowly turned into an anonymous, faceless herd that kept growing.

People around him saw opportunities and adapted, but Asmi's father clung to the past and stubbornly refused to change. When he started working with the bank, he was one of the most admired people in the Wadi. Now, he was just an employee of one of the many banks in the town. He was no longer a rising star but a tired old man. People had lost their admiration for him many years ago, but he did not realise that for a long time. He first saw it in their eyes, which no longer looked at him with rapt attention, then in their voices, which were no longer sweet and mellowed, and then in their words, which no longer carried the same

6

deference they once did. It happened so slowly, so imperceptibly, that he never noticed until it was too late. He tried to resist the change in people's attitude towards him. He thought people had just forgotten the person he was, and if he reminded them of his former glory, they will start treating him with respect once again. But when memories of glory in the past failed to fetch him admiration in the present, he turned into a bitter man. He blamed life for having abandoned him through the lanes of time. He clung on to the past, started worrying about what people thought of him, and became very careful of not damaging his image in their eyes, because his former image was the only thing that now gave meaning to his life!

He had married Asmi's mother a year after joining the bank. After three years of childless marriage, the couple went to a reputed astrologer who told them they would have a baby daughter within a year if they carried out a *yajna*, a sacrificial offering to the Gods. It was no coincidence that Neha was born exactly a year from that date. They celebrated her birth, but not even a year passed before they visited the astrologer again. They wanted a son. The astrologer prophesied that they would get what they wanted and prescribed a bigger *yajna* this time, but the prophecy did not materialise. Five years later, when Asmi was born, her mother cried, and her father stood by watching silently. He, nevertheless, treated both daughters well. He raised them in comfort and provided them with all necessities. He sent them to college to get their art degrees. But engineering?

"What's the need to spend so much and live in a shabby hostel in the city away from family when she would have to stay at home and take care of children after marriage? Neha happily studied arts at the local college and so would Asmi! Let her grow older, and she would herself realise that it was much better to leave the money invested with the bank rather than spend it on foolish endeavours!" he would say to his wife.

7

"Hello, Aai!" Asmi greeted her mother cheerfully as she walked in.

"I'm so happy to see you! Come, let's have lunch! We were waiting for you," Aai replied with a smile on her face.

Abba usually had food in his room. He had difficulty moving in and out of the bed. But, today, Asmi coaxed him to have food with the rest of them at the table. Aai had prepared Asmi's favourite dishes, and the family ate well as they listened to Abba sharing some old stories.

"Aai, Shweta is coming home for tea. She is leaving back for the city today. I'll go see her off at the bus stand," Asmi said to her mother. They finished their meal, and Aai cleaned up the table.

"Will you stay for dinner?" Aai asked.

"No, I'll go home. Sunil will be back by evening, and I have to cook dinner," Asmi lied.

Her parents retired for their afternoon nap, and Asmi helped Abba back to his room. She was very close to her grandfather. They had spent a lot of time together when she was a child. Asmi was eternally grateful to him for inculcating in her a fondness for books. She loved reading. Books helped her escape her mundane existence and travel into the realm of possibilities. While Neha would be busy with her singing classes and Aai would be buried in housework, Asmi would find haven in her world of books. Abba would take her with him for evening walks around the Wadi often taking the winding path going up the hill that ended at the quiet temple at the top. She would tell him what happened at school, and he would tell her about his former life in the city. She would tell him about the new book she read recently, and he would tell her about the old one he had read years ago. She would tell him about her dreams of what she wanted to do when she grew up, and he would just stare at the road ahead saying nothing!

It was the day after Asmi's graduation. She had studied arts at a local college in a neighbouring town. The college was poorly staffed, but she had been an outstanding student. She had taken a keen interest in history, and her passion for the subject had helped her get over the disappointment of not studying engineering. She was sitting with Abba in his room telling him about the things she had learned when Baba walked in.

He said, "Asmi, we have found a wonderful boy for you! His family is coming home tomorrow. You should wear your best clothes and…"

Asmi had stopped listening. Her heart had stopped beating.

"Baba, I don't want to get married!" she exclaimed.

"Don't want to get married? What do you mean?"

She took a deep breath and, regaining her balance, slowly said, "I was one of the best students in my college. All my teachers were very impressed with me. I'm really interested in history, and I want to study archaeology. I spoke to the people in my department, and they told me that the university in Pune offers an excellent postgraduate program in archaeology. I will even get a scholarship for it. We will not have to spend much money!"

Baba was looking in her direction, but his eyes were focussed at a point far beyond. When she finished talking, he turned to Abba and said furiously, "Are you happy now? This is all your fault. See what you have done to her! You and your books have put these weird ideas inside her head. Archaeo-something, she says! Your insistence on forcing your sisters to college ruined my mother's life, and now your books and ideas have ruined my daughter's! When will you recognise that you don't understand women? Why can't you just let them be the way they have been for thousands of years?"

Asmi tried to speak but words didn't leave her mouth.

9

Baba continued, "Listen, Asmi, I'm going to get you married, and then my responsibility is over. You convince your husband to let you do engineering, archaeo-something, or whatever else you want!"

He stormed out of the room and banged the door behind him with such force that the frame of the door cracked. The passage of years had led them to forget the crack in the wooden frame, but the other cracks that were formed that day, those in the family fabric, between son and father, between father and daughter, only widened with time and haunted the house like unforgotten, unforgiving spectres!

Sunil's family came to their house next day to see Asmi. The customary round of questions and answers took place, and they instantly liked Asmi; she was pretty, well educated and knew how to take care of the house. Sunil's mother called Aai later to make their formal offer, and Asmi was given some time to decide. The next morning, Asmi went to talk to Abba and, for the first time, expressed her desire to leave the house. She asked him if she should run away. She asked him if she should not run away. But Abba didn't answer!

When she pushed him, he told her, "What Baba said is true! I am responsible for planting ideas in your mind. If I had not encouraged you, you wouldn't have had 'unwomanly' dreams, and instead of being disappointed, you would have been an excited bride looking forward to her wedding! I am sorry, Asmi, but you should listen to your parents!"

Asmi went to talk to her sister, but Neha did not take her seriously. When she spoke to her mother, Aai told her, "You fancied engineering, and you moved on. Now you fancy archaeology, but you will forget that too! The wellbeing of your children and your family will bring you real happiness, my dear, not these fleeting fancies! Sunil will make a nice husband. Marry him!"

Driven to desperation, Asmi turned to t
She had always been supportive of Asmi, but o
spoke like one of them, "What's wrong in ge
Everyone does that! That is how it is supposed
revolting, because nothing good will come out of it. I
make us unhappy!"

Once again, Asmi decided to forgo her passion and not
back. She married Sunil with a smile on her face and joy in he
heart. She did her best to keep her new family happy. Sunil's
father owned a large clothes shop in the Wadi. Sunil spent the day
in the shop with his father, while Asmi took care of the house. She
would wake up before the men, make morning tea, and cook
breakfast. Once the men left, she would have a bath, get ready,
and prepare lunch. The men would come back for lunch. Lunch
was followed by a short afternoon nap. She would then make
evening tea and cook dinner. The only me-time Asmi got for
herself was in the evenings between tea and dinner. She thought
she would get to use this time to read books, meet her friends,
visit her parents, or pursue some hobby. Alas, that was not to be!
Some evenings, women from the neighbourhood would come
over, and Asmi was expected to attend to the guests. On other
evenings, her mother-in-law would bring up long pending work
such as cleaning closets, sorting and disposing off old household
stuff, reorganising cupboards etc. It's a part of being a family,
Asmi would tell herself. But over time, she began to see a pattern
that such long pending work always came up when she was doing
something of her own. She would pick up a book to read, and her
mother-in-law would walk in to tell her that a lot of dust had
settled in the overhead cupboards, and they needed cleaning. She
would make plans to meet her friends in the evening, and her
mother-in-law would invite guests. Asmi started feeling
suffocated. She spoke to Sunil about these things, but he refused
to listen or even acknowledge the problem.

11

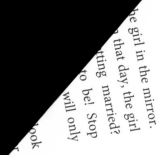

:upboards once in a while?" he

her mother-in-law asked her
one with your books?"
g!" Asmi replied.
itching! At least it will be

hat day, for the first time,
und her, a slimy creature
∪ she could not see but knew
…who wanted to destroy her will! She was furious. Reading was the only thing that allowed her to keep her sanity. She had avoided confrontations so far, but she could not control her temper anymore. That night, when Sunil came back, when he found out what had happened, he slapped Asmi. "How dare you yell at my mother like that?" he said.

Asmi had never felt so humiliated, and she stormed out of the house. She went to her parents' house and told them everything. They listened to her and consoled her. Next morning, however, Baba took her back. He apologised to her in-laws for her behaviour. The propriety of his daughter's upbringing was at stake! Her character was at stake! The family name was at stake! She helplessly looked on with disbelief as he promised them that she would not behave like that again. Asmi was cornered, and there was nowhere to go. Her husband did not stand up for her. Her father was more worried about the image of their family. Her mother was too meek to do anything. Asmi turned to the one person in her life whose advice she trusted. She went to see Abba a few days later and told him everything. She told him she felt like running away. Abba wanted to say something, but he kept quiet. She could see his lips contort as they struggled to prevent those words from leaving his mouth, but his eyes spoke them anyway.

"Go! You are not meant to live this life!" they seemed to say.

Shweta called last morning. They had not met for years, and Asmi went to see her after evening tea. They hugged each other with tears in their eyes. They went for a long walk like they used to after school, along the edge of the Wadi, along the edge of the river. Asmi told her about her difficulties, her helplessness, the lack of meaning in her life, and finally her thoughts of running away.

"Why don't you leave?" Shweta asked.

"How can I just leave? I have no money of my own. I have never worked or earned before. For two years since my wedding, I have been a housewife doing nothing but cleaning and cooking. If I had studied engineering, I would have had a well-paying job in the city. If I had pursued archaeology, I might have been able to get a scholarship to fund my education. Both doors are now closed!"

"Come to the city with me! I'll help you find a job!"

"I am not sure I can work! I don't feel confident. I feel I'm sinking and losing the battle…"

"Battle? With whom?" Shweta asked.

"I don't know!" Asmi answered, but she knew! She knew she was losing the battle with the dragon and could feel his grip tightening around her.

The two friends walked along the winding path going up the hill. Seldom getting a chance to vent, Asmi spoke out her mind. Shweta listened patiently. When she finished, Shweta asked her questions that forced her to think hard and introspect.

"Why don't you fight back?" Shweta asked.

"I don't have the strength to start a fight that will never end. They have been taught to believe that a woman's life is to take care of the house and listen to her husband and elders. My parents believe that. Sunil's parents believe that. Sunil believes that. I'm all-alone. I depend on them more than they do on me.

13

My life is already miserable. I can't imagine what it will be like if I pick up fights with them!"

"Then, if you cannot fight back, why don't you just accept it?"

"I tried to accept it. I killed all my dreams. I did everything that I was expected to do thinking that it will make them happy. Things go smoothly as long as I conform exactly to their wishes. But how long can I suppress myself? I have feelings, emotions, likes, and dislikes. I like reading, and I don't want to learn to stitch! I don't want to entertain fat, old women on evenings! I don't want to cook day in and day out! Aai tells me I'll get used to this life, but I don't see how that will happen. Look at her! Even after thirty years of marriage, she still has to struggle. I don't want to spend all my life battling my instincts in order to squeeze myself into a mould society has created for me only to realise, when I'm old, that it simply wasn't worth it!"

"You must do something! How long will you live like this?"

As they walked up the road, Asmi felt her lack of identity stronger than ever. She was a faithful wife. She was a dutiful daughter-in-law. She would become a loving mother someday. Her life was now defined by the roles she played in society, and she had forgotten that she had an independent existence that went beyond them. In her struggle to fulfil expectations of others, she had buried her own expectations deep down in her soul, so deep that she had almost forgotten them! Asmi knew that, in her heart, she yearned for a life where she could be just herself: not somebody's daughter, wife, or mother, but just herself!

"Asmi, I don't want to push you into doing something drastic, but I want you to be happy. I stay in an apartment with my roommate. If you come to the city, you can stay with me as long as you like. I will help you find a job!" Shweta said in a muddled voice.

They had reached the top of the hill and were standing outside the small temple. Asmi could see the sun peeking out at

14

them from below the edge of the horizon. The clouds were washed with fiery red and orange. A flock of birds was flying in a disciplined formation. She could see the whole inhabitation of the Wadi below them. Asmi closed her eyes and took a deep breath. She wanted to feel alive and be herself even if only for a moment. She felt the gentle breeze blowing against her cheek, and heard distant noises of vehicles running and children playing, noises that the wind carried with it from the Wadi. Asmi felt deeply aware of her surroundings. She was aware of the boundary between her body and the fabric of her clothes. She felt the shoes on her feet and the ring on her finger. At that moment, something magical happened! In that split instant, she felt the boundaries of her body disappear. She could not tell where her feet ended and the earth began. She could not tell the difference between her skin and her clothes. She felt she was the wind and the flaming red sky. In that moment, she became one with her surroundings, one with the world, one with God! She said something to her heart, and when she heard her heart reply, she knew that the entire universe had replied in one voice. It was only a whisper so soft that it could have almost been the sound of the wind blowing. She distinctly heard the voice say, "Let's go!"

Asmi slowly opened her eyes. The sky had lost its fire and looked dull orange. The flock of birds had flown across the sky and disappeared beyond the hills. The Wadi below was lit up with splashes of yellow, red, and green. Shweta saw Asmi turn around to look at her. She was smiling, but it was not the resigned smile she had worn throughout the day. Instead, it was the smile that she remembered seeing on Asmi's face every time the school bell rang. Her face glowed with quiet serenity in the soft light of the setting sun. In a calm voice, she said to Shweta, "Let's go! I will come with you to the city tomorrow!"

Abba thanked Asmi for helping him settle in his bed. He was about to close his eyes when he noticed she had remained standing there. There was a smile hiding on her lips waiting to show itself, but there was also fear in her eyes.

Abba broke the silence saying, "So what does Shweta do in the city?"

"She works as a software engineer in a multinational company."

Another moment of silence; she knew that he had understood.

"Abba, I'm leaving! I cannot live this life!" Asmi blurted out.

He said nothing and continued to look at her blankly.

"Abba, I know I'm running away from my responsibilities. I'm sorry for the disrepute my actions will bring to our family. I am leaving all of you behind. Please forgive me!"

Abba sat up. Tears welled up in his eyes. He wiped them with the edge of the towel he kept at his bedside. With red eyes, he looked at her for a long time. Then, he said, "*Mazya pakhra*, my little bird, I'm happy you are fleeing from your cage!"

Recovering from the initial shock, he let out a laugh and said, "My child, you are about to do something that I and your father could never do. We were cowards, and life made us pay a heavy price for it. I'm happy that you are brave and are not afraid like we were!"

"Cowards? What do you mean? What were you afraid of?"

He looked around the room dreamily and said, "I worked as a lawyer in the city. I worked very hard and was quite successful for my age. I had big dreams and was excited about my life ahead. But when my parents fell sick, I had no choice but to leave my job and come back to the Wadi. I valued family more than my career, and I don't regret coming back, but the difficult sacrifice of leaving my job and my dreams weighed heavily on my mind. It troubled me for a few years till I gradually accepted it and settled in my new life in the Wadi. A few years later, after my parents passed away and my sisters got married, your grandmother suggested we sell our house and go back to the city. My heart filled up with hope and excitement as I realised I could go back to my abandoned dreams!"

Abba took a deep breath and continued, "But I could not do it! Life had given me a second chance but I did not go. How could I leave everything and go? I was afraid of change. Going back to the city meant turning my whole life upside down once again! I had suffered when circumstances forced me to return, and I had worked very hard to rebuild a new life here. There were problems, and I was not completely satisfied with it, but I was comfortable. I didn't have the heart to leave everything and start all over again. I convinced your grandmother that it was better to stay in the Wadi. My heart told me to go, but I stifled its voice. Sometimes at night, when I try to fall asleep, that voice comes back to haunt me!"

Asmi never knew Abba felt this way. "What about Baba?" she asked.

"He was an exceptionally bright student. In those days, getting that bank job was truly an achievement. He was rightly very proud of it. But things changed when the industries came. His friends quickly left their mediocre jobs to start businesses. Your father was much more capable than them and could have done any business better than them, but he too was afraid of change. He had worked hard to get his job, and leaving it would have meant wasting that effort. His friends asked him to join them, but he refused. He made up his mind to stick to his job and, as justification, conjured up all sorts of reasons for not leaving it.

'I will never stoop so low as to sell items to migrant labourers!' he would say when someone offered him a role in their business.

17

As his friends became increasingly successful, he started resenting them and their profession and vowed never to become like them. If he had embraced change, he would have been happier. Instead, he took pride and praised himself for having refused to change!"

Abba had a look of deep sorrow on his face, but mixed up in all that sorrow was a sense of respect he had for his granddaughter.

"People fear change, Asmi, and they go to great lengths to fight it. Every time life shows them the door to a better future, they shut it. They convince themselves that they are happy with the present even if their heart tells them they are not. I am proud of you, because you are not one of those people. You have the strength to walk out of the life you are not satisfied with. I wish we too had the courage you have!"

Abba reached under his bed and pulled out a small cloth pouch that contained a bundle of cash and a couple of gold articles. He took off the ring he wore on his finger, dropped it in the pouch, and gave it to her. Asmi tried to refuse, but Abba waved off her protests saying he was too old to have any use for the money or the gold. Asmi took it and thanked him. It wasn't much, but it would help her survive in the city for a few months. Asmi heard her mother move about outside. It was time to have tea. She hugged Abba tightly and touched his feet.

"*Tathastu!*" he said putting his hand on her head, which meant: "May you get what you wish for!"

Asmi found her mother in the kitchen preparing tea. Shweta was sitting at the table talking to her.

"Where's Baba?" Asmi asked.

"Baba had some work so he left," Aai answered casually.

Continuing her conversation, Aai asked Shweta, "So when will you get married?"

"I don't know! Right now, I don't have time for marriage. I'm just so busy with my work. The management is very impressed with me. They are planning to send me to America next year!"

Aai got three steaming cups of tea and sat down at the table. It was just like the old times when they would come home from school, and Aai would make ginger tea for them. Asmi loved the tea her mother made. She drank it quietly relishing every sip. Ten minutes later, Asmi ran out of tea, and the other two women ran out of things to talk about. It was time to leave. Fighting tears in her eyes, Asmi hugged Aai and started walking.

They picked up Asmi's suitcase from her house and reached the bus stand. Asmi's mobile phone rang. It was Sunil.

"My friends are coming for dinner tonight. Make something nice for us!" he said.

Asmi used to dread Sunil's friends coming over. She would cook dinner and wait for them to finish their drinks. By the time they sat down for dinner, it often got very late. She would then heat the food and wait again till they finished eating. As soon as they finished, Sunil would see them off and go straight to bed. She would clean up, wash the dishes, wipe them dry, and put them back in the cupboard before turning in for the night.

"Sure!" she replied dryly before hanging up. This was the last time she would be hearing this.

As the bus started moving, Asmi felt her vision blur and wetness trickle down her cheeks. She felt a tingling sensation of love in her heart towards everyone she was leaving behind. Overpowering the love, however, was a biting anger she felt for what they had done to her: in blindly and unthinkingly following social expectations, by enforcing upon her life their prejudice and dogma, they had unwittingly become the dragon's soldiers, insufferable monsters wanting to control her life!

19

Chapter 2: The Dragon

AFTER COMING TO THE CITY, Shweta had egged Asmi to take up some work, but finding a job had not been easy. Asmi had no market-worthy skills and no work experience. When she landed at the doorstep of his advertising firm, Jacob Fernandes, the 45-year-old owner, sized her up and quickly concluded that she would be incapable of handling the work. Nonetheless, to test her writing skills, he gave her the assignment to write a copy for a sample advertisement. Pleasantly surprised at what he saw, he offered her the position of a 'Copywriting Intern'. Asmi was teamed up with Namita Agarwal, a quiet girl with an easy-going nature who quickly became friends with her. Namita would design the graphics for the advertisements, while Asmi would write the text. Varun Kelkar, always full of fun and humour, was responsible for communicating with the clients, understanding their requirements, and passing on the relevant details to the duo. Asmi and Namita were of the same age, and Varun was a few years elder.

It was a cloudy morning. After struggling to fall asleep for most of the night, Asmi struggled to wake up and get out of the bed. She lived alone and spent most of her day in office churning out advertisements, blogs, emails, notes, flyers, articles, and websites. She worked tirelessly and diligently, wrote her pieces well, and obeyed instructions without argument.

"Good morning!" Asmi wished Varun as she flung her bag on the corner of the desk and settled down in her chair. By the time he turned around, she was already furiously thrashing the keyboard.

"Hey, hey, relax! Let me get you some coffee!" he said. Varun had made it his duty to get the girls their morning coffee. He returned with a steaming mug of machine coffee, which tasted too watery and too sweet, and kept it on her desk.

"Sorry, I just had another sleepless night! And there's this pile of work on my head that I'm worried about finishing on time," she said turning around to face him.

"Since when have you been bothered by piles of work? Come on, I am sure you will gobble it up like this!" he said snapping his fingers.

"Thanks for the coffee!" Asmi raised her mug and turned back towards her desk.

Varun looked at Asmi with amusement and admiration. He had worked much longer at the job than she had. He too had started as a copywriter, but it was clear to Fernandes that Varun was better at handling clients than writing stuff. To optimise productivity, the artists and copywriters were told not to interact directly with the clients. Varun would do the tedious job of talking to the clients and understanding their requirements. Asmi and Namita would work together to create a couple of drafts and then Varun would show them to the clients. Using his persuasion skills, he would get one of the drafts approved from them. A few corrections and modifications later most clients would be satisfied. Of course, there were some overbearing clients who wouldn't be easily satisfied. Fernandes would stretch his team to satisfy each and every request of such clients and seldom defended them against their excesses.

Fernandes was born in Goa and prided himself on his English. He had studied at a convent school and this, he believed, lent him a pedigree of sorts when it came to speaking English. It didn't matter that Goa had been a Portuguese colony and not a

21

British one! He had meticulously cultivated an accent to impress clients and would cram up 5 new words from the Oxford English Dictionary every morning into his memory. He micro-managed his firm that was now about twenty employees in strength. He had started Fernandes Media almost fifteen years ago. He had worked hard to grow the firm and spared no occasion to remind people of it. As the success of the firm grew, the high-handedness in his behaviour towards his staff also grew in direct proportion. Asmi bore Fernandes better than most other employees. While Varun and Namita were always grumbling their discontent, Asmi quietly handled his criticism. At the end of the day, they were merely his employees doing their job, she would say.

When Asmi came to the city, Shweta was extremely helpful and supportive, and Asmi was grateful towards her for all that she did. She let her stay in her apartment and made her feel at home. She was her pillar of support when her mother called and begged her to return back to the Wadi. She read dozens of job advertisements and shortlisted openings for her. But Asmi soon found out that all good things in life came for a price, often a heavy one, and the world always managed to claim and extract its dues!

Shweta introduced Asmi to her clique of friends: a bunch of young people living fun-filled, carefree lives. They invited her to their parties, movies, and night-outs. Asmi, eager to start a new life, joined in their activities and tried to fit in with them but quickly realised that they were very different from her. Their interests, goals, and priorities were all very different. They did not belong to her world, and she did not belong to theirs! Asmi longed to talk to them about her ideas and beliefs, but they wanted to talk about other friends and the latest celebrity gossip. She wanted to spend quiet time having heartfelt conversations, but they wanted to go to the new club across the city and get drunk. She did not judge them for their actions, but she could not compel herself to adopt their lifestyle and preferences. She would go with them sometimes, but this frequency reduced after a while, and Asmi started staying away.

Asmi felt close to Shweta when it was just the two of them. She could spend hours with her, like their warm childhood days, sometimes talking about everything under the sun, sometimes saying nothing at all. But, in the midst of her friends, Shweta became a totally different person. Something overcame her. She would abandon her convictions and ape the attitudes of the group. She would no longer be herself with her own opinions but turn into one of them: just another person in the crowd, a faceless mirror reflecting the behaviour of those around her. She would cast off her individuality as if it were an unnecessary burden and substitute it with a borrowed one that best suited the crowd. Asmi loved spending time with Shweta, the real Shweta, but she hated the empty shell she became in the company of her friends.

Shweta tried to help Asmi find her way into the group and become a part of it. When Shweta first came to the city to study engineering, she had been a silly village girl amongst sophisticated and suave city kids. She had worked hard to shed this image and get accepted by them. She made compromises, pushed herself outside her comfort zone, and cultivated new habits to match theirs. She had earned her place in the group and wanted to help Asmi do the same. Asmi was intelligent, charming, and attractive, and Shweta thought she would easily get along with them only if she compromised a little and kept aside her stubbornness. She hoped that, given enough time, Asmi would eventually mould herself to fit in with her friends. But, to Shweta's chagrin, Asmi refused to compromise! When Asmi started avoiding them, Shweta stood up for her and told her friends that her behaviour was only temporarily caused due to her personal crisis. She covered up for Asmi's perceived shortcomings, her lack of interest in their parties, her indifference to their gossip, and her seeming rejection of their lifestyle. She did this for a while but started getting frustrated when Asmi did not adopt their ways.

She smilingly asked Asmi once, "Why don't you just relax and have some fun?"

She had really meant, "Why don't you just be like us?"

Asmi did not give in. She took care never to be rude and was always polite in declining invitations, but she declined them none the same! When Asmi left her life behind in the Wadi, she had valiantly fought and rejected the demands of the dragon with a thousand scales. She had seen that there was a Should written on each of his golden scales, a Should that must be complied with, and she had rejected his Shoulds. She had said the sacred no to his Shoulds, a sacred no to the forced expectations of the society, and she was not going to give up now. Asmi remained true to herself. She did not mould herself to their expectations and did not bow before the dragon!

Her friends were initially sympathetic and tried to make Asmi comfortable. But every time Asmi said no, the dragon's strength grew a little. He crept into their minds one by one. The dragon whispered to them that Asmi was a snob, that she thought too highly of herself, that she thought too lowly of them, that she thought their company was beneath her, and that she even looked at them condescendingly! Under the hypnotic spell and the soft whispers of the dragon, they started disliking her. No one knew exactly when or how this dislike started. Or why it started. But they were all convinced that it was for a good reason. It did not matter to them that they could not quite put their finger on what this reason was!

The realisation dawned on Asmi that via some twisted chain of causality, her compliance was the price that was demanded of her to continue her friendship with Shweta. She tried to talk to Shweta to salvage the situation and justify her need to be

24

independent. Shweta said she understood and spoke a few kind words, but Asmi knew that she was far from understanding. One evening, after a long day at work, Asmi came back home and found Shweta dressed to go out.

"I am taking everyone out for dinner to celebrate my birthday. Do you want to come?" she asked Asmi. Something in her tone was not quite right. It was metallic and dry.

Asmi weighed her choices. Shweta's birthday had been last week, and Asmi had wished her with a nice little gift. They had even gone out that evening with her friends. Today, she was tired and wanted to stay home. "Do you mind if I stay back? I want to catch up on some reading," she replied apologetically.

"As you wish!" Shweta said coldly and walked to the door.

At the door, something possessed her. Turning around with an unusual ferocity, she said, her mouth twisted with fury, "You always want to be so different! Why can't you at least pretend to be normal like us?"

As she stormed out, she slammed the door. There was no crack in the doorframe this time, but memories surged forth and flooded Asmi's mind. Rage and the sound of a door slamming! Different doors, different times, and different people, but the same reason, the same failure to comply, the same dragon with golden scales!

Devastated by the incident, she moved out of Shweta's apartment that same week. The separation was cold and mechanical. Asmi thanked her for everything, and Shweta wished her luck. She felt her heart wrenching, but she bravely walked out without turning back. She had made up her mind. She would not make the Faustian bargain with the dragon!

Asmi missed her family. Baba refused to speak to her; in his eyes, she had brought shame to their family and was the reason the whole Wadi was talking behind their backs. Aai furtively

25

called her from time to time. Neha was too bewildered to be of any support. Sunil called her once, and after Asmi refused to apologise and go back, he never called her again.

Aai said over the phone, "Come back, Asmi! I will speak to Sunil and his parents and convince them to take you back. No? You don't want to go back to him? That's all right! Don't worry! We will find another boy for you. Trust me. We will let you do whatever you want. Please, just come back!"

"How is Baba?" Asmi replied.

"He is fine. The work at the bank keeps him busy."

"How is Abba?"

"His age is catching up with him. He finds it difficult to move around. But otherwise, he is doing well."

"Neha?"

"She is the same Neha she always was!"

There was a pause in the conversation.

"*Tu kashi ahes?* How are you?" Aai asked breaking the silence.

Asmi could hear tears well up in her mother's eyes.

"I am fine, Aai. I moved into a new apartment."

"Why?"

"My office is far from Shweta's apartment. I moved somewhere closer."

"Are you staying alone?"

"Yes."

"Do you eat regularly? Good! What? You eat out every day? Please don't do that! Cook something simple but eat at home."

A longer pause. This time, the silence spoke.

"Asmi, will you ever come back?"

"I have to go, Aai! I will be late for office. Take care. I love you!"

Asmi moved into a small, dingy, single-room apartment. With her meagre income, she could hardly afford the rent. She started furnishing it in instalments one month after another. Living alone in the lifeless place started taking a toll on her. She felt the intense pangs of loneliness. It was not the simple loneliness arising out of lack of company; it was the wrenching loneliness of being alienated from the world, of being abandoned by the world, of being not understood and misunderstood by the world! She craved for someone to talk to who would understand her. She wanted an ally: someone who did not belong to this perverted world full of dragon-soldiers following and expecting others to follow the Shoulds they don't even understand! She withdrew far into her world of books, into a world that understood her, into a world she belonged to!

"You did a brave thing leaving Sunil and your marriage. Now that you have put it behind you, what are your plans for the future?" Varun would ask her subtly.

"You should find someone and get married!" Namita would tell her dropping all subtlety.

Asmi tried to explain to them that marriage would only drag her further into the jaws of societal obligations, but they did not understand. She thought of them as great friends, but they could not help her.

As days became months, the hopelessness of her situation started manifesting in her daily activities and the small things that made up the waking hours of her day. She developed apathy towards her surroundings. She didn't care when Fernandes did not like her write-ups or when the client repeatedly complained that the marketing emails were too short. She didn't notice when she skipped dinner. The dead monotony of the office work, the desperate loneliness she felt, and her growing contempt for the world made her life utterly miserable. It was in those dark days that Asmi, due to the lack of an audience, started writing what she felt on loose sheets of paper. They were initially just random thoughts, ramblings written late at night without structure or

27

purpose, fragments that were individually disconnected but were unknowingly parts of a larger whole. She would dash off a few feeble lines, sometimes not even bothering to complete the sentence she had started. Next time, she would continue from the half-finished sentence. It didn't matter. Nothing mattered. Time itself did not matter. Time was just a progression of discrete events, and if the discrete events in her life did not matter, then why would time?

It was late evening. Asmi and Namita were sitting in the office putting the final touches on a brochure they had designed for a new hospital. Sanjeevani Hospital, the biggest and swankiest hospital in the city, was a short walking distance from their office. It was named after the Sanjeevani herb in Hindu mythology purported to have magical healing properties so powerful that, if used correctly, could even bring back the dead!

"Is it not obscenely commercial?" Namita said looking up from her screen.

"Well, it's business at the end of the day!" Asmi retorted.

"I am fine with a hospital being a commercial enterprise, but I think this crosses the line. Which hospital has an indoor sports complex, games rooms, and private swimming pools?"

Asmi shrugged. The hospital was owned by the mammoth Satyashah Group of Companies: a sprawling network of companies and subsidiaries whose businesses included manufacturing, chemicals, retail, hotels, hospitals, real estate, and much more. One of the biggest business houses in the country, it was common knowledge that they unscrupulously worked hand in glove with politicians and bureaucrats with the single-minded purpose of seeking profit. The Group was headed by Charvak Satyashah, the hedonistic, narcissistic, charismatic, corrupt, shrewd, and successful grandson of the founder of the Group, Vallabh Satyashah, who had founded the group fifty years ago.

The girls had designed the brochure beautifully. It was only a small sub-contracted job. Sanjeevani Hospital had hired another bigger media agency for their branding and advertising. Fernandes knew the owner of this agency and often managed to get the smaller bits sub-contracted to his firm. He harboured a long-standing ambition that, one day, he would directly work with the top management of the Satyashah Group. He dreamed of the day when he would stand in front of Charvak Satyashah himself and offer his valuable advice!

"We are done here. My parents are away, and we have the day off tomorrow. Why don't you come over to stay at my place?" Namita invited Asmi. They picked up some food on the way and headed to her house. After dinner, they settled in a comfortable conversation. A warm mood composed of peace and camaraderie enveloped them.

"So, Asmi, tell me about Sunil! Why did you leave him?"

Asmi related bits and pieces of the story.

"Did you love him?"

"Yes, I think so!"

"If you loved him, why did you leave him? Isn't love worth the sacrifices?"

Was love worth the sacrifices? But that question was beside the point! Asmi had not run away from the sacrifices. She had not run away from physical hardships. She had not run away from her husband, her family, or the Wadi.

Asmi replied in a calm steady voice, "Namita, it was not a question of love. I was tired of people telling me what I should do or should not do! I was tired of playing the roles of a daughter and a wife, of fitting myself into society's expectations, of doing this all the time, pleasing everyone at my expense, and adopting their likes and dislikes. I did not run away from my husband. I ran away from the life others expected me to live!" She had really meant to say, "I ran away from the dragon!"

29

"But, Asmi, how long will you keep running? You have to face life! And this is life!" Namita said with an urgent conviction.

How long could she keep running? Asmi did not know. The first time she had sensed the presence of the dragon, she had seen a pitiful creature with slimy scales that disgusted her. But as she grew older and acquired more responsibilities, the dragon too had grown stronger. What had she achieved by leaving the Wadi and coming to the city? The dragon had followed her here. She did not know how to lose him or to fight him. She kept looking at Namita speechlessly. Helplessly. Namita walked over to her and took her head in her hands.

"Asmi, my dear, what do you really want?" she asked.

Fernandes was in a foul mood. His accountant had just handed him his monthly statement of profit and loss. It was the same story. His firm was making money and spending money. The more they made, the more they spent, and little was left for him to line his own pockets. The only way to make more money was to cut spending and increase revenues. He followed this chain of reasoning to the conclusion that he had to fire some employees. He quickly pulled out a blank sheet of paper from the printer tray and started making a list titled 'List of Employees to be Terminated'.

"But sir, we can't fire these people! We need them!" pleaded Ganesh Shinde, his Creative Director, when he saw the list.

"No? Then goddamn it! Find a way to make more money!" Fernandes screamed, crumpled the list into a ball, and threw it towards the waste paper bin. The ball hit the bin and fell outside next to it.

"Am I safe, or will I be fired?" Asmi asked Varun.

Varun had seen the list. "No, your name is not on the list! You are one of the least paid employees, and there's no reason why Fernandes would fire you!" Varun remarked cheerfully.

"But yours is?"

"Yes!"

Fernandes did not fire anyone, but his theatrics ensured that his staff worked doubly hard. Varun now spent more of his time doing business development and pursuing new clients instead of working on existing projects. His work of communicating with clients fell on Asmi. She did not like the work one bit, but she had to do it. She met clients in their offices, in restaurants, in her office, or sometimes even in public places. Most of them were individual entrepreneurs or small-time businessmen: a bakery coming up in an upscale locality that wanted to print brochures, a dentist's clinic that wanted to publish blog articles on the importance of dental health, a boutique clothes store run by a 60-year-old lady who wanted monthly emailers etc. These clients were extremely fussy, and she hated every minute she spent with them.

Asmi's life consisted of long monotonous working days and lonely sleepless nights. A thick miasma of helplessness began to form a tight layer around her heart. She lost interest in and became indifferent to everything, even to herself! They were initially just words or part-sentences floating in white space on loose sheets of paper, desperate half-baked thoughts, ramblings written late at night, bleak words soaked in depression and reeking of hopelessness. Slowly, the words and fragments evolved into complete sentences, and these sentences became paragraphs. The loose stack of papers suddenly found themselves stapled one day, and they became a coherent letter. A suicide note? Did she mean it? Was she really contemplating killing herself? She did not know!

It was Diwali, the festival of lights, a day when a billion people celebrated the triumph of good over evil with their families and friends. Varun and Namita were away visiting their relatives.

31

Asmi was alone by herself. She could see people on the street parading themselves wearing colourful clothes. She opened the cupboard, and put on her best clothes, but that didn't make her feel any better. With no one to talk to, Asmi turned towards the mirror. She started taking off her clothes, one by one, till she stood naked in front of it. She looked at her pretty face, slender body, and long legs. The two girls stood in awkward silence not knowing what to say to each other, almost as if they were strangers. Asmi smiled to break the ice. The girl in the mirror did not smile back. They stood face to face for some time. Asmi sat down on the bed, and looking into the mirror, she screamed! She screamed at that girl with uncontrollable rage. She screamed at the top of her voice, for the world to hear, "Why are you doing this? What are you punishing me for?"

Her voice was drowned by the noise of firecrackers outside the window, and the world did not hear. The girl in the mirror smiled. She smiled with contempt. She looked at Asmi's body from head to toe with derision. Asmi closed her eyes. When she opened them again, the girl in the mirror had transformed into an ugly old woman with golden teeth, wrinkled skin, and white hair. The woman glared at her, and suddenly, without warning, let out a shrieking laugh. Terrified by her, Asmi recoiled to the edge of the bed and stared in horror at the mirror. The woman stood there looking at her for a few minutes and then slowly disappeared back into the glass. As soon as it seemed safe, Asmi got up and smashed the mirror by flinging it on the floor. She threw utensils at it. She hurled her shoes and clothes at it. She stamped on the broken glass with her feet till she bled. She stabbed the small glass pieces with a knife and banged the big ones on the desk. After she was done, the glass splinters were everywhere: in her clothes, in her hair, all over the room, all over her life. She sat down in the middle of the room and burst into tears. Without hope and utterly alone in her nakedness, she cried through the whole night. She did not buy a new mirror.

Varun kept a steaming mug of coffee in front of Asmi. It was a month after Diwali.

"Hey, come on, have the coffee! You will feel better!" he said.

"I don't feel like having it!"

"Are you sure?"

She shrugged and picked up the mug. The warmth it afforded to her hands felt nice, but she did not reward him with her usual smile.

"So, what's up for the day?" he asked glancing at the post-it notes stuck to the bezel of her computer screen.

"I have to finish off a blog article on health benefits of lemongrass!"

"Well, good luck!"

He walked away sensing she did not want conversation.

In the evening, just as she completed the blog article, Fernandes showed up at her desk.

"There's a new client you have to meet!" he said and stuffed a note in her hand.

Asmi sat in the auto-rickshaw. It was a thirty-minute rickshaw ride to the university campus; she was to meet the client in the coffee shop outside the university. She had survived the last few weeks burying herself into any activity that kept her mind occupied. Sitting idle in the rickshaw as it trudged through the dense traffic, all the terrible thoughts she had managed to stave off flooded back to her mind: the ugly woman in the mirror, the golden-scaled dragon, the crack in the door, empty laughter, Shweta's twisted mouth, the door slamming, Baba's anger, Aai's helpless look, the loose sheets of paper now stapled together. She did not want to meet this client or any client. Fernandes had left hurriedly without giving her any background of the project. She glanced at the note. 'Agastya Shastri,' it read and had a phone number on it. She did not know who Agastya was or what he wanted. She took out her mobile phone and typed a text message: "Hi! I will reach in 5 minutes. I am wearing blue jeans and a black shirt - Asmi from Fernandes Media."

"Blue jeans and black shirt! There might be half a dozen other women in the coffee shop fitting this description!" she thought. She didn't care. She almost expected him to reply that he too was wearing the same colours! Her phone buzzed. The screen read: "Hi! You will find me sitting inside reading from a book in my hand. See you!"

Chapter 3: The Timeless Treasure

ASMI WAS FOURTEEN YEARS OLD. It was the month of May, and the school holidays had begun. The thick, sweet smell of mangoes pervaded the hot and humid air. Asmi would sometimes accompany Abba for his routine evening walk. They would walk around the Wadi, often taking the winding path up the hill that ended at the quiet temple at the top. She would tell him what happened at school, and he would tell her about his former life in the city. She would tell him about the new book she read recently, and he would tell her about the old one he had read years ago.

"Abba, I finished reading a nice book yesterday!" she chirped.

"What is it about?"

"It is a story about a man called Edmond. He is in love with a girl. His three friends cheat him and send him to jail, because one of the friends is also in love with the same girl. Edmond goes to jail. There he meets a mad priest who is very intelligent and tells him about a secret treasure. Edmond escapes and finds the treasure. He becomes rich, comes back, and takes revenge on all of them. And the girl falls in love with him again!"

"Did you like the book?"

"Yes, Abba, I liked it."

Edmond, in Asmi's story, was fortunate, because he knew who had implicated him. He knew who had conspired against him. He was fighting men with faces, names, and bodies. They were real people.

Abba said, "I had read a book once, a long time ago. There is a bank clerk named Joseph. One fine day, two policemen come to

35

arrest him. He does not know what crime he has committed. Even the policemen don't know what charges he is being arrested on. Joseph is made to stand trial in court. Even the judges of the court don't know what crime he is being accused of. Yet, all of them are convinced that he must have done something terrible and deserves punishment. After a while, even Joseph himself starts believing that he must have done something terrible!"

"Nobody even knows what he has done wrong?" Asmi asked incredulously.

"Nobody knows! But they are all convinced of his guilt!"

He knew she was too young to understand it then, but he foresaw that her fiercely independent nature would lead her to a similar trial one day where she would be accused of and made to stand trial for vague, undefined charges.

Asmi was quiet. She thought about this strange story. When they returned home, she went to Abba's room.

"Abba, I also want to read that book. Do you have it?"

Scanning the bookshelf, he said, "No, I don't think we have it but..." Taking out a slim book hidden between two fat ones, he said, "...but we have another book by the same author!"

Asmi looked at the unappetizing cover. "I don't want to read children's book!" she said petulantly. The book had a picture of a strange insect-man on its cover: a bug with a man's head. It must be a horror story for kids, she thought.

"It is not a children's book, but maybe you should not read it now; you should read it when you grow older."

"I want to read it now!"

Abba gave her the book, and she happily took it. She started reading it enthusiastically but got bored of it after a few pages and kept it away. Some days later she asked him, "What happens to Gregor Samsa in the end?"

"You should read the book again when you grow up. Then, you might like it and not get bored."

36

"Why?"

"Because you would be older and wiser, and you would understand the story better!"

Asmi had not forgotten the incident. She remembered the picture of the insect-man and the long word the book had as its title. And that she would first have to become a little wiser if she wanted to understand the book! Asmi stepped out of the rickshaw and walked into the coffee shop. She saw Agastya sitting, as he had said, reading a book. He was slightly dark, tall, and well built. He wore a pair of thin-rimmed glasses and a seemingly expensive watch. But Asmi did not notice any of these things. She only noticed the cover of the book in his hand. The strange but familiar insect-man was dancing on it! They exchanged cordial greetings and settled down. Asmi could not take her eyes off the book.

"Have you read it?" Agastya asked sensing her obvious fascination for it.

"Umm... No. Not really. How is it?"

"It is a nice book. Do you like reading?"

Do you like reading? She could not have described what that innocuous question meant to her! "Yes, I like to read!" she eagerly replied knowing well that the answer was hopelessly inadequate.

"Would you like some coffee?"

Agastya went to get coffee. Asmi sat motionless staring at the insect-man. She tried to calm herself down. Her heartbeat had quickened, and she felt jitters running through her entire body. He had asked her a simple, innocent question, but that had changed everything! She knew it the moment he asked that question, knew it instinctively, felt it as surely as her beating heart, that Agastya belonged to her world!

He returned with two cups of coffee. They spoke about the project. Agastya was working with the university library. Asmi had heard that the library was famous throughout the country for its vast and carefully curated collections. They wanted to upgrade their website. A new website had been developed, and Fernandes Media had been hired to populate it with graphics, images, and text. Agastya spoke in a calm manner with rounded spaces between his words and a clarity that emphasised every syllable he spoke. She thought it was lovely to hear him speak. His movements were smooth and confident. He looked a little too polished and intelligent to be working at a university library. On finding an appropriate moment during the conversation, she asked him about his work. Agastya was pursuing his Ph.D. in Physics at the University of California at Berkeley. He had come to India taking a semester-long break from his studies and was doing some organisational work at the library.

"So, what brought you here? I mean, why work at a library?" she asked curiously.

"That's a long story!" he said with a smile.

They had been speaking for a while, and their conversation had run its course. Asmi had stretched it as far as she could. She did not want to leave, but she could not stay there forever. She got up.

"I will prepare some drafts soon. Should we meet tomorrow evening to go over them?" she asked waiting for his reply with bated breath.

"You could also just send them over email if it's inconvenient to come all the way."

"I have to be in this area for some other work so we could meet here," she lied.

Agastya looked at her. It seemed like she would cry if he said no. "Sure! See you tomorrow then!" he said.

Asmi walked into office the next day. Varun noticed her cheerful 'thank you' when he kept her coffee on her desk. She started working on the website content for Agastya. She pushed Namita more than usual for the graphics.

"Can't we do this tomorrow?" Namita asked perplexed by this sudden need for urgency.

"No! We must do this today!" Asmi said.

"What's the matter, Asmi? What's up?" Namita asked mockingly.

Asmi blushed. It was the first time Namita had seen her blush.

Asmi and Agastya had a delightful conversation that evening. She asked him many questions: about his life in America, his studies, and work. She told him about Abba and her love for books. They discussed why so many classics were tragedies and if sorrow moved our hearts more than joy did. They spoke about physics and the nature of time, about food and places. The conversation flowed easily and comfortably.

"It's dinner time. Want to eat something?" he asked.

They had dinner at a nearby South Indian restaurant. It was noisy, but the food was good. It was late, and he offered to drop her home. They sat in the car, and as the doors closed insulating the noise outside, an awkward, intimate silence enveloped them. The doors and windows blocked out the world, and now it was just them!

"Whom do you stay with?" he asked on the way back.

"I stay by myself. I like the privacy!" she replied. "Alone!" she had really meant.

"Where does your family live?"

For a long time, she struggled to say something. Then, she revealed, "I lied before. I did not come to the city to look for jobs. I ran away from home!"

She told him her story. He remained quiet letting silence do justice to her tribulations. She told him about the crack in the door, Shweta's twisted mouth, the golden-scaled dragon, her feelings of utter loneliness, despair, and helplessness. She knew he understood her perfectly. Asmi did not hold back. She told him what she felt when she saw him in the coffee shop, and that he belonged to her world. She recited all of this in a calm and composed monologue. He could make out that she was fighting valiantly, fighting to remain in control, fighting not to cry.

In a genuinely concerned voice, he asked, "Asmi, do you need help?"

The tall dams she had constructed in her mind burst open, and she was drowned in a surge of emotions. She cried like a baby. She cried softly, then hysterically, howled like an animal, and then cried demurely with innocent tears dripping from her eyes. She cried with her head on his shoulder. She cried in his arms. Agastya stayed with her for a long time till she wiped the last of her tears and apologised profusely for making a spectacle of the evening.

Before leaving, he looked into her eyes and asked, "Asmi, what do you want?"

"I want to be happy!" she said.

They began meeting often. They met at coffee shops or went for long walks around the university campus. The place or activity did not matter; they carried their magic along! She shared the daily events of her life with him. They laughed over the outburst of irritation Fernandes displayed one morning in office when he lost a client. He joked about his Ph.D. guide who was obsessed with wanting everything over email. They discussed books they had read. "Why does Dominique Francon marry Peter Keating?" she asked him once. He explained to her how time is relative, and mass and energy are interconvertible. She told him about her life in the Wadi and her failed marriage with Sunil.

One evening, when Agastya dropped her back home after dinner, Asmi showed him a stapled collection of loose sheets of paper. Ramblings she had written late at night. It was the month of June, and torrential rains battered the window parapet making a thunderous noise. A power cut had plunged the whole neighbourhood in darkness. In that sombre atmosphere, in that small candlelit room, Agastya read the terrible things she had written.

"Asmi, were you serious about committing suicide?" he asked gravely.

"No, I don't think so!"

"Are you sure?"

"I don't really know," she confessed.

"I need you to meet someone."

"Really? Who?"

"Swamiji. You should meet him!"

Asmi looked bemused. The word *swami* meant a monk. She said, "I don't believe in God. What will I do meeting a monk?"

"This has nothing to do with God! I am also an atheist. Swamiji is my *guru*. I came to India to spend time with him and learn from him. He is no ordinary *swami*. He will change your life!"

"I thought you came to India to work at the library!"

"Why would I do that?"

"I don't know! So why did you come here? How did you meet Swamiji?"

After a brief moment, Agastya started narrating his story. His father was a microbiologist, and his mother was a doctor. His parents spent two decades working in America and returned back to India when he was ten. Agastya displayed an insatiable curiosity as a child. He acquired a fascination for physics early in his school days. His parents nurtured his interests as best as they

41

could. They enrolled him in science workshops for kids and bought him experiment kits, but most importantly, they patiently and lovingly answered all questions he had about the world!

When he was twelve, they took him on a journey across India. They travelled with another family who were good friends and had a son around the same age as Agastya. Agastya's parents did not follow religious traditions or practices. Unfortunately for Agastya, however, their travel companions did, and they ended up visiting many temples on their journey. These famous centres of worship attracted millions of pilgrims every year. Young Agastya, not used to the filth and the crowds, not used to the idea of worshipping a stone idol as God, was utterly disgusted by it all. He was so harrowed by this experience that, for many years later, he refused to even enter a temple. He disowned religion and God and believed only in science!

Asmi cut an apple for them and made a pot of coffee. She kept the plate and the mugs on the table and sat down opposite him. The rains had not stopped, and she insisted on him staying. He continued with his story. It was many years after that journey, after he became an accomplished physicist in his own right, that he realised the fine distinction between religion and philosophy. In his quest to understand the universe, he studied fundamental groundbreaking theories in physics. Schrödinger, Heisenberg, Einstein were his heroes. These were physicists who had pushed the frontiers of human understanding of the world. One day, when he was debating with his father on matters of spirituality, his father asked him, "Why do you not study ancient Indian philosophy?"

"Because I don't believe in that approach! My approach is that of science!"

"But, my son, your heroes of science don't seem to agree! The great physicists you venerate were believers in Vedanta!"

"Vedanta? What is Vedanta?"

"Hinduism is an amalgamation of a set of ritualistic practices and a system of philosophy. Vedanta refers to the philosophical component of Hinduism that consists of ancient texts called the Upanishads along with other scriptures. Many Western scientists and philosophers went out of their way to get acquainted with Vedanta philosophy! Why don't you read about it?"

Agastya started reading about Vedanta. He read about Niels Bohr, the physicist who made pathbreaking contributions to understanding the structure of the atom, who had said, "I go into the Upanishads to ask questions!" Erwin Schrödinger, who developed a number of fundamental results in quantum mechanics, was an ardent student of Vedanta and had read the Upanishads extensively! Oppenheimer, the father of the atom bomb, himself a professor of Physics at Berkeley, was so enamoured by the Bhagavad Gita that he took Sanskrit classes so he could better understand the Gita in her original form! When he witnessed the first live detonation of the atom bomb, he quoted a verse from the Gita where Krishna tells Arjuna, "I am death. The destroyer of the worlds!"

These great scientists knew about Vedanta philosophy and the wisdom of the Upanishads. Whether they were only aware of it or were influenced by it was a different question, and Agastya was cautious to not conflate the two, but it was clear that his heroes of physics, the prophets of science, had found something valuable in this ancient philosophy, valuable enough to acknowledge these sacred texts, take pains to read and interpret them, and in cases even learn Sanskrit to better understand them! If they acknowledged and recognised it, why was Agastya discrediting this timeless treasure of his own people?

"I want to understand Vedanta. Tell me how?" he told his father.

His father had heard Agastya's 'tell me how?' innumerable times. When he was thirteen, Agastya took apart a radio set to find out what produced the sound. When he put it back, the radio did not work. His parents did not rebuke him for it thinking that the cost of the radio set was too little a price to pay for encouraging their child's curiosity. But his grandfather, to whom radio set belonged, scolded him for his behaviour. A hurt Agastya went to his father and said, "I want to learn how to repair radios. Tell me how?" His father gave him printouts of a step-by-step manual to build radios and money to buy the necessary components. Agastya did not repair the original radio but built a new one. The excitement that gleamed in his eyes that day when he played an old Tamil song on his very own radio was second only to the pride that shone in his father's eyes. So when Agastya asked how he should understand Vedanta, his father did not doubt for a moment the seriousness of his intentions.

"Well," his father answered, "you can start by reading books on the topic!"

Agastya read the Bhagavad Gita often heralded as the purest gem of Hindu philosophy. He read the Upanishads, and books and commentaries on them. He read Western authors and Indian philosophers, but he could not overcome his scepticism. He understood the technicalities well, but he could not come to terms with some concepts, especially the concept of rebirth and recurrence. All Hindu texts appeared to assume the concept of rebirth. It was described and explained, but nowhere did he find an argument for its existence. Unable to overcome this hurdle, he again turned to his father. His father knew of a monk living in Mumbai. His name was Narayan, but people called him Swamiji. He had heard stories of his wisdom and advised Agastya to see him.

"Swamiji, I cannot accept the idea of rebirth. If I die, I die, and that's it! How will I be reborn?" Agastya asked Swamiji when he first met him.

Swamiji smiled and said, "My child, I understand your scepticism, but to understand rebirth, you must first understand what is it that is being reborn. Is it your physical material body? No! Is it your mind and memory? No! Then what is it? Who are you? Without understanding who you are, without understanding what is being reborn, the question of rebirth is meaningless! The whole of Upanishads addresses the fundamental question 'Who am I?' and once you find the answer to that, you will see for yourself that the question of rebirth does not even arise!"

They spoke for a long time at their first meeting, Swamiji and Agastya, tutor and pupil, *guru* and *shishya*, and Agastya realised that the waters he was trying to fathom ran very deep. Swamiji did not ask him to believe anything at face value. No blind faith. No unquestioned acceptance. He encouraged Agastya to question everything he said and attempt to find the answers himself. There was no mention of a personal God. No religion. No prayers. No rituals. Only questions and answers! The logical, unorthodox method of Swamiji appealed to Agastya's spirit of scientific enquiry. Thereafter, every time Agastya visited India, he went to see Swamiji. Now that most of Agastya's coursework at the university was complete, he had taken a semester-long break to come to India. Swamiji was the librarian at the university library. Agastya was staying at the campus acquiring wisdom from Swamiji and helping him with library chores.

Asmi heard Agastya's story with rapt attention. She loved to hear him speak like this. When he spoke of something he was passionate about, of books and stories, of science and physics, like now when he spoke of Vedanta, words flowed out of him like a slow, calm stream of clear water. He spoke word after word, each

45

word methodically chosen for its subtle shade of expression, like an artist composing his masterpiece, ups and downs of pitch and volume carefully modulated to add layers of meaning that the simple sum of words could never express. Agastya spoke with the supreme confidence of a man not afraid of knowledge, a confidence that did not stem from a lack of doubts but, on the contrary, embraced doubts and questions!

Ever since she first met him at the coffee shop, she had idolised him. She respected and admired his intelligence. If Agastya said he found wisdom in Swamiji's words, she believed him.

"How come your *swami* is a librarian?" she asked chewing on a piece of freshly cut apple.

"Swamiji used to be a member of the well-known international organisation Saraswati Mission. He held workshops in India and abroad preaching and popularising Vedanta philosophy. A great orator and fearsome in debates, he was one of the Mission's rising stars. People flocked to him to seek his blessings. I don't know why he did that, but one day, he abruptly left the Mission! He does not preach anymore or hold workshops or lectures. He lives mostly by himself and has discussions only with people who come to him with questions. He took up the work of managing the library and has done a fantastic job making the library one of the best in the country. Many of his old followers still go to him. Some go for advice. Some go to seek solace and spend time in his company. Others, like me, go to him for knowledge."

There was a pause in the conversation.

"So, when you will come to meet Swamiji?" he asked breaking the silence.

"Soon!" she said smilingly without committing.

Agastya looked at her beautiful face, into her large enchanting eyes that were intently seeing him, at her inviting lightly parted lips and felt his eyes irresistibly glued to her. With a forceful effort, he wrenched them away. Asmi sensed his struggle. Smiling to herself, she got up from the table, picked up the empty plate and mugs with a deliberate movement, and carried them to the kitchen sink. She heard him get up from his chair and walk towards her. She stood still, with her back towards him, with her eyes closed, holding her breath for a brief moment that seemed to contain eternity!

Then, she felt his arms around her. With one hand on her slender waist and the other in her hair still soft and moist from the rain, he gently pulled her towards him and kissed her on her lips. First, a light kiss; then, a deep, firm one. He moved his hand gingerly over her fragile body and felt her heart beating under the thin shirt covering her. Slowly, his grip tightened, and his caresses became bolder. He took off her clothes and watched her standing naked in front of him. He lifted her in his strong arms and carried her to the bed. They felt each other's bodies intimately. Without awkwardness. Without holding back. Without guilt. In the light of the candle, under the sound of the pouring rain, they made real, passionate love to each other. It was not frantic, impatient, or turbulent like the mountain stream. It was intimate, soulful, and powerful like the ocean!

"Agastya, thank you!" she said afterwards. They were sitting on the bed in a loving embrace.

"For what, my dear?"

"For just being! It means a lot to me!" The simple fact of his existence, the very existence of someone who understood her and belonged to her world, meant a lot to her, because it told her that she was not alone!

Agastya looked tenderly at the lovely girl in his arms. She was strong. He knew how difficult it was to remain true to yourself in a society that tried its best to mould you according to its expectations. He knew how society was like Procrustes, the innkeeper in Greek mythology who would invite guests to his inn and, in the middle of the night, stretch them or cut off their heads and limbs to make them fit exactly into the bed he had! He admired Asmi, because she had not let the Procrustean world cut, twist, and fold her into what it wanted but had fought resolutely without giving in!

Chapter 4: The Chains of Causality

ASMI LOOKED AROUND HER ASTONISHED at the massive collection of books. They were walking through shelves and shelves of printed knowledge; their musty smell imparted a feeling of comfort and belonging in her mind.

"Aside from thousands of reference books, we have some really valuable manuscripts, old precious books that are now out of circulation, and local literature almost extinct in the outside world!" said Agastya proudly exhibiting the collection.

"Wow! This is really something! I had not imagined the library to be like this!" Asmi replied.

"Swamiji has taken great pains over the years to collect and curate all of this."

"What work do you do here?"

"I am helping out with modernizing the library, digitizing old directories, implementing software systems to simplify and expedite processes, and so on."

They had reached Swamiji's office. Agastya went in followed by Asmi. Swamiji was very unlike what Asmi had imagined. She thought he would be a traditional *swami* wearing saffron robes and sporting a flowing white beard. To the contrary, Swamiji had a very unassuming appearance, almost an ordinary one. He looked between fifty and sixty years of age, was of medium height and complexion, and wore a plain white *kurta*. He had grey hair that had been cut short. The office was sparsely decorated. There were no photos or idols of Gods. There was only a bronze 'Om' on one side of the wall and a round wall-clock on the other.

"How are you, Asmi?" Swamiji asked. He had a broad disarming smile on his face. She had been asked 'how are you?' thousands of times, and she had never really thought before answering instinctively; but today, in front of Swamiji, she hesitated, because she sensed that his question had not been a formality or a routine greeting, but it had been a genuine question, and he really wanted to know how she was.

As they spoke in the small and cosy office, Asmi realised that Swamiji's ordinary appearance belied his extraordinary nature. She felt an instant connection with him, a deep trust that she could not logically explain. She told him her story as Agastya sat silently beside her. She told him about her running away from the Wadi, the crack in the door, Shweta's twisted mouth, the golden-scaled dragon, and her abandoned suicide note. She spoke in a plain honest manner devoid of all pretenses. She told him everything that mattered without hesitation or awkwardness; it felt only natural to do so. Many days later, she wondered what had made her so comfortable with him that she felt no hesitation in sharing her deepest emotions and thoughts with a complete stranger!

"Swamiji, I'm tired of running. How can I be happy?" she asked.

Swamiji looked at Asmi, the smile not having left his face even for a moment. He replied in a deep, powerful voice, "You ask me how you can be happy, but I see no question in that; you are already happy! You were born happy, and you will always remain happy. Happiness is not a temporary state of mind; it is a permanent state of your being. Happiness exists in your heart at all times. No one can take it away from you except yourself. It is unfortunate that people bind their happiness to all sorts of conditions. I will be happy when I get a promotion. I will be happy when my exams get over. I will be happy after I purchase a new car. I will be happy when I have a child. They create lists of conditions for their happiness. What do you think happens when these conditions are fulfilled? Do they become happy? No, they simply replace those conditions with new ones! As soon as one item gets checked off the list, another takes its place. Success and failure are not in your hands. Emotions and reactions of people are not in your control. You can do nothing to fulfil the conditions except do your part in performing the actions required of you. The secret to happiness does not lie in blindly chasing the fulfilment of your desires. It lies in realising that you are already happy, and you only need to liberate your happiness from those conditions that you have yourself imposed. My child, do not let desires affect your happiness. Liberate your happiness, and you will find lasting peace!"

It was a hot afternoon in office, and Varun was in a foul mood.

"What does a man like Charvak Satyashah want more in life? God only knows why he keeps starting new projects!" he grumbled. Asmi and Namita looked at him waiting for him to further elaborate his outburst.

He continued, "He has everything he wants! He owns one of the biggest businesses in the country. He is rich and famous. He has the fanciest cars and sleeps with the sexiest models. He owns half the city. You name it, and he has it!"

"Relax! Why are you getting so worked up?" Namita said.

"What does Fernandes want me to do?" he almost screamed the question at her.

It was extremely rare to see the usually calm and funny Varun get so stressed. Fernandes had stormed into the office that morning. He had gotten wind on the grapevine that the Satyashah Hotels Company was looking to hire a new media agency for marketing, branding, and advertising for their latest luxury hotel 'The Palazzo'. The construction of The Palazzo was in the final

51

stages. Except for the much touted revolving restaurant at the top, everything else was ready. Fernandes saw this as an ideal opportunity to get his foot in the door with the Satyashah Group. He immediately summoned his partner and second-in-command, Ganesh Shinde, and told him to convene an all-hands meeting that afternoon. In the dark, air-conditioned conference room, in the sleepy hours of the afternoon, Fernandes gave what he thought was a motivational talk to his employees. He urged them to use their grey cells and come up with creative ideas. Later, he called Varun to his office.

"Hello Varun, please come in and have a seat!" he greeted.

Varun knew that such politeness from Fernandes meant something unpleasant was to follow.

"Look, Varun, you know more than all people how important it is for us to get new clients. It has been more than a year since we got a new major client. We have only been servicing existing clients, and we need a break badly. Ever since you started doing business development, I am afraid I must say that your performance has been poor."

"But sir, if I may..."

"No, Varun, I am not asking for explanations!" Fernandes perfectly knew the explanations. Varun had been working under Ganesh Shinde for the last couple of months. His job was to solicit new clients. Shinde had been making Varun do all the difficult sales calls, while he himself quickly claimed the easier ones.

"See, the thing is," Fernandes continued, "you need to step up your game. Now, this is an excellent opportunity for you! If you can work extra hard and get the project with Satyashah Hotels, then we have done it!"

The four of them - Asmi, Agastya, Varun and Namita - often spent evenings together. They would spend hours on the *katta*, a half-broken wall, outside the university canteen having tea one cup after another. Asmi would specifically ask for the ginger tea; the taste of ginger on her lips reminded her of Aai. That day, after work, they went for dinner to a newly opened Italian restaurant.

Varun, unable to get the topic off his mind, said, "I know what Fernandes is doing. He usually leads business development himself for such important projects. But this time, he knows we will fail! He does not want to take failure upon himself so he will pin it on me. We have never managed to get a single contract with any of the Satyashah companies. Why will this be any different? I think he will fire me!"

"He might fire us all. Don't worry! We will start a new media company then!" Asmi said humorously.

"No! He will never fire you! You are his blue-eyed babe!"

"Come on, that's not true!" Asmi exclaimed with a frown, "He categorically told me he was not happy with my performance!"

"Yes, but that was before…"

"Before what?"

"It was before… before the university library project. Ever since then, you have been working top notch. There's no reason for him to be unhappy about your work!"

Namita added, "That's true, Asmi! You are the hardest working person in the firm. These days no project gets completed without your involvement!"

It was true that things had changed for Asmi after she met Agastya, after 'the university library project' as Varun had delicately described it. The smile on her face, the twinkle in her eyes, the liveliness in her movements, the mirror on the wall, all of them were back. It was almost as if she had rediscovered herself.

Varun and Namita left after the salad and pasta dinner. Asmi stayed back with Agastya having some more wine.

"What would a person like Charvak Satyashah be wanting in life? He really has everything he wants in abundance!" she asked thoughtfully remembering the afternoon conversation.

"I am sure there is something he wants that he has very little of!" Agastya replied.

"What does he have very little of that he would want so much?"

"The same thing we all want: freedom! All of us, all of nature, through every living being, and through every single atom ultimately cries out for only one thing: perfect freedom!"

"Why do you say he has little freedom?"

"Look at him! He leads a multi-billion-dollar empire. His every action is tied to so many causes and effects. He will have thousands of dependencies and consequently no freedom."

"But Agastya, freedom from what? What does he need to get free from?"

Agastya had anticipated this question. He answered cautiously, "His own mind! Asmi, he needs to get free from himself!"

Asmi thought for a moment. She had read in the Bhagavad Gita that your mind is your best friend and also your worst enemy. She had read that true freedom meant freedom from your own mind, but she did not quite understand or believe that. She thought these were only clever words that appeared to be full of wisdom, but she could not discern any substance or meaning behind them. What did it really mean to be free from oneself?

Asmi started visiting the library regularly. She would sometimes help Agastya in his work, sometimes Swamiji in his. They were sitting on the *katta* outside the canteen one day when Agastya said, "Our Swamiji has a long history. Did you know he used to be a student at this very university?"

"How would I know if you never told me?" Asmi said with mock anger.

"Swamiji's real name is Narayan Thosar. Many years ago, young Narayan came to Mumbai from a small village in

Maharashtra to study at the university. He was shy but sociable and quickly made many friends. The students often gathered around the *katta* during their free time. He seldom spoke at such gatherings on his own choosing to listen quietly to the discussions. He spoke only when someone asked him what he felt about a topic. However, as soon as he opened his mouth to speak, everyone else would stay still and listen to him with undivided attention. He spoke with sheer brilliance. His depth of analysis, clarity of thought, choice of words, and manner of speaking were such that his popularity spread rapidly throughout the campus. In no time, these informal gatherings became organised lectures, and many students started attending them. The university allowed them to use the auditorium. By the time he graduated, students from nearby colleges and even professors and administrative staff had started showing up at these sessions. Although he spoke about a range of topics from God and religion to politics and war, his primary interest was philosophy. He soon caught the attention of the Saraswati Mission, an international religious society spreading the teachings of Hinduism across the world. He joined the Mission, underwent training, and became a *swami*."

"What does *swami* exactly mean?" Asmi asked interrupting his story.

"The word *swami* means a master. A *swami* is a person who strives to achieve mastery over his mind in his quest for ultimate liberation. However, *swami* also means a member of an ordained order of monks. Our Swamiji was ordained by the Saraswati Mission. These ordained *swamis* can trace their lineage from *guru* to *shishya*, from teacher to student, all the way from Adi Shankaracharya, who was one of the greatest philosophers of Hinduism."

"What happened afterwards?" Asmi asked curiously.

"Narayan, now officially named Swami Narayanananda Saraswati, travelled far and wide. Considering that he was fluent in English and emphasised philosophy more than religion, they sent him to Europe and North America where he became quite popular. However, after a few years, Swamiji abruptly left the Mission and stopped giving public lectures. He gave up his Mission life entirely and, with little money or possessions, embarked on a spiritual journey that took him to the Himalayas. He returned to Mumbai a couple of years later, took up the position of the librarian, and has been here ever since."

"Why did Swamiji leave the Mission? And what did he do wandering in the Himalayas?"

"I don't know why he left the Mission; he does not talk about it. He roamed the Himalayas as an ascetic for many years looking for the *Saptarishis!*"

Asmi had heard the legend of the *Saptarishis*. The world *rishi* meant a sage. Literally meaning seven sages, they were a mystical tribe of enlightened sages of ancient India. It was said that they were immortal and lived in remote inaccessible regions of the mountains.

"Oh, come on! You don't believe the *Saptarishis* exist, do you?" she asked incredulously.

"Asmi, Swamiji met one of them!" Agastya said in a whisper.

"Immortal *rishis*? You believe in immortality?" She was irritated. She could not understand how a trained physicist like Agastya, a man of science, could believe such superstitions!

"No! I certainly do not believe in immortality in the conventional sense, but these sages think very differently of life and death. For them, there is no life and there is no death; there is only being! Their frame of reference is very different from ours, and maybe immortality means something different in their language. We might be missing something in our understanding."

"But Agastya! Life and death are certainties in the natural world. They are absolutes. How can there be any question of interpretation in that?" she asked.

56

"I am a physicist, and let me tell you there are no certainties! Over and over again, we have been proved wrong about our understanding of the world and reality. Through millennia, through the Newtonian era of classical mechanics, we had assumed that time was absolute. We believed that one minute was one minute and would always be one minute for everyone! There was no question of interpreting it in any other way until Einstein came up with his Theory of Relativity that fundamentally changed our understanding of the very nature of time and space. It made us realise that time is relative to the observer's frame of reference. That one minute for one person might not be one minute for another. One metre does not have to be one metre everywhere. There is no absolute time or space! Do you realise what a big shock that was? It shattered our belief in absolute time, in something we had taken for granted for thousands of years! This is only one example. Quantum Physics, for instance, has thrown up so many unimaginable surprises that we, as physicists, genuinely question whether we understand reality at all! In that case, why should life and death be not open for interpretation?"

Agastya took her hand in his. He looked into her eyes and said, "Please be patient! When you begin your quest to understand Vedanta, or any new philosophy for that matter, it always hurts at the beginning. It hurts, because you are so used to thinking in a particular way, and the new philosophy challenges that. Introspecting and updating beliefs that you have held for your entire life is difficult but not impossible. I strongly urge you to keep an open mind. Do not believe anything without questioning it. Question everything, but do not get tempted to prematurely rule out an idea simply because it does not conform to your existing beliefs. Give every new idea a chance it deserves! Reserve your judgment till you objectively analyse it, gather observations, and draw your own independent inferences - this is the only way you can embrace knowledge and wisdom!"

Asmi started reading ancient texts on Hindu philosophy, but she got lost in the morass of different schools of thought. She would read one thing and then, somewhere else, she would read its exact opposite. She would read about the importance of rituals in one book, and then get baffled at the complete absence of them in another. Gradually, she realised that Hinduism was not one religion or a single coherent system of thought but an unruly admixture of more than a dozen schools of thought spanning across millennia. The most ancient texts on Hinduism were the four Vedas. These contained details and specifications of rituals and sacrifices to appease Gods of rain, fertility, wealth, health etc. This was the earliest and the most rudimentary phase of Hinduism. The oldest parts of the first Veda, the Rigveda, were probably composed over six thousand years ago making it the most ancient surviving literature of that scale in the world. For thousands of years, these Vedas had been passed orally from one generation to another, from *guru* to *shishya*, with students memorizing these tomes of knowledge without writing them down.

The ritualistic Vedas gave way to the philosophical Upanishads in the later times of Hinduism. The Upanishads were pure philosophy unadulterated by religion or rituals. They represented one of the deepest reaches of mortal minds into understanding and deciphering the nature of reality. What is real and what is unreal? Who am I? What is the nature of the bondage that binds one to the cycle of life? By answering these questions, the Upanishads, the crown jewel of human philosophy, had inspired ancient and modern philosophers alike from Gautam Buddha to Arthur Schopenhauer, the famous German philosopher, who said about the Upanishads, "They have been the solace of my life and will be the solace of my death!" They inspired scientists from Aryabhatta to Agastya's heroes

Heisenberg and Schrödinger. The term *Vedanta* referred to the collective teachings of the Upanishads. The Upanishads were agnostic, almost atheistic, and believed neither in a personal God nor in theistic concepts like sin, heaven, and hell. They only believed in logically dissecting philosophical arguments, asking questions, finding answers, and reaching the truth through enquiry!

Asmi felt the irony in her life. She would spend the day at her job doing mundane things, writing copies glorifying pickles and hotels, and speaking with fussy clients, while she spent her evenings with Agastya and Swamiji, talking about philosophy and life, understanding what it meant to be free. Things were not going very well for Fernandes Media. Varun had worked hard for the project with Satyashah Hotels, but they did not get it. Fernandes was worried. Financially, they were doing tolerably well with revenues from retainership work for existing clients, but it had been really long since they had bagged a big fish. Varun, now working exclusively on business development and sales, got a few small projects but nothing big enough to improve the situation. The air of general despondency had spread throughout the firm. Last week, Fernandes fired some employees. The headcount of the firm had fallen from twenty to fifteen now, and the sword of further layoffs still hung above everyone's head.

One afternoon, Fernandes called Asmi into his office. For the last few months, she had been silently directing many of the projects, while Ganesh Shinde nominally signed off on them. She made swift decisions and was good with her work. She would quickly grasp what the clients wanted, and with machine-like efficiency, she would finish off the work, deliver it, and close the assignment. She had grown far beyond her modest title of 'Copywriting Intern' and was now practically running projects. While this was wonderful for the firm, Fernandes resented her

59

upstart confidence. He resented the fact that whenever faced with unhappy clients, his employees no longer came to him requesting that he call and pacify them. They went to Asmi, and she, instead of resorting to cumbersome conversations to appease them, would simply give them what they wanted, make them happy, and do all of this in lesser time and effort. He resented the unspoken deference he saw in their eyes towards her, while he, despite being the owner of the firm, got only cold, discontented stares and grumbling.

"Hello Asmi, how are you? How is the work going?" he asked with unusual politeness.

"I am fine. The work is going well!" she replied in a formal voice.

"What are you working on?"

"We have the newspaper advertisement series from Ramachandra Pickles. Then we have the Zen Spa website where we publish a blog article every month. And we…"

"That's great!" said Fernandes rudely interrupted her. He was not really interested in knowing. "What work do you do on these projects?"

"I write for them."

"Yes, you write; that is your job. But I have received complaints about you!" he said leaning forward on the desk.

"Complaints?" she asked dumbfounded.

"As a copywriter, you are not supposed to interact directly with clients. Was that not clear to you? Yet, why do you do that routinely? Please try to understand, Asmi, that you are trampling on the job functions of other employees. You are directly interfering in their work!"

Asmi was perplexed. She wondered what Fernandes was trying to tell her. "Sir, I never wanted to handle communication with the clients. Varun used to do it, but after he moved to

60

business development, there was no one left to do it. I was compelled to start doing it out of necessity!"

"What about last week? Were you also compelled to interfere in the Furniture World project?" he asked.

"I finished writing the copy and handed it to Shinde sir. The client was not happy with the design and visuals. Shinde sir was not able to understand what they really wanted so he requested me to speak to them. I spoke to them and sat with Namita to redesign the layout and images. That's all! I have never interfered in anyone's work! I would not have spoken to the client if Shinde sir had not asked me to. I thought there was no harm in helping out."

Fernandes picked up a folder from his desk and took out a copy of a blog post she had written for a spa. "You need to make some corrections!" he said and started listing out some trivial, needless modifications.

"I am sorry to interrupt, sir, but we submitted this to the client yesterday, and they have already posted it on their blog. They were very happy with the work!" she said politely maintaining an even tone.

Fernandes reddened with indignation but quickly controlled himself. He still needed her. He complimented her to gain some lost ground and then asked her to leave thinking he would have to deal with her conceit some other day!

"This is so ridiculous! Fernandes hates me because my work is not good enough, and he hates you because your work is too good! What's wrong with the world?" Varun exclaimed when she told him the story. Asmi knew what was wrong with the world. She had felt the cold sensation around her inside his office, and the golden scales creeping slowly along her skin!

That night, the four of them went out for dinner. During casual conversation, Namita asked Agastya, "How long will you stay in Mumbai?"

"I have three more weeks here. After that, I will go back to California."

Namita involuntarily glanced at Asmi who was looking elsewhere. Next day in office, she asked Asmi, "Do you love each other?"

"Yes, very much!"

"What will you do when he goes back?"

"Nothing! He goes to California, and I stay here."

"I am sorry for asking personal questions, but I know he means a lot to you. I am worried for you after he goes back."

Asmi smiled. She knew Namita was genuinely concerned. "Don't worry! It doesn't really matter to us whether we are together or apart on opposite sides of the planet. I know he exists, and this knowledge is sufficient to sustain my love for him and his for me!"

Asmi was sitting with Swamiji in his office. Agastya was working elsewhere in the library. Swamiji offered her a banana from a plate of fruits kept on the table. On the way, she had seen a large hoarding put up outside the newly opened 'The Palazzo' hotel owned by the Satyashah Group. It reminded her of Varun's failed efforts to get the project for Fernandes.

"Swamiji, what does it really mean to be free from yourself?" she asked.

As always, with a smile on his face, in his deep and powerful voice, Swamiji answered, "If you ask a random person on the street the meaning of freedom, he will tell you freedom is the ability to do what you want. But Asmi, why do we want what we want? You felt like eating the banana. Why did you feel that? You felt like eating it, because you were hungry. Why were you hungry? Because your blood glucose level was low. Why was it low? Because you had not eaten for a long time. Do you see? You wanting to eat the banana was the effect of the cause that you were hungry, and this cause was, in turn, the effect of another cause that your blood glucose level was low. Behind everything you want, behind every desire and feeling you have, there is an infinitely long chain of cause and effect that we call causality. A cause giving rise to an effect, and this effect becoming the cause of another effect, ad infinitum till a desire emerges in your mind. But can you see this infinite chain of causality? No! You can only see the final desire in your mind. Thus, you erroneously believe that your mind is the source of the desire. However, your mind is only a conduit. Your environment, the whole universe in fact, through the agency of causality, using your mind as a conduit, controls you! Asmi, your mind does not belong to you. It is merely a slave of causality!"

Asmi nodded and said, "So true freedom means freedom from your own mind and freedom from causality?"

"Yes, you are right!"

"But Swamiji, does this mean that everything we do is always determined by causality, and we can never really choose to do anything of our own accord? Does this mean there is no *free will*?"

Swamiji looked at her thoughtfully. He generally avoided giving direct answers to questions about *free will*, because people often misunderstood both the words: *free* and *will*. He said, "Asmi, what does the word *will* mean? Your *will* is what your mind wants you to do. But your mind is bound by causality, and hence, your *will* is only an instrument of causality! There is no *free will*, because *will*, itself, can never be free, but there is something behind that *will* which is free!"

"What is behind the *will* which is free, Swamiji?" she asked.

"To find the answer to that is what we have the wisdom of the Upanishads for!" he replied.

63

That evening, Asmi and Agastya went for a quiet walk in the university campus. It was a large campus about four hundred acres in size. The academic buildings were spread throughout the campus with lots of open spaces and dense trees between them. The university was a serene and clean zone in the middle of the otherwise bustling and crowded city.

"Agastya, I don't understand! If freedom means being free of your desires, does it mean we should just give up all our desires? Life would become so meaningless then!" she said.

"No, Asmi, freedom does not mean giving up all your desires!"

"But that is what I read in the Bhagavad Gita!"

"What did you read?"

"It says you should renounce your desires."

"Aah, I see! The problem is with the word *renounce*. I think it is the most misunderstood and abused word in all of Hindu philosophy! No, Asmi, the Upanishads do not preach that you should give up all desires. They do not tell you to live like a vegetable! They teach you how to be a master of your desires rather than being a slave to them! They teach you how to rejoice and live a fulfilling life without getting caught in the endless conditions that bind your happiness. They teach you how to achieve lasting happiness and freedom from *Samsara*, the cycle of bondage!"

Later in the night when Asmi returned home, she called her parents.

"Hello Aai, *kashi ahes?* How are you? *Baba kase ahet?* How is Baba?"

"We are fine, Asmi, but good you called! Abba is not keeping very well. He is sick and we fear he will not be with us for long. You should come home to see him!"

64

That Sunday, Asmi went to the Wadi for the first time after she had left. Agastya offered to go with her.

"No, Agastya! I need to go alone!" she told him.

Even before she entered the house, even from a distance, she could tell something was different. Aai opened the door for her. She came in and looked around. Paint coming off the wall, a thick layer of dust on the window sills, a broken door handle, cushions torn at the edges, the house had all the telltale signs of the neglect the inhabitants had for it.

Sensing her dismay, Aai said, "Since you left, it has been very different! Your father does not talk to Abba. Nowadays, he seldom speaks to me either. He leaves the house in the morning and comes back only at night. Neha visits sometimes but very infrequently. It is just Abba and me. He is too old and sick. So it is just me living alone like a ghost in this house!"

"Where is Baba?"

"He had to go out for some important work," Aai answered averting her gaze.

Asmi went inside Abba's room. Abba saw Asmi, but she could not tell if he recognised her. She spoke to him nonetheless and told him about her life in the city. She sat there silently holding his hand till it was lunch time. Neha came over for lunch. Asmi wanted to meet Saurabh, her nephew, but Neha did not get him along. After lunch, as Aai kept steaming cups of ginger tea on the table and sat down, she put on a serious expression on her face.

"Asmi, have you found someone?" she asked nervously not knowing how her daughter would react. She had noticed Asmi's modern attire of jeans and a thin shirt. She had noticed the nail paint on her fingers and the way she had made her hair. She had noticed the confidence in her movements and words. She was happy for Asmi for all of these things, but as a parent, she was worried about her future.

"Yes. His name is Agastya," Asmi replied.

"Do you love him?"

"Yes."

"And he? Does he love you too?" she asked timidly.

"Yes."

"What does he do?"

"He is a scientist and lives in America."

"Do you know Sunil remarried?"

"Yes."

Neha had told her. Asmi had never met Sunil after that day. Their divorce proceedings had been quick and uneventful since there had been no disputes.

"Are you planning to get married to Agastya?" Aai asked.

"No!" Asmi replied looking straight at her. Aai looked away.

"Why? Does he not want to marry you? Have you at least asked him? Or is he already married?" Horror dawned on Aai's face as she contemplated the latter possibility.

Asmi felt a tremor of anger growing in her heart. Even now, after all that had happened, Aai had assumed things and had not bothered to ask what she wanted! "No. He is not married," Asmi answered in a frigid voice.

"Then why not get married to him?"

"Because I don't want to get married!"

"Why?"

How could she explain to her mother that neither she nor Agastya wanted to torture and subject their beautiful, intimate, and real relationship to society's Procrustean Bed? Asmi chose to say nothing in reply.

"Asmi, get married to a suitable husband! That is the proper thing to do! It is the only way you will get a respectable place in the society! Asmi, please, for the sake of my love for you, do not be stubborn and get married!"

"Aai, enough!" Asmi said furiously, "This is blackmail! You talk about a place in the society! What place did your society give

66

me when I married Sunil? A respectable place of slavery? Wash utensils, cook food, clean the house, keep the men happy, is this what I was born for? Where simply wanting to do something I liked was a crime? Where asking for a little space and time for myself was a sin? Really? Is this what you want for your own daughter? That I should trade my happiness for propriety? That I give up my life for social values? Not only did you not stand up for me when I most needed you, but you tacitly supported my suffering, and now you still want the same thing for me? Why?" Asmi's face turned red as tears streamed down her cheeks. She had borne everything patiently until now, but she could not take it that her own mother had sided with the dragon!

Aai was devastated by Asmi's outburst. Through bouts of sobbing, she managed to say in broken fragments, "I am only doing what I think is best for you!"

They lay together that last night in each other's arms. He liked holding her like this: his arms tightly wrapped around her body, his feet touching hers, her back towards him, both facing in the same direction, thinking the same thoughts, feeling the same feelings, their hearts beating together as if they were one!

"I will miss you, Asmi!" he said.

She did not move or reply. It was not necessary.

"You hate them, don't you?" he asked.

"Yes. My parents, Sunil's family, Shweta and her friends, Fernandes - all of them!"

"You know you don't have to. They are not in control of their actions. They cannot help it. But you can!"

"It is not my fault that they are not in control. Why should I pay the price for it? And it certainly does not excuse them from owning responsibility for their actions!"

"You will not be free till you stop hating them. Rise above all this, and let it go. Forgive them. Don't do it for them, Asmi, but do it for yourself!"

Chapter 5: The Choice

FERNANDES AND ASMI HAD A strained relationship after the last incident. He left no opportunity to assert his authority and show her 'her place' in the organisation; she, on the other hand, tried her best to stay out of his way. Fernandes stormed into the office one morning. He had gotten wind on the grapevine that Charvak Satyashah was after a huge new real estate project. Menaka Park was close to two hundred acres in size and was to be developed on some of the prime land in the city. At the all-hands meeting, he roared at his team the motivational quotes he had read on the web. His employees had heard them too many times, and they ignored him. Besides, in spite of trying for so many years, they had not been able to get a single contract from any of the Satyashah companies! Varun was tensed and sat upright expecting Fernandes to make a scapegoat of him yet again. He was surprised when Fernandes did not take his name and, instead, exclaimed, "Asmi, this is an opportunity for you! For a long time, you have been wanting to do things other than copywriting. This is your chance to prove yourself!"

"But sir, I have never done any business development before!" Asmi replied defensively.

"Do not let us down, Asmi!" he growled before concluding the meeting.

Asmi felt utter contempt for Fernandes. Too taken aback, she had found herself unable to respond and had remained a meek spectator through the meeting. Once the meeting got over, however, she felt anger slowly rising in her.

She tried to control it remembering what Swamiji had once said to her, "Why do you get angry at people? Do you also get angry at objects? If you are walking on the road and accidentally trip over a brick, will you get angry at the brick? Why not? Because the brick has no mind of its own? The brick did not choose to do anything; it simply happened to be in your path due to a chain of cause and effect. How are people any different? Yes, they do have a mind, but their mind is a slave of causality too! It is causality that brought the brick into your path, and it is causality that made the person behave in a certain way. If you want to get angry, don't get angry at the brick, don't get angry at the person, get angry at causality herself! But do you know what it means to get angry at causality? It means to get angry at the whole universe! Asmi, anger corrodes the soul. Every time you get angry, you make deep cuts into your soul. Think! Can you really afford to get angry at the universe?"

Asmi had no idea how to go about creating a proposal and sending it to the Satyashah Group. "What am I exactly supposed to do? I can write, come up with ideas, and make a presentation, but I don't know anyone in the Satyashah Group; whom do I speak to?" Asmi asked Varun.

"Don't worry! When I was working for the hotel project, I made hundreds of cold calls to them. Finally, someone gave me the contact details of Ritesh Sundaram, the person who heads marketing for the entire group. I emailed him our proposal. After many follow up calls, I finally got to speak to him. Sundaram told me he would go over my proposal and get back. He never got back to us, but now we at least have a way of communicating with them. You work on drafting a proposal, and I will ensure it gets across!" Varun said reassuringly.

"Thanks, Varun! What can we pitch to them?"

"Frankly, nothing! They are a huge conglomerate. They work only with the best media agencies. What can we offer them that they do not have? Your job here is to show Fernandes that you worked hard and gave out a decent proposal. He also knows it is going to fail!"

When Charvak Satyashah's grandfather, the venerated Vallabh Satyashah, founded his business empire, he had begun by building a humble textile mill on his family's ancestral land. In those days, this Satyashah Mill, as it was called then, was located outside the city limits. With rapid urban expansion in the last few decades, however, this land and the mill were now right in the heart of the city. The old, abandoned mill building stood on one corner of this land, but the rest of it was heavily fragmented: shanty houses where families of servants and mill workers had lived for decades, plots temporarily leased to relatives and acquaintances without legal agreements that they now claimed as their own, dense undergrowth, piles of garbage and industrial wastes, and streams of dirty sewage water were scattered across it. With so many claimants having squatted there for generations, consolidating this ancestral property was a legal nightmare. Charvak's father, Ravindra Satyashah, had given up. When Charvak assumed the reigns, he reinitiated the efforts to consolidate it. He bought out some of the squatters by offering them money; others, for whom money was not sufficient, were lured by non-monetary temptations; and those who rigidly refused were driven out by force, blackmail, and coercion. Charvak doled out millions in bribing police officers, bureaucrats, and ministers to expedite the process of clearing the titles and legal hurdles. Having fought for years, the whole of the land, all two hundred acres, was now fully available to him, and he started developing it into the most sought after residential and

71

commercial address in the city. The first phase of the project was nearing completion and would soon be opened to public for sale. This project was dear to him, and he had taken a personal interest in it. His marketing team had given him numerous concepts, but he was not satisfied with them.

Sitting in his office, he picked up the phone and dialled Sundaram, the head of the corporate team that handled marketing, advertising, and branding for most of their companies.

"Good evening, sir! How may I help you?" Sundaram said.

"Send me all designs and concepts you have considered for Menaka Park!"

"Yes, sir!"

"Sundaram, Menaka is the ultimate expression of exclusivity. It is a tribute to my grandfather and father. Your target is the cream elite of the society. Make something that will appeal to them."

"Yes, sir!"

Some time later, a clerk walked in and kept some files on Charvak's desk in a neatly arranged stack. The stack lay there unattended for two days.

Now in his late thirties, Charvak had been at the helm of the Satyashah Group of Companies for almost twelve years. When his father died of a sudden heart attack, he was thrust into the world of business, which he knew very little of, and given charge of companies that were suffering from multiple ailments. Over the last decade, he had managed to expertly steer the ship out of difficult waters. Analysts, shareholders, and the general public alike hailed him as a visionary and a great business leader. The Group's oldest and most established businesses were textile and manufacturing. Later, they had expanded into chemicals, hospitality, healthcare, real estate, and retail. As recognised as he was for his business acumen, Charvak was also infamous for his lack of morals and debauchery. He was notoriously unscrupulous in his business dealings and let nothing come in the way of his desired outcome. He was the most lascivious playboy the country had seen and made no efforts to hide that proudly wearing his hedonism on his sleeve.

Charvak's office was on the top floor of the Group's corporate headquarters. Two sides of the massive office were glass walls. One side overlooked the sea, and the other overlooked the city. He often stayed back late after everyone else left. Solitude helped him think clearly. During the day, his attention would be flooded with constant interruptions, phone calls, emails, visitors, and irksome subordinates reporting some or the other emergency. It was nearly midnight when his gaze fell on the stack of designs and concepts Sundaram had sent over for Menaka Park. He pulled the files closer and told the night attendant to get him a bottle of beer. The real estate market was booming, and there were thousands of construction projects throughout the city. He wanted this one to be unquestionably special. None of the concepts he had seen so far lived up to what he wanted. One of them described the bespoke luxury the project offered. Another emphasised the prestige of having an address in Menaka Park. A third spoke of simplicity and sophistication. All beaten up ideas, he thought disdainfully! He shut the file in his hand and carelessly dropped it on top of the stack causing it to cascade down on the desk. As he was about to get up, his eyes went to a thin folder in the middle of the stack. He pulled it out. In the centre of the cover page was a single word printed in small but bold letters: Freedom!

Next morning, Asmi came to office at the usual time. She flung her bag on the desk and went to make herself a cup of coffee. The changing times had taken their toll on Varun and drained him of his fun and humour. Most employees had not turned up yet. Fernandes was in Goa at his family home and would not be back for a couple of days. His absence meant a relaxed atmosphere in the office. As she sat down at her desk, her phone rang. The woman on the line said she was calling from the Satyashah Group's Marketing Division and asked if Asmi could visit their office the following day to discuss the proposal she had sent. Asmi called Fernandes. He was probably still in bed and sounded irritable. She told him about the call.

"Sir, if you want I can go with Varun for the meeting. I will handle it!" she offered.

"No, I will come back. Prepare and send me some presentation slides. I will work on them tonight," he said. He could not afford to sit out on this!

Fernandes, Asmi, and Varun sat quietly in the reception lobby of the corporate headquarters of the Satyashah Group. Nobody spoke to one another. Asmi had prepared a presentation and sent it to Fernandes the night before. In the morning, when she saw what he had done with it, she was utterly dismayed. He had taken her idea of personal freedom and disfigured it into something completely different. Invoking the Indian Freedom Struggle against the colonial British rule, Fernandes had themed the slides saffron, white, and green, the colours of the national flag, and proposed that the marketing campaign be launched on 15th August, the day India celebrated Independence. She tried to tell him while they waited in the lobby that the proposal she had sent referred to a different idea of freedom, and there was no mention of the Indian Freedom Struggle, but Fernandes did not listen. He scowled at her, "Can't you see I am trying to concentrate?"

Someone came to escort them to Sundaram's office. Fernandes delivered a lacklustre pitch to a periodically nodding Sundaram who was clearly not paying attention. As soon as it was over, Sundaram picked up the phone and spoke to someone on the other end.

"Well, Mr Fernandes, we now have to go to Mr Satyashah's office. Please follow me!" he said and got up.

Fernandes leaped out of his chair and stood between Sundaram and the door. "Sir! Meeting Mr Satyashah would be a great honour! But, sir, do you think our presentation is good? Do you have any inputs for us? What should we say to him?"

Sundaram waved him off casually, almost rudely, saying, "Your presentation is fine. Let's go!"

In the elevator ride to the top floor, Asmi exchanged a glance and a furtive smile with Varun. This was exciting for them. Neither of them had ever been inside a corporate office like this. It was humongous. There were fully grown trees inside the office with special glass roofs to let in the sunlight! Busy people, looking smart in their business attires, scurried around everywhere. The elevator stopped, and they entered another reception room. This was smaller but much more elegant and posh than the previous one. Sundaram went inside the office and the three of them sat down on a sofa in the reception room. An extremely attractive woman sat on the reception desk looking at them with conspicuous condescension in her eyes. After a few minutes, she told them to enter. As they went in, they saw Sundaram sitting in front of a giant desk. Behind the desk, sitting upright in his chair, was Charvak Satyashah himself! There was an air of undeniable authority around him. He wore an expensive shirt with his sleeves rolled up, no tie, and sported a stubble that suited him very well. Fernandes had imagined that he would walk up to Charvak, shake his hand, and offer him his business card, but something in Charvak's demeanour told him that was not a good idea. Before Fernandes could introduce himself, Sundaram told him to start explaining the concept. Varun stepped forward to set up the laptop and presentation, but Charvak gestured him away without looking at him. His eyes were intently fixed on Fernandes.

"You have one minute to tell me how you will brand Menaka Park on the theme of freedom," Charvak said in a strong calibrated voice. He had not even as much as glanced at Asmi or Varun.

Without his slides to support him, Fernandes faltered. Freedom had not been his idea. He did not think freedom had anything to do with a real estate project. He blurted out, his cultivated accent sounding contrived and out of place, how Menaka Park would be the ideal location to get freedom from the daily hassles of traffic, dirt, noise, and pollution, and drew up a far stretched analogy with the Indian Freedom Struggle.

Before Fernandes could finish, Charvak raised his hand. "Thank you for coming over! We will get back to you in a few days," he said brusquely indicating that the meeting was over.

Fernandes got up, muttered a thank you, and started walking towards the door followed by Varun. Charvak, without waiting for them to leave the room, started speaking to Sundaram about something else.

"I am sorry to interrupt, sir! May I please speak for a moment?" Asmi said cutting Charvak mid-sentence. Everyone turned to look at her. Time stood still. Varun nudged her and whispered, "Asmi! Let's go!" but she did not move. Charvak turned his gaze towards her.

Without waiting for an answer, she continued, "By freedom, we do not mean freedom only from worldly things such as noise and pollution nor are we referring to the Indian Freedom Struggle. We are talking here about freedom from something much deeper. Menaka Park provides exclusively designed spaces that bring out the real you! They offer you a chance to find true freedom - freedom from yourself! This is the central theme around which we propose to build the marketing campaign."

She finished speaking. Charvak did not move. He continued looking at her with a fierce intensity that made her acutely uncomfortable, but she did not blink or look away. Their eyes met as they held each other's gaze at an unbreakable impasse, for a moment too long, before he broke it. Turning towards Fernandes, he said in a whisper that turned his blood cold, "Get out of here!"

There was utter silence in the car on the way back. When they reached office, she started walking towards her desk when Fernandes called out, "Asmi!"

"Sir?" she said.

He was standing in the middle of the workspace with his face flushed with anger. "What the hell did you think you were doing?" he asked loudly.

"Sir, it was the only chance we had! I thought we should at least put across our point correctly!"

"You blew up the opportunity, goddamnit!"

She could sense his temper rising.

Varun broke in, "Sir, Mr Satyashah had made up his mind. We had already lost the deal before Asmi spoke!"

"No, we had not! He said they would get back to us later. Did you not hear that, you fool? I have been in this business for decades. I know how it works. You know nothing, you brats! What is she? A mere intern and she thinks she is smarter than everyone else to speak like that? We had a chance! They might have called us back only if this bitch here had held her tongue!"

In the fifteen years of existence of Fernandes Media, nobody had heard him swear at an employee like that. He had never sworn at a woman before. Later, Fernandes was himself shocked at the vehemence with which those words had left his mouth. It was almost as if a foreign power had possessed him. Asmi felt the same sickly feeling in her stomach that she knew so well and the same icy scales creeping along her skin. But this time, she was

77

stronger! Unlike the previous times, she did not feel her heart wrenching. She did not feel scared. She did not feel her eyes moisten. With her head held high, without affording Fernandes even the courtesy of her glance, without offering the dragon an acknowledgment of his victory, Asmi walked out of the door calmly and confidently!

Asmi went to see Swamiji that evening. He was not there in his office, but she knew where to find him. She made her way to the well-maintained garden behind the library where he took his evening walks. He had finished his walk and was sitting on a bench below an old, patriarchal banyan tree. She gently sat down next to him looked at the leaves dancing in the gentle breeze. Something in their dance mesmerised her. As the upper rim of the sun was about to dip below the horizon, Swamiji joined his palms in the form of a *namaskar* and said his brief evening prayer. The sunrise and the sunset were the only times she had seen him say something akin to a prayer. He never mentioned God so she wondered whom he prayed to. She would ask him someday, she thought.

"Don't worry, Asmi, you are strong! Bad things happen, and people cause you hurt, but you must not hate them. Learn to forgive them, my child!" he said when she told him about the incident.

"I try to, but I cannot! For how long can I keep letting things go? I am tired of dealing with people!"

Swamiji looked at her with benevolent eyes. He knew she had not finished.

"Swamiji, the dragon follows me everywhere, and I am tired of running. I want to be free of the dragon. Teach me how to fight him!"

"My dear, do you not see the contradiction in your statement?"

"What contradiction?"

He shifted his posture to face her. He was not smiling; it was the first time she had seen that perpetual smile leave his face. "Asmi, listen to me carefully! You can either fight this dragon, or you can be free of him, but not both. If you fight him you cannot be free of him! You must choose your path. Do it wisely!"

"How can I make this choice?" she said, but she saw Swamiji was not listening.

His smile had not returned. His eyes were focussed at the point of infinity, not seeing anything in front of him but seeing something beyond from another time almost twelve years ago. The same university garden and the same bench under the giant banyan flashed before his eyes. They were sitting on the bench, *guru* and *shishya*, Swamiji and his young pupil, quietly watching the leaves dancing to the tune of the gentle breeze.

"Isn't it late?" he had said glancing at his wrist to see that the old, golden-coloured watch he wore had stopped ticking. "The batteries must be dead," he had thought.

"Give it to me, Swamiji! I will get the batteries replaced tomorrow," the young *shishya* had said cheerfully.

As Swamiji walked back with Asmi towards the library, his glance went to his hand - his watchless hand! His *shishya*, whom he loved like his son, had never come back. Before leaving, he had asked him the same question that Asmi asked today: about fighting the dragon!

Asmi did not know what she would do next. She would have to start looking for another job. She barely had enough money to pay the month's rent, but she was not scared. She reached home and found Varun and Namita sitting outside the door.

"Let's go for dinner!" Namita exclaimed.

"I was thinking I will just rest at home," Asmi said.

"Come, sweetheart! Have dinner with us!" Namita coaxed her.

Asmi gladly obliged; she felt lucky to have these two friends in her life.

While having dinner, Varun asked, "Asmi, are you all right?"

"Yes, Varun! I am fine!"

"Listen, I spoke to Fernandes. He had no right to swear at you like that, but he is ready to apologise. He needs you. We all need you. So let's put this behind us, all right?"

Asmi did not answer.

"So, you will come to office tomorrow, right?" he asked.

"No," she said.

"What do you mean by 'no'?"

"You know what I mean. I will not set foot in that office again!"

"Come on! Don't do this! Things got hot and he lost his temper. I am sure you understand he did not really mean that!"

"I understand it only too well Varun. Which is why I am not going back!"

Namita interjected, "Varun, you heard how he swore at Asmi! How can you expect her to go back? Asmi, damn that bastard! Don't see his face again!"

"Namita! Be practical! This is not about ego!" Varun said.

Turning to Asmi he continued, "Listen, Asmi, you start looking for other jobs immediately, but you also know that it will take time before you find one. Till then, continue working with Fernandes. The money won't hurt!"

"Varun, I have made up my mind!" Asmi said with finality.

Varun resigned. He looked up at her and, in a genuine voice, said, "If you need any help, financial or otherwise, please tell us!"

Charvak realised he had held his breath for too long. He eased his tensed muscles and breathed again feeling better as fresh oxygen entered his lungs. Fernandes and the other man had scurried out of the door immediately, but the girl had continued to stare at him insolently till she turned around and walked out. People seldom looked straight into his eyes, and nobody ever interrupted him!

"Sundaram, the girl? What's her name?" he asked.

Sundaram fished out the proposal and said, "Asmi from Fernandes Media. Sir, I think the concept of freedom is…"

"I want her on our marketing team!"

"Sir? Yes, sir!"

After Sundaram left, Charvak picked up the proposal. Freedom, the bold lettered title, stood out of the paper mocking him. The word meant nothing to him. Many years ago, he had banished and buried that word deep inside the darkest pits of his soul and had never thought of it again; until now, when the girl brought it up and dared to talk to him about it! One glance at that faltering man speaking in his artificial accent told him that his media agency could never handle the work. But one glance at that girl who looked him in the eye told him he wanted her! He tried to recollect how she looked. How tall was she? Was she fair? What colour were her eyes?

The next morning, Asmi got a call asking her to come for interviews to the corporate headquarters of the Satyashah Group. She had two rounds of interviews and a third one with Sundaram. He said they liked her idea of creating a campaign around the theme of freedom and offered her the post of a 'Content Writer' with a salary many times of what Fernandes paid her. She was pleasantly surprised and happily accepted the offer!

Chapter 6: The Garden of Life

CHARVAK'S SPEECH AT THE GRADUATION ceremony that morning at the National Institute of Management (N.I.M.), the premier business school in the country, had been a success. Sundaram called to tell him that the speech had gone viral on the web and social media, and his Web Engagement team was working hard to maintain the momentum it had generated. He looked out through the glass window of his office at the city spread out before him. Reclining back in the chair, he closed his eyes. It was four o'clock in the afternoon. He told the attendant to get him his tea.

It had been six months since Asmi started her new job with the Satyashah Group. She worked in what was called the Marketing Division, although the division did a lot more than that: it handled all functions related to marketing, branding, advertising, corporate communications, and public relations. It was headed by Ritesh Sundaram, but Asmi never needed to directly interact with him and had met him in person only twice since joining. Her immediate manage whom she most interacted with, Akash Patel, was around forty, had an MBA degree from one of the pedigree schools, and led the team that was responsible for content creation including text and multimedia. Unlike her previous job where her responsibilities were broad and flexible, she now worked exclusively on content writing. She wrote things, and that was pretty much all she did. Even the research for her writing was done by someone else; she was given an outline, and she wrote the text to fill it up. However, after a few months, Patel became more confident in her capabilities and started according her more autonomy. But even then, her work was extensively reviewed and edited before any of it was approved. The freedom theme she had envisaged for Menaka Park was eventually scrapped. When she asked Patel about it, he just shrugged and told her that the decision had been taken at higher levels beyond him.

Namita had burst out laughing when Asmi told her about her new job.

"So much for his tantrum! Fernandes beware! I am coming to personally rub this in your face!" Varun had exclaimed with sadistic delight.

Asmi was amused by their reactions, but Fernandes didn't really matter to her. Agastya was happy, but he gave her a reaction that was more contained than Namita or Varun. He asked her practical details about her work and if she were happy to take it up. The reaction that most puzzled her, however, came from Swamiji. He congratulated her, but for some inexplicable reason, he seemed worried. She asked Agastya if he knew why Swamiji might be worried, but he was as clueless as her. She decided to ask him directly.

"Swamiji, you do not seem to be happy about my new job. Is there something wrong? Am I missing something?"

"Asmi, you have embarked on a difficult journey on the path of Vedanta. It will not be easy. Seemingly insurmountable obstacles will come in your way. They will make you doubt yourself. They will make you question the path and your understanding of it. But never doubt yourself, and never lose hope, my child! I know you are strong, but I am worried if you know it yourself!"

"With you as my *guru*, there is nothing I worry about!" she said with a confused smile.

Swamiji was worried for her. Ever since he returned from his spiritual pilgrimage across the country and started working at the library, he had mentored many students. He had been a *guru* to many disciples who came to him for advice. Some of them were interested in Vedanta for theoretically understanding its philosophy, while others, the more serious ones, made efforts to practise it in their daily lives. Understanding a philosophical concept was very different from realising it and applying it. Asmi could now grasp concepts easily, but she still had a long way to go before she could fully realise them. The dragon was powerful and would do his best to deflect her from her path. He saw in her an immense potential to realise the truth of Vedanta in all its might but not yet! She was still only a beginner and very vulnerable to the machinations of the devious world. He was worried, because she was now working for a man who represented all that was wrong with the world!

Swamiji remembered what the *rishi* had told him. On a cold afternoon, dying of starvation, wandering without direction, lost in the harsh and unforgiving reaches of the Himalayas, he had met one of the *Saptarishis* who told him to repay a debt. Asmi was his means of repaying that debt. She would be his deliverance, and he could not afford to let the world corrupt her. He was well aware that when someone as capable as her makes a wrong choice, makes a choice to loathe and fight the world instead of forgiving and embracing it, a monster like Charvak Satyashah is born!

"Swamiji, I am hopeless at meditation! I don't think I'll ever learn to do it correctly!" Asmi exclaimed one evening as they were having tea at the canteen. For the last few months, she had been actively practising meditation. Swamiji had said that in order to apply her knowledge of philosophy to her daily life, she needed to master meditation. She meditated regularly every morning for fifteen to twenty minutes before going to office.

"Why do you say that?" he asked dipping a glucose biscuit in the teacup.

"I cannot keep my mind free of thoughts for a single minute. I can do it, maybe, for a couple of seconds, but then the thoughts surge forth, and I lose control. Must we learn to meditate?" she asked coyly.

"Yes, Asmi, we must learn to meditate!"

"Why must we meditate?"

"Asmi, what we see around us is not reality but only a perception. What we see, feel, taste, hear, and smell are artefacts that our senses create on the canvas of our mind, and it is through these that we interpret the world. So, you see, it is always our mind that creates our experience of the world. Meditation teaches you to master your mind and hence direct your experiences. You must learn to observe your mind. Where do your thoughts arise from? How does one thought lead to another? The first requisite to understanding your mind is to detach yourself from it. Meditation enables you to observe the inner workings of your mind by becoming a detached observer."

"But how can I observe my thoughts if I focus my full attention on preventing them from arising? Isn't meditation about shutting down your thoughts and being at peace?"

"No, Asmi, it is not! The goal of meditation is not to block your thoughts."

"But that is what you told me to do!"

"No! That is only what I told you to begin with!" he said correcting her. "To observe your mind carefully, you need to focus. You cannot focus if your thoughts jump around wildly, which they usually do if you don't have practice. When you begin meditation, sit still and calm your mind. Let thoughts arise, but do not feed them. Do not entertain them. When you entertain a

85

thought, it gives rise to another thought, and then to another one, and this leads to a cascade that soon goes out of your control. The key is not in preventing thoughts; the key is in not entertaining them! When you don't entertain a thought, it automatically dissolves back into your mind. This is how you learn to control your thoughts!"

"What does this achieve?"

"You learn a very important thing by doing this. You learn that you have the power to choose when to entertain a thought and when to let it go. You learn that you are not a slave to whatever pops up in your mind, but you can control your actions and own responsibility for them. Thoughts are extremely powerful. Do you know what Mahatma Gandhi said about thoughts? He said, 'Watch your thoughts, because your thoughts become your words; your words become your actions; your actions become your habits; your habits become your values; and your values become your destiny!' Asmi, a person who masters his thoughts masters his destiny!"

"Namita, the women in my office are so chic! They look at me as if I am an animal!" Asmi told Namita laughingly during her first week at work. Coming to the city had been a big change for Asmi. At Fernandes Media, she had mostly worn jeans and informal shirts to work. But now, at the Satyashah Group, she shifted to a more formal attire wearing trousers and collared shirts. She learned how to do her hair and makeup, and use the right shades of lipstick. Her accent, which had been quite provincial when she first came to Mumbai, had now become slick and refined. She had completed the transformation, and nobody could tell by looking at her that she came from a small, forgotten town in rural India.

It was a Sunday morning. Asmi was woken up by her ringing phone.

"Hi, sleepyhead! Wake up!" Namita greeted her.

Namita asked her if she were free that evening. She wanted company for shopping so they went to a shopping mall. They were meeting after weeks and had a lot of catching up to do. Fernandes Media was not doing well. Some more people had been fired. There were no new clients, and the old ones were slowly dropping out.

"How long will you continue to work there?" Asmi asked.

"Till the end of the year! I will leave the job in December!"

Namita had a strange smile on her face suggesting there was something more.

"Namita, are you getting married?"

Namita blushed. Yes, she was getting married! Asmi knew that her parents had been looking for a suitable boy for a while.

"Congratulations! That's great news!" Asmi hugged her.

Her husband-to-be was from Delhi, and Namita would shift there after her wedding.

"You must convince Agastya to come to India for my wedding!" Namita said.

"Yes, I promise to try my best!"

Asmi asked her about the groom, how they met, what they said to each other, and all sorts of questions. It was an arranged-marriage facilitated by common friends of their parents. They had a light dinner at a small sandwich place.

Just as they were about to leave, somebody called out, "Asmi? How are you? It's been so long!" It was Shweta beaming with joy.

"Hi, Shweta! Yes, it's been long. I am good. How have you been?"

Asmi was happy to see her. They decided to meet the following evening after work.

Sipping on his afternoon tea, Charvak Satyashah read the report the Web Engagement team had emailed. It had snippets from online posts and blogs. People raved about the speech he had given. He was amused at the whole incident. He was not even supposed to be in India. The dean of the National Institute of Management had called him last month inviting him to be the commencement speaker, but he had declined due to his scheduled business trip to Europe. In his place, the institute later invited Rahul Sharma, the leading Bollywood actor. Charvak's business trip got cancelled. Yesterday afternoon, he remembered the invitation. It was a good opportunity to whip up some attention in academic institutes, especially at a fertile recruitment ground like the N.I.M., so he called the dean and expressed his desire to be the speaker.

"I am so sorry, Mr Satyashah, but we already invited Rahul Sharma. We would love to have you as our speaker next year!" the dean had said.

Within a few minutes, the dean got a call from Rahul Sharma informing him that he was down with a terrible flu and, unfortunately, would be unable to attend the commencement ceremony! However, he strongly recommended Charvak Satyashah in his place.

One of the comments in the report caught Charvak's eye. It read, "I was very surprised with the speech. He does not seem to be the kind of person who would say those things!" That was true, Charvak thought. A younger version of him, in his early twenties, might have said those things. But who cared about this incongruity? The speech was a big success!

"Sundaram, your team did a good job of putting together that speech at such a short notice!" Charvak said to Sundaram over the phone.

"Thank you, sir!"

"Who wrote the speech?"

"I will have to find out, sir!"

"Please find out and send him to my office!"

"Yes, sir!"

Shweta was late for their coffee meeting. She saw Asmi sitting in the coffee shop reading from a book in her hand.

"Hey, I am sorry I am late!" she said. She asked Asmi how she was.

Asmi told her the happenings in her life. She told her about Agastya, Fernandes, and her new job.

"How are things back home in the Wadi?" Shweta asked.

"Not good. I have not spoken to my family in months!"

Asmi's relations with her family had become very strained after her last visit. Neha had called a month ago to tell her Abba passed away. She did not go home to attend his last rites. He had passed away in his sleep. Asmi cried that night. But, in a way, she was happy that he was liberated from this world where he too did not belong!

"Asmi, you have changed! You look so nice!" Shweta said stretching out her hand to touch hers. She had noticed Asmi's changed appearance, her new clothes and shoes, her changed behaviour, the confidence with which she carried herself, her manner of speaking, and the smooth sureness of her movements.

"You tell me! How are you Shweta?"

"I am good. I am now waiting for my next promotion. I should have got it this April, but my manager is a bastard! I will have to wait till next April now. I must get that promotion! Why am I calling him a bastard? Because he promoted another girl who had joined after I did! It had been my turn to get that promotion!"

"Why do you want to participate in this rat race?"

"I don't like it either, but I must get that promotion. Without it, I will not be eligible to go abroad for work, and I really want to go. And a promotion would mean a hefty increase in my salary! My parents are now looking for suitable marriage proposals for me. A larger salary greatly improves my prospects in the arranged-marriage market!" she said with a wink.

Asmi listened to all of this quietly and only smiled in response.

Charvak had not read the complete speech that he was to give. In the car, on the way to the graduation ceremony, his executive assistant handed him the copy of the speech. It was a four-page long document. He glanced through the first two pages and, satisfied with the content, lazily put away the rest. Besides, Sundaram's signature on it meant that it had already been scanned for sensitive statements. Charvak was good with public gatherings. The students seemed excited, and he started his speech to a loud thunder of applause. He read from the page in front of him, but he spiced it up with his own flavour of wit and charisma.

He had finished the first two pages. He flipped open the third page and continued, "Imagine you find yourself in a beautiful garden. You walk along a cobbled-stone pathway. On both sides, there are lovely flowers and lush green trees. There is a stream of clear water running alongside making a soft gurgling sound. You can hear the melody of birds singing at a distance. This is the garden of life, and trust me, it is beautiful!

"Suddenly, you find your colleagues, your friends, your classmates running wildly through this garden. They have a map in their hand, and they are frantically trying to reach some destination. 'Where do you want to go?' you ask them. 'The finish line!' they yell back without stopping. They are not looking at the flowers. They have not even noticed the sparkling stream. They cannot hear the melody of the birds. 'What if I take a wrong turn?' one of them screams. 'It doesn't matter. It's a garden. Just enjoy it!' you want to tell him, but he has already gone far away. Do you see the absurdness of this?

"Friends, your life is like this garden - breathtakingly beautiful - but you will know that only if you stand still for a moment and appreciate it. Do not rush through it like madmen. Enjoy the flowers, taste the fruits, and marvel at the beauty! When you reach crossroads, do not fret over the choice. Pick one, and keep walking. All the roads and pathways are equally beautiful. They are just different. If you do not like what you see, turn around and go back. And if you cannot find the way back, keep walking till the next crossroads. There is no destination for a walk in the garden. There is no finish line. You have been granted the privilege of spending a day in this beautiful place. Spend it well!"

Charvak waited for a moment to let the thoughts sink in. The writing was very good! He continued, "Before I say farewell and wish you luck, there's one last thing I want to say. You will all now start your careers. Through your life, you will change your jobs. You will change your professions. Your bosses, colleagues, customers, interests, passions, cars, clothes, everything will keep changing. Money will keep coming in and going out of your bank account. People will keep coming in and going out of your life. Old things will continuously be replaced by new things except for one thing! There is only one thing that will be with you throughout your life, and that is your self! You will be involved in hundreds of projects: projects related to work, projects regarding hobbies; your family, children, friends are all projects! But do you know what is the most important project you will ever work on? The one project that all other projects depend on? Your self! My friends, your self is the most important thing you have. It is your only possession that truly belongs to you. It is the only thing that will be with you till your dying breath and beyond. Take care to nurture it. Do not neglect it. There is nothing more important I can tell you than this!"

The phone rang. It was his receptionist.

91

"Sir, Asmi from the Marketing Division is here to meet you," she said.

"What for?" he asked. He did not remember any Asmi.

"She says Mr Sundaram told her to meet you regarding the speech."

"Let her in."

In the last six months of working in the same building, Asmi had never seen Charvak. She used to work on the fifth floor; his office was on the eighteenth. She opened the door and came in.

"Good afternoon, sir! Mr Sundaram said you wanted to see me."

He looked at her. Their eyes met. The same insolent eyes! He had met her before!

"You wrote the speech for me?" he asked.

"Yes," Asmi replied.

"It was beautiful!"

"Thank you, sir! I am glad you liked it!"

An awkward silence. She did not move or look away. He kept looking at her. Yet again, an unbreakable impasse!

"Was it not you who had proposed the theme of freedom for Menaka Park?" he asked breaking the impasse.

"Yes!"

He now remembered the day clearly.

"Sir, if I may ask, why did you hire me if you had disliked my idea of freedom so much?" she said.

"Who told you I disliked the idea?"

"Why would you tell us to get out if you had liked it?"

She was not afraid to be frank. He had instantly liked her then, and he liked her now. She was young and full of hope like so many people of her age. He could almost feel the innocence about her. He wondered how little she knew of the twisted and wicked world. "I liked your idea. I just did not like your boss!"

"Neither did I!"

92

They exchanged a smile.

"Very well! Thank you for the speech!"

"Thank you, sir!"

She turned around and started walking towards the door.

"Asmi?"

"Yes?"

He did not know why he had stopped her; he just wanted her to stay a little longer. "Your ideas! It is wonderful that you can think of them and believe in them at such a young age!" he said.

"Thank you, sir, but I cannot take full credit for them."

"Why? Where did you get them from?"

After wondering for a moment whether she should tell him, she said, "I often talk with my *guru* about life and freedom."

"Guru?" he asked suspiciously.

"I go to him for guidance. His name is Narayanswami. He lives in the university and…"

Charvak had stopped listening. Memories, consciously repressed and relegated to the darkest depths of the mind, can erupt without warning due to a trigger. Charvak remembered a day, from a long time ago, when he was sitting on a bench in the university garden under a giant, patriarchal banyan tree, mesmerised by the leaves dancing in the gentle breeze. He must have been around the same age then as the beautiful girl standing in front of him now. He had the same hopeful ideas about life and freedom. The scene from his memory faded, and he regained his composure. He looked at her and knew that she had seen his change of expression. She had seen, only for a moment, the composed, strong businessman mask drop from his face. She had seen behind the mask a young man looking at her with large eyes, with an expression that a child lost in a crowded street would have when he spots a familiar face.

He felt embarrassed at his display of weakness. When Asmi left, Charvak bent down and opened the lowest drawer of his desk. From a cardboard box inside, he took out a round golden-coloured wristwatch that had stopped ticking many years ago!

Chapter 7: The Grand Illusion

AGASTYA BREATHED A SIGH OF relief. The days leading up to his Ph.D. preliminary examination had kept him busy. His advisor, Professor Dr Richard Warnock, was not an easy man to please. Warnock won the Nobel Prize in Physics when he was only thirty-five for his discoveries of equations governing the oscillations of certain subatomic particles. He was an ambitious man and expected the same ambitiousness from his students. Although he was direct, too direct at times, and lacked all forms of social euphemisms and politeness, Agastya liked him. The two of them had a very healthy relationship with Warnock trusting Agastya with his work, and Agastya trusting Warnock with his guidance. Agastya was required to undergo the preliminary examination where he was evaluated for his competency and knowledge of the field before he could begin independent research. Now, having cleared the examination, he was to select a research topic and begin the process of original research that would culminate in his doctoral thesis.

"Motion of subatomic particles? Rate of expansion of the universe? Aren't all these things too abstract? Too big or too small to have any bearing on our lives?" Asmi often asked him.

"These are our feeble attempts to understand the universe!" he would say. He spoke of physics with a deeply felt affection and enthusiasm. For him, an elegant mathematical derivation was equivalent to a lovely poem, variables analogous to words, operations similar to grammar, statements to sentences, both the derivation and the poem offering the elation of discovering beauty and truth in symbols!

One day, Asmi asked Swamiji the question that had been bothering her for a while, "Freedom from what, Swamiji? I try to break free from my mind, but I don't understand. Am I and my mind not the same thing? No? If I am not my mind, and I am not my body, then who am I?"

Swamiji smiled. She had, for the first time, directly approached the fundamental question 'Who am I?'. They were sitting on one of the benches in the garden after their evening walk.

"Asmi, what you see around you - the trees, the ground, the people - all of these are only illusions. They are not real. They do not exist!"

"Then, what exists?" she asked.

"Only the ultimate truth! Reality, as we see it, is an illusion and does not exist. What exists are only vibrations that pervade space and time! We call these vibrations the *Brahman*! All material things in the world are only temporary manifestations of the eternal *Brahman*. Nothing in this material world is permanent. All of it arises out of the *Brahman* and will later dissolve back into the *Brahman*. All mentions of God you read about in the Upanishads refer to this *Brahman*!" Swamiji added, "The word *Brahman* is pronounced as 'Bhruh-mun'. Do not confuse it with *Brahma* the God or *Brahmin* the caste. The *Brahman*, formless and unattached, is the ultimate reality!"

"Agastya, how is this possible? The things I see and touch, are they not real? I cannot assimilate this thought. This is superstition! How am I to believe it?" she asked him. It was a lazy Sunday morning. She had just woken up and was sitting in the bed wearing an old t-shirt and pyjamas. He had finished dinner with his lab colleagues and returned back to his apartment.

"Sweetheart, I would like to tell you something but only if you promise me that you will listen patiently. You must understand the reasoning without frolicking to the conclusion"

She muttered some promise. Knowing well what was to come, she got up from the bed to make coffee; if she were to follow Agastya's train of thoughts, she needed to be alert.

Agastya started his explanation, "Modern science has made strange statements in the last century but nothing as outrageous as those that Quantum Physics makes. Quantum Physics says that reality does not exist on its own, but you create reality when you observe it! Let us take a moment to see how it reached these conclusions. For a long time, physicists had been debating whether light is made of particles or if it is a wave. Newton believed it was made of particles, while his contemporary Christiaan Huygens supported a wave theory of light. On the turn of the twentieth century, a consensus started building up within the scientific community that light has a dual nature; it is both particles and waves! Discoveries made by Max Planck and later built upon by Einstein confirmed this dual nature of light."

"So light is both particles and waves?" she asked to make sure she understood. She poured out the coffee in a mug, picked up an apple and a knife, and sat down at the table.

"Yes, but not only light! In his Ph.D. thesis, a physicist named De Broglie postulated that even electrons have this dual property. Until then, atoms and subatomic particles including electrons were believed to be solid balls of matter. Three years later, experimental physicists confirmed his hypothesis that electrons are also both particles and waves. A beam of electrons bouncing off a solid metal plate demonstrated diffraction, a property thought to belong only to waves, confirming that electrons exhibit what is now called wave-particle duality. But the shocking fact is

97

that wave-particle duality is not restricted to electrons but to all matter! Asmi, all matter is essentially formed out of waves!"

"You mean to say that the apple I am eating is a wave?"

"Yes! From the smallest subatomic particle to a Boeing 747, everything is a wave! Schrödinger developed an equation that represents particles of matter in their wave form. He unequivocally stated that all matter exists fundamentally as waves. A wave is not located at a precise point in space but is spread across like a hazy cloud. Is this not bizarre?" he asked.

She had been listening to him attentively and had followed him closely knowing that he had simplified things for her understanding. Yes, she had to admit, this was indeed bizarre.

He continued, "Scientists performed what is called the 'Double Slit Experiment', which is often referred to as the experiment of the century. The experiment begins by firing a beam of electrons using an electron gun at a screen on the wall. The electrons hit the screen forming small dots that can be observed in the lab. Now, a plate with two parallel slits is placed between the electron gun and the screen. If electrons were only particles, you would see two clear lines on the screen corresponding to the two slits. But instead, since they are waves, you see an interference pattern on the screen similar to the ripples you would see in a pond if you threw two stones in it. This again proves that electrons, and indeed all matter, behave like waves. So far so good?"

"Yes!" She had followed him till here.

"Coming to the strangest part, now, instead of a beam, only one single electron is fired. What do you expect happens? The single electron should pass through one of the two slits and leave a dot where it hits the screen. But what you see is not a dot but the same interference pattern we get for a beam of electrons! This can happen only if the single electron passed simultaneously through both the slits and interfered with itself to cause this pattern! How can this happen? After multiple runs of the experiment and years of analysis, physicists reached the conclusion that the electron indeed passes through both the slits simultaneously creating the interference pattern!"

"Wait! Are you saying that the electron passes through both the slits at the same time? That it exists at two places at once?" she asked incredulously.

"Yes, Asmi, because it is a wave!"

Asmi had finished the apple and was still hungry. She took a bowl and filled it with cornflakes and milk. "Agastya, so basically you are telling me that not just electrons but all matter is formed out of waves!"

"Yes, matter is formed, at the most fundamental level, out of nothing but vibrations! This is the basis of Quantum Physics!"

"Swamiji said the same thing: everything in this world is a manifestation of *Brahman*!"

"Vedanta philosophers reached these conclusions thousands of years ago through the depth of their contemplative introspection. Modern physics has reached these conclusions through the rigor of the scientific method. Their means and goals were very different. Although the conclusions are similar, they are still different things, and I will not encourage you to draw hasty parallels between Vedanta and Quantum Physics..."

"But there are parallels, right? These parallels are what attracted your heroes of science like Schrödinger and Niels Bohr to the wisdom of the Upanishads?"

"Yes, that is true! These physicists who developed the fundamentals of Quantum Mechanics were avid readers of Vedanta!"

It was past midnight in California. Agastya was sleepy and Asmi would soon have to figure out what to do for lunch.

"Agastya, I miss you! Will you come for Namita's wedding?"

"I miss you too! Yes, I spoke to Warnock today morning. I will come for a few days." He could almost hear her smile.

"Good night!" she said and hung up.

Asmi went to see Swamiji in the afternoon; she had to clear her thoughts. She told him about her conversation with Agastya about Quantum Physics and wave-particle duality.

"Asmi, do you know what Om stands for?" Swamiji asked.

Om was the single-syllable word that was said before the beginning of every Hindu prayer. It was a mantra on its own. It was the most sacred symbol in Hindu religion and culture. She said Om every morning before starting meditation and had chanted it hundreds of times but did not know what it meant.

"No, what does it stand for?" she said.

"Vedanta says that reality exists as vibrations and the music of these vibrations pervades the universe. Everything, from electrons to galaxies, dances to the tune of this cosmic music. Om represents the music of the fundamental vibration. It represents the sound that was produced when the first of these unmanifested vibrations manifested itself as reality. Om is the sacred sound. Om is the music of the *Brahman!*"

"So when we chant Om, we invoke the *Brahman* to become one with it?" she asked with a questioning furrow on her eyebrows.

"You are already one with the *Brahman*. You are the *Brahman*. Every atom in your body is the *Brahman*. You only have to realise it! When you realise that you are the one stainless reality, that you are beyond the chains of causality, that you are God Himself, you attain *Moksha,* the ultimate freedom!"

"Swamiji, we have spoken so much about freedom, but do you know any living person, a person who walks and talks, who has attained it? Have you attained *Moksha*? Are you liberated?"

"No, Asmi, I have not attained *Moksha,* but I have met someone who has. I have spoken to him. He has spoken to me."

"Who? Where did you meet him?"

"The *Saptarishis!* I met one of them in the heart of the Himalayas!"

Asmi stood in the office lobby patiently waiting for the elevator.

"How much of our lives do we spend simply waiting?" she thought. "Waiting for the bus to arrive, waiting for the phone to connect, waiting for someone to turn up, waiting for the tea to boil, waiting to fall asleep, waiting to grow up, waiting to get married, waiting for a promotion, waiting to have a child, waiting for the child to grow up, waiting for the child to get married..."

She was glad that the arrival of the elevator put a brake on her chain of thoughts. It was almost five in the evening and most people were leaving office. It was a Friday, and she looked forward to the weekend. She would get up late, laze in the bed, catch up on her reading, and meet some friends. Only on weekends could she talk at length with Agastya, maybe even video-chat with him. There were only two weeks left for him to come. After stopping at a couple of floors in between, the elevator finally reached the top floor. Asmi went inside the office and sat down in the reception room. The attractive receptionist looked at her and smiled; the condescension in her gaze had mellowed after each successive visit.

"He is in a meeting with someone. You might have to wait for a while," she said.

"Sure!"

Rachana had been the receptionist for almost two years now. She had been a model before she was hired for this job. She had appeared on a couple of print advertisements and once for a TV advertisement, but by and large, her modelling career had been unsuccessful. Her work as the receptionist was simple: she had to look pretty, speak charmingly, answer calls, and reply to emails for appointment requests. The door opened and an old man, aged around sixty, came out. Asmi looked at him with mild surprise. He seemed completely out of place in the corporate environment of the office. He wore a faded white shirt and had a provincial uncouth air about him. As he came out of the door, she heard Charvak say, "Ramu *kaka*, please inform mother about this."

Ramesh Kadam, whom Charvak called Ramu *kaka*, had no formal designation in the organisation. Ramesh's father had worked as a driver for Vallabh Satyashah. Ramesh Kadam and Ravindra Satyashah grew up together. When they were children, they often played together and were good friends. However, Ravindra inherited the business empire, while Ramesh inherited the job of a driver. Ravindra sent Ramesh to a local business school to get a degree, but he failed the examinations. Not giving up hope, he gave Ramesh odd tasks to do around the house. Ramesh did them efficiently. Over time, he became the off-the-books troubleshooter for the Satyashah family. He kept in touch with local politicians, criminals, police officers, and government officials and was exceedingly good at dealing with their lot. Although he was never formally employed by any of the Satyashah companies, he held an unspoken position of influence in the organisation. He had never married and lived alone in the humble quarters behind the Satyashah Mansion. He had been a close confidant of Ravindra Satyashah and had been with the family for so long that he was almost a part of it. When Charvak took over the responsibilities of the business after his father's death, Ramesh had been of immense help. The senior management of the Group disliked Ramesh and never approved of his involvement in the affairs of the company. They pressurised young Charvak to remove Ramesh from any position of influence. However, during the first year of Charvak's management, a massive labour strike affected all their manufacturing units. Ramesh's role in diffusing this strike had been so indispensable that nobody raised any protests after that. The word *kaka* meant uncle.

Asmi entered the office.

"Hello, Asmi, please sit down!" Charvak said. He seemed relaxed and a lot less formal than their previous meetings. He shuffled around some files on his desk and looked up. "Will you have some tea?" he offered. Without waiting for her reply, he picked up the phone and instructed someone to send tea. "How are you?" he asked, this time waiting for her reply.

"I am doing well, sir! Thank you!"

"Asmi, there is some work for you. The team at Business Forum, the magazine, wants to publish a story on me in their next month's issue. I had initially refused, because I did not have time for an interview. But they sent over a list of questions and said they would publish the story if we answer those questions for them." Giving her a list of questions printed on an A4 sheet of paper, he added, "I want you to compose answers to these questions. I really liked the speech you wrote, and I think you are the right person for this."

"It would be my pleasure," she said. She was surprised at the request. Such tasks would usually be passed to Sundaram, and he would get the work done from his team. They were general questions about his beliefs, his style of working, his childhood, what motivated him etc.

"Sir, I would be able to answer some of these questions by talking to people in the organisation. But for others, which are more personal, I am afraid I would need a bit of your time."

"How much time?" he asked.

"Maybe an hour!"

He looked at the clock mounted on the wall. It was 530 in the evening. "I have a meeting now. Would you mind staying back for a while? We can speak about the questions after my meeting."

"Sure!"

"Great! You can go back to your desk. I will call you."

Asmi came out of the office and saw some people waiting in the reception room. They went inside as she came out. The article for the magazine was a part of a series they did on successful businessmen. Some of the questions were regarding Charvak's working style, timings, and habits. She thought she could talk to Rachana about these.

"Rachana, do you mind helping me out a bit?" she asked.

Asmi told Rachana about the article and asked her a few questions. What are his usual work timings? How many visitors does he get daily? How often does she see him upset or stressed? Asmi jotted down a few things and thanked her. As she turned to leave, Rachana spoke, "Asmi?"

"Yes?"

"Nothing! Just be careful!"

In the elevator ride down, Asmi wondered what Rachana had meant. She had heard stories about Charvak's playboy lifestyle, his hedonism, and his alleged objectification of women. She had heard he slept on a regular basis with attractive models and movie starlets. She looked at herself in the mirror on the inside of the elevator. She was in her regular office attire of a formal white shirt and black trousers. She did not think herself to be particularly attractive. She did not, even for a moment, consider herself to be in the same situation as those models and starlets. It was unusual for him to directly reach out to her for this work, but he said he thought of her because of the speech she wrote, and his compliment for the speech had been genuine. She sat down at her desk and started working on the questions. Around 715, Charvak called her, and she went up to his office. Rachana was not there and had probably left for the day. She knocked on the door and entered.

"It's a bit late to be working in the office, don't you think?" he said. "It will take us some time to answer all the questions. Why don't we do this over dinner? Unless you have other plans, of course!"

She looked at him. The expression on his face was friendly and sincere. "Would that not be a bit removed from protocol?" she asked.

He leaned back in his chair and said, "Asmi, I am tired of this office. I know you would be wondering why I am asking you out for dinner. It is just that, while I am in here, I have a lot of things on my mind. If we go out, I can relax, be myself, and give you more honest answers. Let's go!"

The Aurea was an unabashedly opulent revolving restaurant on the top floor of The Palazzo hotel. She had never been there. It was by far the most exclusive and expensive restaurant in the city. It was about ten minutes from the office, and they had been driven there in his unnecessarily long, silver Rolls Royce. As they entered the hotel, Asmi gawked at the grandeur. They were greeted at the restaurant entrance by an elegant, elderly manager who made a small bow to her and wished her a pleasant evening in a tone full of deepest courtesy. She muttered a thank you and closed her eyes feeling overwhelmed with the lavishness. She looked at Charvak and saw him move around with the ease of a man walking in his own house. The manager asked her politely which table she would like to sit at. Without much thought, she indicated a table in the corner. The assistant manager who had been following behind quickly went to the table and removed the 'Reserved' tag that had been kept on it; they would accommodate the guests who had reserved that table elsewhere. He held the chair for Asmi to sit down. Charvak sat across her. A couple of waiters came and quickly put 'Reserved' tags on all immediately adjacent tables and removed the cutlery and plates from them. Nobody sat on tables adjacent to Charvak Satyashah - that was the standard protocol. When they had settled down, the chef de cuisine came over, introduced himself, and presented a leather-bound menu card to them. He spoke in a refined accent, gave them a quick explanation about the dishes they would be happy to serve, and then receded into the background waiting for them to make their selection.

"What would you like to have?" Charvak asked.

She opened the menu card and looked at the long list. "What will you have?" she asked weakly.

Sensing her discomfort, he smiled and said, "Why don't we let the chef decide for us? I am sure he will serve us something edible!"

She nodded.

"Do you eat non-vegetarian food?"

"No."

"Would you like some wine?"

"No."

On his signal, the chef came over. While Charvak spoke to him, Asmi composed herself. She had not been prepared for this. Coming from conservative rural India, she had never been in the midst of such luxury before.

"Will you not have some wine, madam? We have an excellent collection of exquisite French wines. Would you like to try?" the chef offered.

"Umm... ok! Thank you!" she replied not having the will to refuse.

The whole charade had taken up some time. Now that it was over, they were left alone to themselves. Except for a waiter standing attentively at a distance, everyone else had gone back to work. Asmi relaxed and let out a deep breath. She looked around and noticed the finer details of the restaurant for the first time. When they sat down at the table, she had seen from the window a bridge lit up in splashes of yellow and red. The revolving restaurant had shifted by a couple of degrees, and she could now see a tall skyscraper at a distance.

"It is the first time that I am coming to a revolving restaurant," she said opening the conversation.

"Do you like it?"

"It is fascinating!"

"Do you know what was the first revolving construction in the world? It was a revolving dining area the Roman Emperor Nero built atop his luxurious palace called Domus Aurea."

"Is that why you named this restaurant Aurea after the palace?"

"I do not know much about Nero or Roman history. The marketing team came up with the name. It seems Nero was an emperor who was rich and powerful and enjoyed luxury. These brats from the media accuse me of my lavish lifestyle, but I am not ashamed of the fact that I am rich and powerful and enjoy luxury too! In a way, I identify with Nero and thought this was an apt name!"

Asmi looked at him and asked in a careful voice, "Did your marketing team also tell you that Nero committed suicide?"

Charvak swirled his eyes towards her. No, he had not known that Nero committed suicide, and the revelation had shocked him, but he quickly recovered. A waiter came and served them soup. He told them it was *bhendi* or okra soup prepared in a traditional Nigerian recipe. Asmi missed the *bharli bhendi* Aai used to make. She had never had a *bhendi* soup before. She tasted it; it was delightful!

"Do you like history?" he asked.

"Yes, I used to like history a lot in my college days!"

"Is that how you know about Nero?"

Asmi smiled to herself. She had studied history at a local college in a nearby town close to the Wadi. The college was severely understaffed and had taught her nothing; she did not remember even one faculty member whom she looked up to! Whatever she knew, she had taught herself by reading books. "I came across Nero somewhere in my reading. I like to read," she explained.

"What do you like to read?"

"Well, presently, I am reading philosophy. Coming to think of it, I now remember how I came across Nero. I read a book about Seneca, the Roman philosopher, a wise man who served as the tutor and imperial advisor to Nero. Somewhere in that book, I read about Nero's suicide."

"Why did Nero commit suicide?"

"His decadent lifestyle led him to commit some serious political mistakes."

"But if Seneca, his advisor, was a wise man as you say, why did he not counsel Nero and prevent the suicide?"

"They had a complicated relationship. During Nero's early years, Seneca was almost a *guru* to him. Under Seneca's tutorship, Nero ruled competently. But Nero got carried away under influence from other advisors at court and had a falling out with Seneca. They parted ways. Without Seneca's guidance, Nero lost himself in decadence!"

The chef came up to the table to see if they had finished the soup. The next course was ready. "How was the soup, sir?" he asked respectfully.

Charvak was lost in his thoughts and did not hear the chef who stood there waiting for a response.

"Thank you! It was delicious!" Asmi replied.

With a bow, he left. A waiter came and cleared the soup bowls. Charvak remained still. Her story had stirred something deep inside him. He remembered the last time he had seen his

108

guru almost twelve years ago. They had sat on the bench under the giant banyan tree. Asmi glanced at her watch. It was already late, and she had work to do. She took out the list of questions from her bag.

"Sir, should we start?" she said looking at the list. He did not respond; he was clearly not interested in that list.

"Asmi?"

"Yes?"

"How is Swamiji? Does he ever speak about me?"

She looked at him quizzically. "No," she answered and then added, "Do you know him?"

A waiter came and arranged clean plates along with the next course, an assortment of delectable kebabs. He returned to refill their wine glasses. Her question remained unanswered.

"Sir..." she started speaking but he interrupted her.

"Not here! Outside of the office, please call me Charvak!" he said simply as a matter of fact.

"When I worked with Fernandes Media, we had tried really hard to get the project for marketing and advertising for The Palazzo," she said looking around.

"Was that your first job?" He noticed the curves of her slender body accentuated by the plain white shirt she was wearing. He looked at her sensual lips and felt something in the pit of his stomach. He shook his head and wondered if it was the wine having its effect.

"Yes, that was my first job."

"You are not from Mumbai, are you?"

"No. I am from a small town in Konkan. We call it the Wadi."

"How did you end up here?"

The ambient light was dim, and the mood was relaxed. She deliberated with herself whether she should tell him; it was not an appropriate story to narrate to your boss, but the two glasses of wine had diminished the social distance between them. She told him her story of leaving behind the narrow lanes of the Wadi and the narrower minds of its inhabitants. Of wanting to do engineering and the crack in the door. Shweta's twisted mouth. Her work at Fernandes Media. Despair, loneliness, and the abandoned suicide note. Her meeting Swamiji. She did not tell him about the golden-scaled dragon or about Agastya. She did not think he would understand; after all, Charvak did not belong to her world. Their glasses were refilled again. A chef's special consisting of Burmese noodles in coconut sauce generously flavoured with garlic, red chillies, and caramelised onions was served for main course.

Charvak listened to her intently. He admired her easy frankness, which stood in stark contrast to his own modulated behaviour. Since years, he had been training himself to be a leader. He believed that a great leader projects and epitomises strength at all times. Being strong meant standing upright in the face of battle. But, all this while, he had also believed that being strong meant not showing your vulnerabilities to others, because vulnerabilities were signs of incompetence and weakness! He had carefully developed his image of a supremely confident leader, and to keep up and sustain this image, he had to wear his mask of strength at all times. He went around doing things with bravado, eliminating any hint of vulnerabilities, and people around him followed his example and learned to do the same thing. He dealt with hundreds of people every day. His subordinate CXOs of individual companies of the Group, division heads, employees, customers, partners, politicians, bureaucrats, servants, acquaintances, relatives, friends, prostitutes, the list could go on. All these people wore a façade that magnified their strengths and hid their weaknesses.

He looked at Asmi across the table. She was innocently toying with the last remaining noodles in her plate. She had told him things that were deeply personal. She had spoken of her most intimate thoughts, and she had done this with confidence in a genuine honest manner without worrying, even for a moment, how it would make her look. He realised, at that instant, that he was looking at a woman who wore no façade, who was truly authentic to herself, and accepted herself, every part of her, the way she was, without hiding any of it! He realised, then, that real confidence came when you wholeheartedly embraced your weaknesses and acknowledged them as your own instead of hiding them from others or, worse, from yourself! He felt a deep respect for her for doing something he had never been able to do. By being so completely genuine, without pretense or mask, she had shown him that confidence was not about exhibiting your commendable parts while stowing away the unseemly ones; it was about loving yourself, showing yourself to others completely, without shame or guilt, embracing yourself the way you truly are, without censoring or moderating your image for others, and staying authentic to your true self!

After the waiter cleared the plates, the chef came with dessert: honey and date ice cream made of dates specially imported from Arabia and honey sourced from Turkey. They enjoyed the ice-cream in silence. The list of questions printed on the A4 sheet still lay there on the table. Asmi glanced at the watch. It was a few minutes past midnight.

"Charvak, when shall we do these questions?" she said remembering not to address him as 'sir' outside the office.

He smiled but did not answer and waved off the question with a gesture.

They had finished the food. The chef came to ask them if they wanted anything else. They were the only ones left in the restaurant. They got up to leave. The manager was waiting at the door. He usually left once the last order for the day was taken, but today he had to wait back. He knew how these dinners ended; it was not the first time that the boss had come with a date. When Asmi went to use the restroom, the manager came up to Charvak and said, "Sir, if you wish, your suite is ready!"

Charvak looked at him and said feebly, "Make arrangements for a car to drop her home."

"Yes, sir!"

"And, inform me when she reaches back safely!"

"Yes, sir!"

Chapter 8: Neti Neti

"ASMI, WHEN DID YOU CHANGE your job?" Neha asked excitedly. "Why didn't you tell me?"

It had been a long while since they last spoke. Neha was the only extant link Asmi had with her family. That day, when Baba came home and saw Aai sitting and crying in a corner, he forbade her to speak to Asmi again.

"Our daughter does not exist for us anymore!" he firmly declared.

Aai did not call Asmi again and neither did Asmi call her. Neha made helpless attempts to remain in touch.

"Asmi, why don't you come and visit us? No? All right! I will come to Mumbai to see you!"

Asmi was waiting at the bus stand to receive Neha. The crowded terminal was bustling with morning activity. A battered red bus drove in. Neha climbed down from it and hugged Asmi tightly. They had shared a healthy sibling relationship in their childhood but had never been particularly close to each other. Their temperaments and interests were very different. Neha had always been a pragmatic person, grounded in practicality, and had no time or patience for idle dreams. Her childhood had been filled with studies and playing girly games with her friends. Singing was the only hobby she ever had. Aside from performing on stage with her music group, she had never harboured any other ambitions. It was a Friday, and Asmi had taken the day off. Neha would stay with her for two days and take the afternoon bus back on Sunday. They got into a taxi.

On the way to her house, Asmi pointed to a tall building and said, "I work there!"

"Wow! That looks like a really fancy office! Can I see it?"

"Sure. Let's drop your bag home. After you freshen up, we will go to see my office!"

After leaving Fernandes Media, Asmi had moved into a new apartment, a more recent construction in a better locality closer to her office.

Asmi entered Neha's details in the register at the entrance of the office building. Due to security restrictions, she was not able to show Neha her desk, not even the floor where she worked, but she took her to the reception lobby and the cafeteria on the ground floor. As they walked in, Asmi could see the astonishment on her sister's face. Neha looked around at the enormous lobby, which was nothing like anything she had seen before. There was an indoor garden next to the reception desks. Many people, smartly dressed men and women, walked around briskly carrying laptops and folders. There was a giant screen on one side showing a video about the Satyashah Group.

"Asmi, what work do you do here?"

Asmi explained what she did as they proceeded towards the cafeteria. It was almost lunchtime. "Shall we have lunch here?" Asmi asked.

Neha looked around uncomfortably. She felt awkward and jarringly conscious of her small-town bearings. Her *salwar kurta* dress, one of the better ones she had, looked old fashioned and shabby in comparison to what others were wearing. Her rural hairstyle with simple braids was a straight giveaway that she did not belong there. She looked at Asmi who moved around effortlessly, almost gracefully!

"Can we go somewhere else?" Neha asked meekly.

"Sure. What would you like to have?"

"Anything. You decide!"

They went to a nice Italian place overlooking the sea. As they settled down in their seats, a waiter came, poured out water in their glasses, and kept a menu card on the table. They decided to order pasta and pizza. The captain came with a notepad to take their order. He looked intimidating in his black suit and red tie.

"Good afternoon! What can I get for you?" he asked.

Asmi spoke to him with ease in a friendly, pleasant manner and told him what they wanted. Neha wondered if she knew anyone from the Wadi who would be as comfortable as Asmi in a situation like this: a big city, a fancy restaurant, and a towering man wearing a suit! After lunch, they went to a nearby ice-cream shop.

"What will you have?" Asmi asked.

Neha read through the flavours printed on the menu card along with their prices and said, "Should we go somewhere else?"

"Why? They have really good ice-cream!"

"It's expensive!" Neha blurted out hesitatingly.

"Neha, this is Mumbai! It will be expensive. Trust me, it's delicious. Come on, just pick a flavour!"

Neha offered to pay, but Asmi refused.

They went to the university in the evening. Asmi introduced Neha to Swamiji, and the two sisters went for a walk on the campus. They had not had a heart-to-heart conversation since the day Asmi left the Wadi. Their infrequent phone conversations had been factual and devoid of emotions; they told each other what happened in their lives, but they did not speak about how they felt about those things. On that day, walking amongst pathways lined with trees, talking face to face instead of talking into an electronic device, Asmi told Neha about her feelings for the first time. She told her about the resentment she harboured against society. She did not tell her about the suicide note, but she told her about her falling out with Shweta. She spoke about Fernandes, her friends Varun and Namita, and her new job. She

115

told her about the speech she wrote for Charvak, and their lunch at the lavish Aurea. She spoke about Agastya and Swamiji, and her practice of meditation. Neha loved listening to Asmi sharing details of her life, but she was quiet and stared at the path ahead. What could she tell Asmi? Her life had been practically the same for years, and Asmi knew all about it.

As they started walking back, Neha asked her, "What shall we do for dinner?"

"What would you like?" Asmi asked.

"No, it is your turn! What would you like?"

Asmi laughed and said, "You know what I would really like? The *bharli bhendi* Aai makes!"

"I can make it the exact same way! Let me cook dinner for you!"

After a delicious home cooked dinner, they sat in the balcony enjoying the cool breeze. Neha looked at her little sister. Asmi was wearing a cotton three-fourths with a sleeveless pale-yellow t-shirt.

"Asmi, I am very happy for you!" Neha said, "You did the right thing by leaving your life in the Wadi! I did not realise it then. I feel ashamed that I could not understand or support you in any way. I was just a helpless bystander. But I am sure of it now that you did the right thing!"

"Thank you, Neha!"

"We were so similar two years ago, you and I. Stuck in *Samsara*, the trap of life, busy fulfilling expectations, you were like any other woman in the Wadi. But you shunned all that and moved so far ahead in life! You have become so confident! You have a wonderful job and are probably earning more money than what Baba earns now at his age! I am so proud of you!"

Next day, they spent the afternoon at a newly opened shopping mall. They went for dinner to a garden restaurant with Varun and Namita. Asmi had deliberately selected it, because on

116

Saturdays, they had live music consisting of Hindi *ghazals,* which Neha was very fond of. Halfway through the dinner, Asmi brought up the topic of Neha's singing and told Varun and Namita how well she sang. The three of them urged Neha to sing. Neha reluctantly agreed. Asmi went with her to the stage and announced to the crowd that her sister would like to sing for them. Neha took the microphone in her jittery hands. It had been years since she last performed on stage. She still used to sing at small functions in the Wadi but always for an audience whom she knew personally. Looking at anonymous faces waiting to hear her made her nervous, but as soon as the first note found expression in her voice, all the nervousness disappeared. She sang a slow, melodious *ghazal* reminiscent of longing and sadness. Her voice was charged with emotion. As she finished, there was a loud applause from the crowd. With closed eyes and a smile on her lips, Neha soaked it in. She would remember that day for a long time to come!

It was late afternoon, almost time for tea, when Charvak walked into the office. He crashed into his plush chair and cursed angrily under his breath. He was supposed to come two hours earlier, and Rachana had scheduled meetings for him. There were visitors waiting in the reception area outside, but he was in no mood to entertain them. It was the eighty-fifth birth anniversary of his grandfather Vallabh Satyashah. After attending a small formal function in the office that morning, he had gone home for lunch with the extended Satyashah family. He hated these family gatherings. His mother, Sumitra Satyashah, had invited Charvak's uncle and his family: Manoj, who was Ravindra's younger brother; Poonam, his wife; Devika, their daughter; and Prateek, their son. The two families shared a frigid relationship. In the last thirty years since Vallabh died, they had met only during board meetings, corporate functions, and such obligatory familial

117

occasions. Ravindra's death and Charvak's succession had only exacerbated the conflict.

Ravindra and Manoj were born exactly six years apart and had the same date as their birthday. Their mother died three years after Manoj was born leaving Vallabh alone with two young children, a fledgling textile mill located outside the city, and a burning ambition. Vallabh raised his two sons well. On attaining the appropriate age, Ravindra married Charvak's mother, Sumitra, and a few years later, Manoj married Poonam. When Vallabh Satyashah's illustrious life abruptly ended due to a stroke, Ravindra was 32 and Manoj was 26. For 26 years, the two brothers had celebrated every single birthday together, but they would never do that again. Manoj went to London to study Business Management, and Ravindra took over the affairs of the Satyashah Group of Companies. Charvak was only 6 years old at that time, but he still remembered going to the airport to say goodbye to Manoj *kaka*, Poonam *kaki*, and a two-year-old Devika.

Charvak dialled Rachana and said, "Send them all back. I cannot see anyone today!"

"But sir, they have been waiting for quite some time!"

He did not reply to her question and simply hung up the phone. She should have learned by now not to make him repeat instructions, he thought. He glanced at the pile of documents awaiting his perusal and approval on the desk. Next to them, lay the latest issue of Business Forum. On its cover was a full-page photograph of him and, below that, a bold caption that read: 'Is Charvak Satyashah the businessman of the decade?' He took the magazine and flipped it open. The article claimed to be an exclusive interview with him. He remembered the list of questions and his subsequent dinner with Asmi. She had done a pretty good job at answering the questions without his help. He picked up the phone and told Rachana to send Asmi to his office. When Asmi stepped into the reception, Rachana gave her a caustic look before beckoning her to go inside.

"Hello, Asmi!" he greeted.

"Good evening, sir!"

Pointing to the magazine, he remarked, "You have done a fine job!"

"Thank you!"

"How is it going?"

"Good! I just finished some work for Menaka Park."

"Have you visited the site?"

"No, sir, I haven't, but I would love to go there!"

"That's great, because I am just about to go there now. Would you like to come along?" he offered.

"I am sorry, but I have to go somewhere in the evening."

His face fell. After the family lunch, he had no appetite for work and had really wanted to have her company.

Sensing his disappointment, she added, "I have to meet Swamiji. I don't want to cancel that!"

"Well, another time then!" he said with a resigned smile.

Asmi went to the university directly from office. She had been practising meditation regularly every morning and had become proficient at holding her mind steady. She would wake up, make herself a cup of tea, and have a bath. After that, she would meditate sitting on the floor in a cross-legged position. Initially, she had used mental imagery to focus her thoughts. She would imagine the steady flame of a candle, which would flicker whenever a thought emerged on the canvas of her mind; she would concentrate and try her best to keep the flame steady without flickering. Gradually, on Swamiji's advice, she did away with the mental imagery. She could now sit motionless with an absolutely still mind for 15-20 minutes.

"What should I do now, Swamiji?" she asked. She was excited about her progress. A month ago, she could hardly hold her mind steady even for a minute.

Swamiji replied, "What you have achieved is called *Manolaya*, a temporary stillness of thought, and this is the first stage of meditation. You have already progressed a lot, my child, but you must not stop here. There is nothing to be gained in stilling your thoughts alone, is there? You must use this steadiness of mind to ask yourself the fundamental question '*Koham?* Who am I?' and continue this self-enquiry till you find the answer. The answer is the ultimate truth!"

They were sitting on the *katta* outside the university canteen. It was the same *katta* where Swamiji, as young Narayan in his college days, had given his first discourses on philosophy.

"How do I find the answer to that question?" she asked.

"There are many methods, but the most direct and efficient of those, the one most suitable for you, is *atma vichara*, the method of self-enquiry. You have experienced *Manolaya*. Ask yourself who experienced it? When you get thoughts, who gets them? Who feels hungry? Who feels lonely? Who is the one feeling these things?" he asked.

"I feel them!" she said cautiously.

"And who are you?"

Asmi did not respond. She had tried answering this question before and failed. She was tired of trying again and again.

Swamiji continued, "When you introduce yourself, what do you say? I am Asmi; but Asmi is just a name! It is just a word that society gave you for conveniently addressing you. You mention your profession saying you are a content writer, an engineer, or a doctor; but does your work and profession give you an identity?"

Making an attempt to answer, she said, "No, I am much more than my name and place in society. But why am I not my body? My brain, heart, limbs, and organs? My brain thinks and feels

120

owing to the neurological circuitry in it. That is also how it stores memories. It is supported by my physiological system of organs, bones, and tissues. I am my body!"

Swamiji took her hand and, touching a point on her palm with his finger, said, "Imagine this cell. It is a part of your skin. Is this cell you?"

"Yes, it is a part of me!"

"Now, imagine I remove this cell from your hand and keep it on the table. The cell starts walking around on its own. Is it still you?"

"Maybe, yes!"

"Now, if a bird swoops down from the tree and eats that cell, the cell will become a part of the bird. Will it still be you?"

"Maybe, no, not anymore!"

"Asmi, your physical body is just a collection of billions of cells. Each of those cells is a living being in its own right. Cells in your body continuously die and get replaced by newer ones. Due to this continuous replacement, it is likely that the body you have now is composed of an entirely different set of cells than your body a few years ago. If you have a completely different body today than what you had then, how can you say you are still the same person?"

She was aware of the Ship of Theseus paradox. She said, "I am still the same person I was a few years ago, because I still have the memories I had then. I think the same thoughts. I know the same things. I have lived in a continuum without interruptions. So, even if every cell in my body has changed, I am still the same person, because my memories and thoughts have remained intact!"

"If I clone you, and this clone has the same memories and thoughts, would you and the clone be the same person? You two would have the same name, memories, thoughts, and feelings, but would you have the same identity? A single ego?"

"We would be different people," she conceded.

Asmi was exasperated. She had discussed this question endlessly with Swamiji many times. Every time, the discussion went the same way. He asked her 'Who are you?' and she did her best to come up with answers. She had proposed dozens of different explanations, but he had shot down each one of them with a logical argument that she could find no fault in. Frustrated with repeating the same cycle over and over again, she said in a high-pitched voice that barely concealed her irritation, "I follow your reasoning. I know I am not my physical body. I know I am not my thoughts and memories. I know I am not formed out of my name, profession, or societal relationships. What else do you want me to say? I am not this, and I am not that! If I am none of these things, then nothing remains! There is no answer!"

She calmed down and quickly apologised for the outburst, but Swamiji did not seem offended. He seemed rather amused and was smiling at her. In a mocking voice, he said, "*Neti neti*! I am not this, and I am not that! Then who are you?"

Like the water flowing downhill has only one place to go, like a falling apple can fall in only one direction, as if there was only one natural answer, almost as if someone put that answer on her lips, she said involuntarily and automatically, "I am not this, and I am not that. I am nothing! I do not exist!"

She was shocked by her statement, but she knew that it was the answer he had been waiting for all along.

Looking at her tenderly, with pride in his eyes, he said, "Yes, Asmi, you are right! You do not exist! Your ego, your 'I', is only an illusion! You are none of the things that you normally identify yourself with. Your name, personality, memories, thoughts, emotions, feelings, profession, designation are only appendages. Your physical body is only an accessory. Wrongly identifying your true self with this false illusion of an ego is the root of all suffering! Ignorance about the true nature of the self is what binds you to *Samsara,* the trap of life! Dispel this ignorance, realise that the ego is only an illusion, and you will achieve *Moksha,* the ultimate liberation!"

The sun had set, and it was getting dark. They had been sitting on the *katta* for a long time. As they started walking back towards his office, Swamiji told Asmi a beautiful Zen story: "There was an immensely strong and skilled wrestler in Japan named Onami, which meant 'great waves'. In private, he defeated his master, but in public, even his pupils could throw him. He went to see a famous Zen master at a nearby temple. The master heard his troubles and said, 'Your name is Great Waves! Stay in this temple tonight and meditate. Imagine you are the waves of the great ocean. Forget that you are a wrestler. Become those waves and you will become the greatest wrestler ever!' Onami sat in meditation but many thoughts disturbed him. He persisted, and slowly he began to think only of the waves. Gradually, the waves became larger and larger. They swept away all the flowers and the vases. They swept away even the bronze Buddha in the shrine. By the break of dawn, Onami had become the ocean! When the master came in the morning, he saw Onami with a light smile on his face. No one ever defeated Onami again!

"Asmi, this is a story of losing your ego. Everyone, like Onami, is immensely strong, but they do not know it. They think they are weak and find synthetic ways of feeling strong. They think power, money, recognition, and possessions will make them strong. Onami was strong in private, because in private, he was himself. In public, he was easily defeated, because he was afraid of being judged. He was afraid of being judged, because judgment disturbed his ego. We are all great waves of the ocean, but what happens when the wave forgets that she is a part of the ocean? She becomes weak and powerless. She thinks she exists independently, becomes selfish, and identifies with an ego. Once she has an ego, she fears being judged and forgets that she is not a mere ripple of water but the mighty ocean itself! This is what had happened to Onami! When the wave drops her ego, she loses her weakness, and she becomes the infinitely powerful ocean!"

They had reached the library. Asmi waited outside the entrance and did not go in.

"Swamiji, just one more thing! The correct answer to the question 'Who am I?' is 'I am the *Brahman*', isn't it?" she asked.

"Yes! The correct answer to the question '*Koham?* Who am I?' is '*Aham Brahmasmi!* I am the Brahman!'"

"I know the answer, but it doesn't help me!"

"Because knowing, understanding, and realising are very different things, aren't they? Tomorrow, if Agastya tells you the equation 'E = mc^2', you will ask him to explain it to you. He would say, 'It is very simple. It means that energy is equal to mass multiplied by the square of the speed of light'. Now, you know the equation, but does it mean you have understood it?"

"All right! Now that I know I am *Brahman,* how do I fully understand and realise it?"

"Keep practicing meditation and self-enquiry. Focus your mind inwards and ask yourself '*Koham?* Who am I?'. Persist in your efforts, and one by one, the false appendages of your ego will drop away. When, at last, your ego itself drops away, your true self will shine forth. You will realise that you are *Brahman*, that you are God! When that happens, all the frailties of human nature that arose because you believed in the illusion of the ego will also disappear. Like Onami, you will become one with the universe!"

It was almost 10 o'clock in the night when she reached back home. As she fished out the keys to open the door, she saw a woman and a boy sitting on the staircase. They got up when they saw her. The woman was wearing an impoverished *saree.* The boy, probably her son, was in his late teens and hid shyly behind his mother.

With folded hands conveying respect, the woman spoke, "Asmi *tai*, Neha *tai* gave me your address. This is my son. He has passed his twelfth standard examination."

Hearing the conversation, Mrs Deshmukh, Asmi's neighbour, opened the door and said, "They have been waiting here since afternoon!" The Deshmukhs were an elderly couple that lived in the house opposite. They were friendly and accommodating neighbours, and Asmi got along well with them.

Looking at the woman, Asmi could tell that she came from a poor farming community. Asmi opened the door and invited them in.

"What can I do for you?" she asked.

"*Tai*, my son wants to study further, but his father refused. He said he should work on the farm, but I told his father that my son will study! I told him, 'Let him finish his studies and then you do whatever you want!' Neha *tai* gave me your address. I have come to you for help!"

"What do you want to study?" Asmi asked the boy.

"Commerce," he said looking at the floor.

"Why don't you enroll him in a college in some nearby town?"

"No *tai*, he must come to the city. It is only here that he will be able to pursue his dreams. The local colleges hardly have any teachers. If he goes there, he will lose interest, and his father will take him back to the fields. I have also saved money for him. I will pay his fees. Please, help us find a college for him! I don't have anywhere else to go! I cannot go back to the Wadi till my son gets admission here!"

Chapter 9: The Veils of Maya

ASMI SAT DOWN ON A bench in the arrival lobby of the airport waiting for Agastya. He would be in Mumbai for two weeks before returning back to America. His parents were in Australia for work, and he would not be able to meet them during this visit. It had been a year and a half since she last saw him. She had taken a leave from work for the time he was here. Sundaram had been reluctant to approve her leave, but she had firmly put her foot down. She looked at people around her. Most of them were waiting for someone to arrive and were busy with their phones, emptily engrossed in dabbing the screens with their fingers.

She had helped the mother get admission for her son in one of the city colleges. Swamiji introduced Asmi to a retired couple running a non-profit organisation called Sahyadri that helped underprivileged rural children get education in the city. Mr and Mrs Joshi were former schoolteachers who started Sahyadri after their retirement eight years ago. They gave Asmi information about different government scholarship schemes and student hostels and provided her references to key people; all of this proved very helpful in getting the boy financial assistance for both tuition and hostel residence. There were still a few weeks left for the term to begin. Before leaving, the mother profusely thanked her with tears in her eyes, and the boy touched her feet to seek her blessings.

She had missed Agastya. They had a lot in common. They shared a mutual fondness for abstract concepts. He would talk to her about thermodynamics, and she would tell him that language was not only a medium for expressing ideas, but it also directed and shaped our thinking. Both of them avoided crowds and liked meeting their friends in smaller groups preferring a few intimate relationships to many distant and impersonal ones. They shared these common bonds, but they were fundamentally different in other ways. Agastya was a man of science. He trusted logic and reason above all else when making decisions. Asmi relied on her intuition. When provided with solid reasoning, she would still wait for intuition to show up, but when she felt something intuitively, she did not need the support of reason.

He would sometimes get exasperated at her for prematurely jumping to conclusions. "How do you know it? You don't have evidence!" he would say. "I just know it!" would be her reply.

She would sometimes get impatient with his obsession for rigour and would say, "You don't need to explain every detail! Just tell me the result!" He would answer, "No! If you take away the reasoning, then the result is just superstition!"

They respected these differences in their personalities and even cherished and nurtured them. He believed reality was something to dissect and understand; she believed reality needed to be experienced. For him, truth was to be known; for her, truth was to be felt. His quest was for knowledge; hers was for realisation. They loved each other deeply and powerfully. She was his mind-mate with whom he shared the most precious of his thoughts! He was her soul-mate who belonged to her world!

Asmi got up from the bench and walked to the arrivals exit door. People had started coming out carrying their luggage. In a few minutes, she saw Agastya. She waited patiently for him to come up to her, and they embraced each other tightly. No words were required to be spoken. They took a taxi back to her apartment. The first week of his stay was filled with the multitude of functions and celebrations for Namita's wedding. They were meeting Namita and Varun after a long time. They enjoyed the days of the wedding eating sumptuous meals, playing catch up, and making fun of each other!

It was evening, a gentle breeze was blowing, and Asmi and Agastya were sitting at the sea-front on Marine Drive looking into the vast expanse of water in front of them. She was enjoying the feeling of the cool air brush against her cheek while idly listening to the hum of the city traffic. He was thinking about the city's millions of inhabitants and what lay beyond the sea on the other side. The wedding was over, and now they had more time for themselves.

Agastya, having completed the requisite coursework and cleared the preliminary examinations, was now free to pursue independent research. He was yet to select a topic for his dissertation, but Warnock was a reasonable advisor and did not pressurise him. Agastya had chosen Warnock because he was an expert on the motion of subatomic particles; a field that Agastya was himself fascinated with. He was working with Warnock and another researcher to publish a paper presenting new equations related to plasma acceleration. If they succeeded, their equations would allow construction of more compact and affordable particle accelerators for medical applications. The deadline for submission of the paper was next month. Agastya would have only two weeks after getting back to Berkeley, so he was carrying his work along and spent early mornings and evenings working on it. He would sit on the floor engrossed in his laptop while Asmi used that time to catch up on reading.

Looking at the pile of books at her bedside, he said, "Why don't you use an e-book reader instead of creating this mess of books?"

"The sight of a book in front of my eyes is alluring. I cannot resist the temptation to pick it up and open it; an e-book cannot evoke the same feelings in me. I wonder if I would read as many books if I read them as e-books!"

"Well, on the contrary, I think you would read many more. You can carry a whole library with you on your phone. Whenever you get time, wherever you are, whether in office or in transit, you can pull out your phone and start reading. Imagine, you could have read a book while you were waiting for me at the airport!"

"And deprived myself of the opportunity to think of you?" she said coyly and winked at him. He looked away rolling his eyes. He pretended to dislike overt displays of affection, but she knew he liked it when she did that.

Asmi and Agastya had *vada pav* at the canteen while they waited for Swamiji who was talking to some visitors. People from all professions and socio-economic backgrounds came to Swamiji for guidance. Some of them were his disciples from the time he used to be a part of the Saraswati Mission. Others had come in contact with him after he returned from his pilgrimage and joined the library. Asmi got acquainted with a few of them. She noticed that most of them came to him just to talk. Swamiji had an uncanny ability that made people trust him quickly and deeply. His powerful presence dissolved deep-seated pretenses within them enabling them to be honest with themselves. He could magically form intimate bonds with complete strangers who had never met him before. Later in the afternoon, sitting in his office, Asmi said, "Swamiji, I am sorry if my question seems silly, but I have been thinking about it. Suppose I practise meditation and I realise that 'I am *Brahman*', what happens then? How does this help me in real life?"

Swamiji, his kind smile never leaving his face, said softly, "My dear, do you know the origin of Shaolin Kung Fu? Legend has it that a Buddhist monk from South India named Bodhidharma created this system of martial arts to protect the Shaolin

Monastery in China from bandits and raiders. If you ask a layman on the street to punch a bag and watch him do it, you will see he punches using only his arms. The power of his punch originates in his shoulder and triceps muscles and gets transmitted through the extension of the elbow joint. But ask a trained martial artist, and he will tell you that this is a wrong way to punch. He will tell you that a real punch draws power not just from the shoulder and the arms but from the entire body! He will tell you to rotate your hips and torso towards the target and feel the weight of your body go into the punch. For a trained martial artist, the power of his punch originates from his legs and the torso and involves the entire body.

"During my numerous travels, I stayed at many Buddhist monasteries in Nepal and Bhutan. In one much monastery, I had the opportunity to closely observe a Shaolin teacher; that is how I know about punches! Dressed in the maroon robes of a Tibetan monk, he taught Kung Fu to his disciples. During a demonstration one day, he stood in front of a thick block of solid wood. He invited his students to try and punch through the block, but no one volunteered. I saw and felt the block with my own hands and thought it would be impossible for any human to punch through it. The monk then told the students a secret. A real warrior, he said, knows he is one with the universe. The source of his power does not lie in his body. When he throws a punch, he draws energy from the earth! The energy of the universe flows from the earth, through the muscles of his legs, shoulders, and arms, and hits the target delivering a devastating impact. Saying so, he took a stance in front of the block and closed his eyes. Without intimation, without any sign of hesitation, as quick as lighting, he delivered a single fatal blow that shattered the block into pieces."

Swamiji continued, "You do not want to be a Kung Fu warrior? Fair enough! You must have heard of Tansen, one of the finest singers ever, a jewel in the court of the Mughal Emperor Akbar. One day, during a performance, the emperor lined up his court with unlit oil lamps. When Tansen sang *Raag Deepak*, the song of fire, the intensity of his singing set those lamps alight. Tansen would get so absorbed in his music that, like Onami who became one with the waves, he would become one with sound. He did not just sing musical notes; he became them!

"You may not want to become a singer either, but you do want to be a scientist or a writer. Ramanujan, the great mathematician, had famously said 'An equation means nothing to me unless it expresses a thought of God!' Agastya, you are a scientist, and Asmi, you are a writer. Both of you play with symbols. One composes a proof with variables, and the other composes an article with words. Only when you dissolve your ego, you can become one with the universe. And when you become one with the universe, nothing can stop you. You can then punch through a solid block of wood, light lamps with your music, derive equations that help us understand the world, or write literature that stirs our souls!"

Asmi said, "Swamiji, have you ever experienced this feeling of being one with the *Brahman*?"

"You have seen me say a short prayer at sunrise and sunset, haven't you?" Swamiji replied.

"Yes," she said.

"I chant the *Gayatri Mantra*. Do you know it?"

ॐ भूर्भुवः स्वः
तत्सवितुर्वरेण्यं ।
भर्गो देवस्य धीमहि
धियो यो नः प्रचोदयात् ॥

Asmi knew the *Gayatri Mantra* as one of the most revered mantra in Hindu philosophy. During the *Upanayan* ceremony, when a *guru* accepts a young student as a *shishya*, the *guru* tells the *shishya* to meditate on this mantra. She loosely remembered reading that the mantra was a prayer to the Sun God, but she was sure there was something more to it. "I know the mantra but not its meaning. What does it mean?" she asked.

Swamiji took a moment. He joined his palms in the form of a *namaskar* and then said in a sacred voice, "I pray to you, the infinite energy that keeps the Sun burning, the vibrations that sustain all life; I pray to you to reveal to me the understanding of the universe and the understanding of my self!"

Asmi was astonished at the simplicity and beauty of this mantra. It was not a plea to wipe off sins. It was not a supplication for material gains, success, or mercy. It was a simple prayer to the *Brahman,* to God, to reveal to the seeker the ultimate knowledge - understanding of the self!

"Coming back to your original question," Swamiji continued, "I will tell you how it happened for me for the first time. After I left the Saraswati Mission, I wandered from place to place searching for spirituality and freedom. My journey carried me to many places and offered me strange experiences. One evening, I reached a small village on the banks of river Narmada. I was carrying some food with me and had a meagre meal. For most part of my journey, I took shelter in temples, so I found a small temple next to the river. Peering inside, I saw a stone idol of Krishna looking back at me. I had not prayed for a long time since leaving the Mission, but for some reason, I felt like saying something to the idol. I was tired and fatigued. I had spent thirteen years with the Mission and had not found God. I had spent another three years wandering aimlessly and had not found God. I was losing hope of ever finding Him. After sitting in silence for a while looking at the idol, I folded my palms, did a *namaskar*, and said the *Gayatri Mantra*. It happened abruptly without warning. As I opened my eyes, I could suddenly see! I strongly felt God's infinite power. I saw the brilliance of a thousand splendid suns. But, I did not see it in the stone idol; I saw it in myself! That moment, I realised that the God I was looking for was neither outside me nor inside me. I was God! I was the brilliance of a thousand splendid suns! I realised that I was the *Brahman*! In that moment, I did not associate myself with my body. I had become the air, the idol of Krishna, the walls of the temple, and the trees outside. I had become time, become everything, and was everywhere!"

"Was that your moment of enlightenment, Swamiji?" Agastya asked.

"It was the first time I *saw*. It was the first time I realised the truth which I had only known before. In Hinduism, this state is called *Nirvikalpa Samadhi*. Zen Buddhism calls it *Kensho*. The experience changed my life forever. *Nirvikalpa Samadhi*, however, is only an initial insight and not final liberation. The *samadhi*, the state of heightened consciousness, lasts for a while, and when it subsides, you return to your usual thought processes and behaviours. In this state, your ego is not completely destroyed but only temporarily suspended. You must continue to meditate with the goal of reaching *Moksha*, the permanent realisation that, once and for all, erases your ignorance and frees you from human bondage. *Moksha* is the ultimate liberation!"

It was the first time that Swamiji had told them about one of his personal experiences. He seldom spoke about himself.

"Swamiji, how can I attain *Nirvikalpa Samadhi*?" Asmi asked.

"*Samadhi* is not a destination you need to reach, because it already exists inside of you. You are already free, but you cannot see it, because your vision is obscured due to your ignorance. You live in the realm of *Maya*, the grand illusion! You must burn the seeds of ignorance in the fire of knowledge, and the spell cast by

133

Maya will be broken. Meditate, but understand that attaining an ecstatic trance is not your goal; you can achieve a trance with much easier means like using drugs and intoxicants. Your goal is to lift the veils of *Maya* and see the true reality!"

They left Swamiji to his work and went for a walk in the campus. The weather was pleasant, but their minds had become heavy with the talk.

"Is it really necessary for us to think about life and freedom?" Asmi asked.

"We are thinkers! We can't help thinking!" Agastya replied looking at the road.

"But there are many people who don't think and can go a lifetime without seriously thinking about anything! Sometimes I wish I was one of them!"

"Have you read Viktor Frankl's book called Man's Search for Meaning?"

"No. What about it?"

"Viktor Frankl was a Jewish psychiatrist and a holocaust survivor. In the book, he describes his observations and experiences in the cruel, hopeless environment of the concentration camps. The inmates of the camps came from all walks of life and had to face extreme hardships. You would imagine that inmates who came from backgrounds that were more accustomed to rough life and manual work such as plumbers, labourers, and factory workers would have survived those hardships better than those who led lives in more intellectual professions such as doctors, lawyers, and teachers. To the contrary, however, he says that people who led intellectual lives coped with these conditions better than those who didn't. When the outside world became unbearable, they had a rich internal world sustained by their imagination that they could fall back on, but other inmates who lacked this richness of imagination quickly succumbed to circumstances. They did not die because their physical bodies caved in; they died, because the situation broke their will to live! Don't you think philosophy makes us stronger?"

"Yes, I do think so! I remember Seneca's book on Stoicism. In one of my favourite paragraphs, he writes: 'Philosophy is the only power that can stir us, the only power that can shake off our deep slumber. Devote yourself wholly to philosophy. You are worthy of her; she is worthy of you; greet one another with a loving embrace. Turn to her with all your soul, sit at her feet, cherish her; a great distance will then begin to separate you from other men. You will be far ahead of all mortals, and even the gods will not be far ahead of you!'"

It was the last day of Agastya's stay and he was to leave next morning. They spent the day in the pure unadulterated joy of being in each other's company. She would miss seeing him work, totally engrossed in it, oblivious to his surroundings. She would miss him pulling her close, holding her in his strong arms, and making passionate love that left her wishing it never ended! He would miss having her around him when he worked, her mere presence lending him so much support that made it unnecessary for him to be aware of his surroundings. He would miss playing with her hair and getting lost in her enchanting eyes that could stop the flow of time!

"Distance cannot separate us!" he told her as they sat up in bed cuddled together.

"What about time?" she asked.

"The smile on your lips and the look in your eyes is etched in my heart! You are always with me. Neither time nor death can separate you from me! I love you, Asmi, from the depths of my soul!"

She pressed her face to his chest and could hear his heart beating. She said, "Agastya, I would have been so lost without you! I would have been left alone to fight the ugly world all by myself!"

"You are still alone in your fight. I don't hate them; you do! I am not your ally, Asmi, not in this fight!"

Last week, Mrs Deshmukh, Asmi's neighbour, knocked on her door in the morning. She was always nice to Asmi, almost protective at times, and often invited her for dinner. However, on that day, something had possessed Mrs Deshmukh. In a rude and direct manner unbecoming of her, she told Asmi that it was not morally correct for a single woman to have an unrelated man living in her house. "You have been corrupted by Western influence! Our culture does not allow live-in relationships!" she told her with an unnatural hostility that did not belong there. Asmi could see the dragon circling around her whispering in her ears lessons on moral conduct and propriety. A few days later, when they came across each other, Mrs Deshmukh walked past Asmi completely ignoring her presence. The dragon had claimed another casualty. Asmi had defied her moral advice and gone against society's rules, and this was the price she had to pay: another relationship irreconcilably strained, because she refused to obey the Shoulds written on his scales!

Chapter 10: The Bloodthirsty Flies

WHEN ASMI RESUMED OFFICE AFTER her leave, she was dismayed to see her inbox cluttered with a dozen new tasks. She went to her manager, Akash Patel, and demanded to know why she was given all the work when there were other people in her team practically sitting idle. He shrugged and told her that Sundaram had specifically assigned that work to her. "He could not bear to see me happy, could he?" she said and stormed off to her desk. She had just finished organising and prioritizing her tasks when her desk phone rang.

"The boss wants to see you!" Rachana said and hung up. When Asmi walked into the reception on the eighteenth floor, Rachana sized her up and said, "What are you doing with him?"

"What do you mean?" Asmi asked bewildered.

"Don't mess with me!"

"I don't know what you are talking about. I was on a leave for two weeks. I just came back today!"

"I know! We all know!" Pointing at Charvak's door, she said, "He has been asking for you all this time. I finally found out when you would be back and told him. Now that you are back, he immediately wants to see you! What's up?"

Asmi sidestepped her and entered his office.

Charvak had built a certain worldview standing at the helm of the Satyashah Group. He viewed life as a string of victories and defeats. In his eyes, everything was a competition. Negotiations were to be won, competitors were to be destroyed, employees were to be managed, politicians and bureaucrats were to be controlled, and opportunities were to be exploited. Likewise, for him, women were to be conquered. Whenever he saw an attractive woman, he would see in her a challenge that must be completed through conquest. He had been fairly successful at these conquests, and women were easily seduced by the combination of his good looks, refined manners, wealth, and influence. What made this concoction even more potent was the addition of his brash confidence and über charm. Civilization had created multiple measures of success like wealth, intelligence, prestige, and fame, but millions of years of evolution had not altered the one inalienable measure of success in the animal world: the capacity to attract sexual mates; and Charvak found immense satisfaction in repeatedly proving to himself that women found him irresistibly attractive!

"But Charvak, don't you think what you are doing is fundamentally wrong? Till when will you continue having casual affairs? Don't you feel like settling down with someone you truly love?" Devika asked him once.

Charvak and Devika had been close to each other since childhood. Although she was his cousin, he thought of her as a sibling sister. Devika was married to a businessman settled in London. She was the only member of his family with whom he shared a positive, healthy relationship.

"I do, at times, but I have never met a woman with whom I thought I could fall in love!" he said.

"How will you ever fall in love? You despise women and think of them as your playthings!"

How could he explain to her that he did not despise women, but he despised everyone?

"Hello, how are you?" Charvak said as Asmi entered his office.

"I am doing well. How are you?"

"I just wanted to talk to you!" he said in an even voice. She looked at him puzzled. He continued, "Look, I am not going to cook up reasons. I am not going to tell you that I am going to visit Menaka Park and you should come along, or tell you to write answers for interview questions for a magazine, although I commend you for the excellent work you did! I just want to talk to you!"

"Why?" she asked in a tone that suggested that it was a real question, not a conversational one, and she wanted an answer, and her subsequent response would depend on his answer.

Composing himself, he said, "Asmi, everyone I meet is always on their best behaviour around me. They do what I want them to do. They say things I want to hear. In turn, I am also on my most guarded behaviour around them. I have a reputation to protect: an image that I have carefully constructed and unknowingly enforced upon myself. The constant need to moderate my behaviour drains me; I crave to be just myself and talk freely with someone. When we went for dinner, I realised I can do that with you! That's all I am asking for. Will you come with me for dinner tonight?"

"Why me?" she asked looking straight into his eyes.

"Because, Asmi, with you I can be honest with myself, and I don't have to pretend to be someone I am not! For some reason, your presence makes me feel comfortable being who I really am!"

Asmi remembered how she had felt the same way when she formed an instant connection with Swamiji at their first meeting.

Charvak despised the general obsequiousness of people around him. They always seemed to want something from him. His employees wanted promotions and salary raises. Customers wanted business favours, and vendors and suppliers wanted new contracts. But these wants were simple and tangible, and they did not irritate him so much. What did really irritate him was people desiring intangible things from him. He hated it when they servilely hankered for his attention and admiration. He hated sycophants like Sundaram who lingered on sheepishly after meetings just to be within range of his eyesight. He hated cowards who stole credit from junior employees and stepped over each other's toes, not for money, but for cheap approval and shallow recognition.

Charvak looked at her slender figure in beige trousers and a green shirt. From the calm confidence on her face, he knew she was not one of them! She was looking intently at him, and their eyes met. She saw in his eyes sincerity and frankness, and she knew he was not lying, and he had really meant what he had said.

She answered softly, "Yes, I would love to come for dinner, but I am afraid I am buried in piles of work. Sundaram has assigned me enough work to keep me occupied for weeks!"

At the mention of Sundaram, the world of corporate business gushed back into his consciousness. He regained his composure, the mask came back on his face, and all signs of vulnerability disappeared without a trace. He let out a hearty laugh, in a way glad to be the person he was used to being, and said, "Don't worry about that! Let's leave by 7!"

Asmi returned to her desk and started working. An hour later, when she checked her inbox, she found that most of her excess work had disappeared and had been reassigned.

They were sitting in the revolving Aurea again.

"Did you tell Sundaram to reassign my work?" Asmi asked pointedly; she was not happy about Charvak patronizing her.

"I don't know what you are talking about!" he replied, effectively deflecting her question.

"So, are the rumours true? About you being a womaniser and a playboy?" she asked in a bid to make conversation.

The overt question took him by surprise. He had an answer ready in his mind, one that would neither confirm nor deny her supposition, an answer he would give to a journalist to report, an answer that would be appropriate for the businessman mask he wore; except, he did not want to give her that answer! He looked at her. She was waiting for an answer. Her lips were slightly parted in a smile. He found his eyes glued to her sensual mouth, and he had to force himself to look away.

At length, he said, "Yes, some of them are true. Some of them are not. Which ones have you heard?"

"That you sleep with models and movie stars?"

"I did a few times, but it's not a regular occurrence!"

"I am sorry! I was just kidding! You don't have to answer me. I don't mean to pry into your personal life!"

"No, please continue! I would like to know what rumours are presently in circulation!" he said smilingly.

"Well," she said trying to recollect rumours she had heard, "That you sleep with Rachana?"

"No, that is utter bullshit!"

"That you demanded to sleep with the contractor's wife before giving him the contract to build this hotel?"

"Yes. Where did you hear that?"

"Really? Was she attractive?"

"No. She wasn't."

"Then, why?"

Charvak, 8 years old, sat between his parents holding a cone of ice-cream in his hand. The summer holidays had just begun. School was closed, and he could watch his favourite cartoons all day. But today, he was not watching cartoons, because today was a special day; his father had set aside time to take him to the see the circus!

"Mamma, who is the strongest animal in the jungle?" he asked his mother.

"The tiger!" she said knowing that it was the answer he wanted to hear.

"I am a tiger!" he said and growled at her.

A huge tent had been erected for the circus. Raja, a majestic Bengal tiger, was the star of the show, and young Charvak eagerly awaited his performance. He had been waiting for the circus for days wanting to see Raja perform and move around flaunting his grandeur. When Raja's performance was announced, Charvak stood up on his seat and cheered frantically, only to be disappointed moments later! The splendid, powerful tiger crouched fearfully before a puny trainer holding a whip in his hand. The trainer made Raja jump through a hoop, sit on a stool, and open his jaws so he could put his head inside. When the act ended to a loud applause, Charvak felt a numbing silence engulf him. He had wanted to see Raja's greatness; instead, he got to see a sad spectacle of how a spineless trainer made the magnificent beast dance to his commands! He imagined Raja's pain and despair. He vowed to himself to take revenge on the trainer and set Raja free!

Charvak was 24 years old when his father passed away and the Satyashah family got embroiled in a bitter power tussle. Manoj, his uncle, at 42 years of age, was the frontrunner to lead the organisation. He was a part of the family and was one of the largest shareholders of the Group second only to his brother Ravindra. However, in the 15 years of working with the Group, he had never proved his mettle, and he had detractors. Sumitra Satyashah, Charvak's mother, opposed him and aggressively promoted Charvak as the next Chairman. The only experience in running a business Charvak had was 3 years of training he received directly from his father. Nobody doubted young Charvak's brilliance, but they worried about his lack of experience. Sumitra persisted and got her son elected as the Chairman of the Group. Charvak did not disappoint. He made up for his lack of experience by his sheer intelligence and determination. The massive debilitating labour strike just weeks after he took over hit the businesses hard, but he came out of it stronger and wiser. In the years to come, he proved himself to be a worthy successor to his father and grandfather. He was, perhaps, admired and respected even more than they had been in their times.

Charvak formed a belief, early in his life, that beneath the thin veneer of civilization, man was an unprincipled, egoistic, and greedy savage. When he entered the world of corporate business, he realised that it was not just individuals but also society at large that peddled in these same vices. In the hands of society, however, they assumed far more dangerous proportions, because they were surrounded by layers of hypocrisy and thrust onto people in seemingly innocuous disguises. He saw hideous selfishness routinely disguised as charity and stinking dishonesty regularly packaged in beautiful advertisements. He saw from a close distance how the pressure of expectations could easily turn honest people into selfish monsters. In this jungle, Charvak concluded, you must rule or be ruled. You must conquer or be conquered. Charvak Satyashah wanted to rise above this dirt and filth, and he set out to do it by conquest believing that the only way for an honest, competent man to survive happily in this vile world was through gaining power. He had not forgotten the miserable scene of the magnificent Raja crouching before the spineless trainer. He came across many such trainers who did not hold whips in their hands but were armed with more dangerous weapons they called policies, ethics, rules, norms, conventions, morals, and culture! He had not forgotten his vow to avenge Raja. When he realised

143

that avenging the Rajas around him meant drawing vengeance on the whole world, he started doing just that!

Charvak spoke, "The contractor had worked with us before. He was a pompous brat who went around bragging how indispensable he was to us. He said many presumptuous things that made me extremely agitated. That day, he came to meet me at the Star Regency Hotel, another hotel owned by the Group, with his wife and begged for the contract. I told him to leave his wife behind and take a copy of the contract with him."

"And he agreed?" Asmi asked.

"Yes. His wife spent the night at the hotel. I wanted to expose his hypocrisy and make him admit his own baseness. No, I did not sleep with her! I went to her room but turned away disgusted with myself and the whole affair!"

As he explained to her why he despised the world, she realised that he too was fighting a battle with the golden-scaled dragon. She saw in him a kindred spirit who, like her, was struggling to find a place in society. Asmi told him her story about leaving the Wadi and her battle with the dragon.

When she finished, Charvak laughed out loud and said, "A dragon! My dear, you couldn't be more mistaken! It is no dragon you are fighting. You are fighting only a bunch of flies!"

"What do you mean?"

"The world is full of small, pitiable people. Like blood sucking flies, they sting you. They hate your independence. They cannot hurt you alone so they find strength in numbers. They have no conscience. Their opinions, attitudes, and morals are all borrowed from their neighbours who, in turn, borrow them from their neighbours. They resent you, because you break this chain and do not borrow from them. Being ordinary, like others before them, is their claim to virtue, and being extraordinary is your cause for sin, and they will not forgive you for it. They are cowards and will not see eye to eye with you or fight hand to hand; they will sting when you are not watching. So pathetic are they, that they do this in their innocence, unaware of their vileness. They do this self-righteously and praise themselves for being virtuous. They are the meek who want to rule the world by making it so wretched that the strong cannot survive in it. They feel threatened by you. They are wicked so they will not kill you, but they will kill the spark inside you that makes you different from them. They will stamp out the flame in you and make you mediocre like them. To do this, they will turn to their dogmas and sham morals. They will invoke precedence to force you to do things by arguing that this is the way things have been done for centuries. Asmi, you must realise that you are not fighting a powerful dragon who will deal blows squarely and honourably; you are fighting bloodsucking flies who sting when you are not watching. They will keep stinging till you bleed dry and finally give up and become one of them!"

Asmi shuddered. His words had been violent, but there was truth in them. She had faced these bloodthirsty flies and felt their stings against her skin; they had almost driven her to a point of suicide.

"How do you deal with them?" she asked.

"Power! Show them a sign of weakness, and they will immediately try to tame you. Fear their whip, and you will dance to their tune all your life. But wield power over their heads, roar back at them, and they will cower before you and leave you alone!"

Baba was sitting in the living room with a newspaper spread out before him. It was a Sunday morning, and he had no work. Aai brought two cups of tea and sat down next to him. They sipped on their tea silently. It had been exactly three years since Asmi left the Wadi.

"I wonder what Asmi must be doing," Aai said tenderly.

"Don't talk about her! She has brought disgrace to our family!"

"What family is left to bring disgrace to?"

Baba closed the newspaper and said, "Yes, there is little family left! That is why we wanted a son who would carry our family name into the future generation. A son who would make us and the whole Wadi proud of his achievements. Not a daughter who only brought us shame! People talk behind our backs! I have heard whispers about people saying that our daughter is a whore who left her husband! What is this if not disgrace?"

"Watch your words! She works at a respectable company!"

"And has illicit relationships with other men?"

"What do you know? He is a scientist! They love each other!"

"They are not married, and yet they sleep with each other!"

The doorbell rang interrupting them. There was a woman at the door along with her son. Aai called them in.

Giving a box of sweets to Baba, the woman said, "*Saheb*, my son got admission in a college in the city! The classes start tomorrow, and he has come to seek your blessings! Asmi *tai* helped him get admission. She also found a hostel for him. *Saheb*, her kindness has changed our lives, and we will forever be indebted to your family! Thank you!"

As Asmi was getting ready to leave office, her phone rang.

"Asmi *beta*, this is Kamble *kaka* calling from the Wadi. Do you remember me?"

Yes, she remembered him well. He was the owner of a general store close to her house. Aai used to send her to his store to buy household items. He was a friendly man and often gave her small toffees for free, especially during summer holidays. "Hello *kaka*, how are you?" she said.

146

"I am fine. I heard from Neha that you are doing very well in the city. I wanted your help. My daughter has finished her twelfth standard. She wants to study in the city. Will you help her find a good college and a hostel?"

The week before, Asmi had helped two other children from the Wadi. As the admissions season began, she started getting more calls. She directed them to Sahyadri, and Mr and Mrs Joshi took care of them. Sometimes, on weekends, she went to their office to help them out. They had a son and a daughter her age, but both their children were settled abroad, and the Joshis were happy to have her company. Having been teachers all their life, they were well acquainted with the education landscape in the city. In the past eight years since starting Sahyadri, they had helped hundreds of students get decent education. Now, through Asmi, they were helping many more!

Chapter 11: Selfish Forgiveness

ASMI AND CHARVAK STOOD ON a flattened piece of land inside Menaka Park. The project, still in its first development phase, was all set to become a big commercial success. Menaka Park had been designed to be a completely self-contained township with a mix of commercial and residential buildings. Charvak, through his vision and sheer determination, had transformed a fragmented wasteland into the most sought-after address in the city. The old, abandoned mill building that had stood at the centre of the park had been demolished to make way for a memorial of Vallabh and Ravindra Satyashah.

Charvak said, "My grandfather started his life as a poor man. He was not homeless-poor, but he was also not wealthy. He inherited this land as ancestral property, but in those days, it was practically worthless; it was far outside the city, unfit for agriculture, and had no potential for generating any income. He started his business out of almost nothing and poured his heart and soul into it. In his time, the business was fuelled by his own infinite reserves of energy. There were few standards or processes, and he was personally involved in all decisions. This ensured that everyone worked to their full potential, but it also imposed severe limitations on how the business could grow and scale.

"When my father took over, he realised that lack of processes was a significant obstacle for growth. He established processes and protocols. He depersonalised operations improving repeatability and consistency. He was a true visionary. The strength of my grandfather lay in doing things others could not do, whereas the strength of my father lay in imagining and seeing things others could not see. He grew the business from a young fledgling company to one of the biggest business houses in the country. While my grandfather's achievements and contributions were overt and clearly visible, my father's contributions were more fundamental in nature. They were not publicly trumpeted, and most people do not fully understand the extent of the impact he had."

They walked into the construction site office. He showed her sketches of the memorial complex. The eastern side of the complex told the story of how the Satyashah Group of Companies was established and was dedicated to Vallabh Satyashah, the founder and creator. The western side was dedicated to Ravindra Satyashah, the organiser and visionary.

While Charvak discussed the progress of the work with the supervisor, Asmi sat idly sipping on some tea. A large black car drove into her view. Sumitra Satyashah got out of the car and walked into the office. There was a brief moment of silence when all workers stopped whatever they were doing and stood in attention. Her guard of honour was more solemn than Charvak's or even her late husband's. Nobody knew why. Perhaps, it was because her presence naturally commanded deference! She was wearing a royal-blue silk saree and walked towards Charvak with an air of refined elegance. Behind her followed her old friend and confidante, Rinku Malhotra, a wealthy socialite whose husband left her a huge fortune and no clue what to do with it.

"Hello, mother! Hello, Rinku *massi*!" Charvak greeted them.

"Hello, Charvak, what are you doing here?" Sumitra said.

"I came here to inspect the progress of the construction of the memorial."

Sumitra's gaze shifted to Asmi and stayed on her long enough to signal that she had noticed her presence. Asmi moved forward to greet her, but before she could speak, Sumitra shifted her gaze back to Charvak. She raised her eyebrows and said nothing letting the silence ask the question.

"Mother, this is Asmi. She works in the Marketing Division" he said.

Sumitra once again turned towards Asmi and said, "Asmi! That is such a nice name. How are you, my dear?"

"I am fine. Thank you, Mrs Satyashah! It's a pleasure to meet you!"

She checked out Asmi from head to toe, slowly, making no efforts to hide what she was doing. "What are you doing here at a construction site?" she asked coldly.

"I came here with Charvak."

"I can see that! Why?"

There was something viscerally aggressive about the way she had asked that question. Sumitra did not mind her son's philandering and took it in good spirit, but her instincts told her that Asmi was not one of his ordinary play dolls. She waited for Asmi to look to Charvak for support or mutter a few words explaining her presence, because that was what his play dolls usually did when she confronted them. Asmi remained standing upright in a relaxed pose and did not reply.

Not letting it go, Sumitra repeated with spite, "Are you deaf? I asked you a question. What are you doing here?"

"I came here with Charvak to give him company," Asmi replied evenly.

"How presumptuous! My son does not need your company. And how dare you call him Charvak! You…"

Charvak interrupted her saying, "Mother! We need to go. Why don't you show Rinku *massi* the memorial plans?" He took Asmi's hand and led her out.

We interpret the world through our five senses of vision, hearing, smell, taste, and touch. Human vision is significantly

150

more advanced than the other animals we share the planet with making us one of the few organisms that can see colours. It is probably the sense we most rely on in our daily lives. Vision is closely associated with the higher functions of intelligence, and this makes us relegate other senses to secondary status. Evolutionarily speaking, however, vision is the youngest of the senses and evolved the last. We have a far deeper relationship with the other senses. Music, for example, can stir us in ways that a painting never can. A whiff of smell carried over the air can suddenly trigger long forgotten memories in ways we don't understand. The first sense we develop, the one we have the most complex relationship with, is touch. It is the first sense a baby inside the mother's womb will use to explore her surroundings. Touch dominates the language of intimacy in human relationships and activates neurological circuits in the brain no other sense can.

They had barely stepped outside the office when Charvak suddenly realised that he was holding Asmi's hand in his. Her small delicate hand tightly clasped in his! Every point on his hand where her tender skin touched him was charged with tension. Nerves carried this tension to the limbic centres of his brain overwhelming him with emotions he could not handle. He looked deep into her captivating eyes and was lost in them. He felt as if his heart had stopped beating, and time had ceased to exist. He was riveted in that moment and wished it would last forever. In that instant, holding her hand in his, he realised what love was and knew that he was unquestionably and irresistibly in love with her!

After being thrust into business, Charvak faced an immense responsibility of living up to his father's reputation and fulfilling the expectations of many thousands of people who were in some way linked to the business. He worked tirelessly with a single-minded purpose of developing himself into a true leader. He excelled at his work and not only did he fulfil expectations, but he surpassed them. In this blind pursuit, however, he had forgotten what he truly was. He had unknowingly buried the child in him that yearned for things other than business, for fun and joy, for love and companionship, for the lightness of living; he had buried the child deep inside of him and had forgotten its existence until now, when he felt something move in his heart, when he felt the child struggle inside him to break free and come out. Inundated with a million emotions, Charvak had frozen for a little too long. The construction workers stopped their work and turned to look at them. Rinku tapped on Sumitra's shoulder to bring her attention to what was happening. Asmi lightly nudged him, and he came back to the world.

Using her other hand to gently free herself, she said, "Come, Charvak, let's go!"

At that moment, he would have done anything for her!

Charvak had never loved before. He had a few teenage infatuations, but they had ended abruptly. He had a semi-serious relationship in college, but things did not work out. When he attained a marriageable age, his mother brought to him many suitable brides. Wanting only the best for her son, Sumitra defined a criterion for bride selection and presented only those specimens to him that fit her criteria.

"You must choose a wife that befits your social and financial position in society!" she would say.

After he turned 30, she intensified her efforts. Over the years, she presented him many choices, but Charvak rejected them all. Two years ago, Sumitra made her last serious attempt at this arranged-marriage exercise. Rinku's cousin sister had married an Indian businessman settled in Dubai who had a large import-export business. Owing to better opportunities in India, they had shifted back to Mumbai along with their pretty daughter named

152

Saloni. Sumitra was convinced that Saloni was perfect for Charvak. She spotted Saloni at a grand party that was hosted to celebrate Rinku's fiftieth birthday. Although Saloni was meeting her aunt Rinku after many years and had met her only a few times before when she was a child, she warmed up to Rinku so quickly and so well that Rinku told Sumitra that she could almost have been her own daughter! Saloni was the cynosure of all eyes at the party. Dressed impeccably, she moved through the crowd with such grace and charm that she instantly became everyone's darling. Rinku had winked at Sumitra, and they both knew what that wink meant. Sumitra invited Saloni and her parents to the Satyashah mansion. Later, Charvak and Saloni went for dinner to get to know each other.

"What do you mean you don't like her? She is gorgeous!" Sumitra fumed when Charvak said he would not marry her.

"I got bored with her. I don't think I can have a decent 30-minute conversation with her!"

"That's rubbish! She is a talkative girl and can hold conversations quite well. At the party, I saw her talking to everyone!"

"Smiling at people and asking them 'how are you' is not the same as having a conversation!"

"Listen to me! You are my son, and I know you well. You are great at business, but you lack social skills. You cannot connect and maintain bonds with people. You don't know how to organise and host functions. She is charming and adept at social mannerisms. She will complement you perfectly!"

"I don't care about hosting functions!"

"You should! Why do you always have to be buried in your world of business! She will help you loosen up, and you will learn how to have fun!"

"How will I have fun with her if I can't stand one dinner with her? She is not interested in anything. I spoke to her about numerous topics, and I got nothing in return! She is empty and hollow from the inside. I doubt if she is capable of anything more than doing small-talk and charming people!"

"You are just like your father! He had no social sense, but I made up for it. The way your father needed me, you need someone like her. She will stand by your side. You will spread your influence in the corporate world, and she will spread it in the society reaching places that you cannot reach. She will make other men, your peers, jealous of you, and they will squirm in their sleep. She will make you more human. She will complete you. Listen to me: Saloni is the perfect wife for you!"

"No! She is not the perfect wife for me; she is the perfect daughter-in-law for you! Don't confuse the two!"

Sumitra stopped looking for brides after that and resigned to the fact that her son may never marry. Saloni had come closest to being the perfect match for him. If he rejected her, he will never choose anyone, she told herself. She ignored the occasional tabloid gossip about his philandering. He never got his play dolls home, and she never enquired about them knowing they were only passing affairs. Occasionally, if she happened to come across them, she amused herself by making them severely uncomfortable, and he did not seem to particularly mind that. But Asmi did not look like one of his play dolls; she had unwaveringly stood her ground. Sumitra had seen her son take her hand and lead her out of the office. And she had seen, like everyone else saw, how he had stupidly gawked at her face outside the office! Sumitra was a strong woman and knew how to get what she wanted. She knew how to deal with people. When her husband passed away, it was assumed that Manoj would be the next chairman. She had fought for her son tooth and nail. She had gathered the support of board members and senior management. She had campaigned in the media. And she had won! She had won, because she excelled at the art of understanding people and accurately measuring their strengths, weaknesses, preferences, fears, and motivations. She had made it her business to know things about people, and her son was no exception. When Sumitra came back home that day, she called Rachana and got to know everything she wanted to know about Asmi.

Asmi's meetings with Swamiji had become less frequent since she started spending more time at Sahyadri's office with the Joshis. In the last few months, she had worked with them to accommodate dozens of rural children in the education system in the city. Seeing the delight on their faces gave her deeply felt satisfaction. She remembered her struggle, the cracked door, and her helplessness. For her, helping these children was like doing justice to her own younger self. Swamiji supported and encouraged her work. Asmi and Swamiji were sitting on the *katta* outside the canteen after their evening walk. She told him about her strange meeting with Sumitra Satyashah. Swamiji smiled lightly but did not reply.

"Swamiji, why do you never say anything when I speak about Charvak?"

He still said nothing.

"He asks about you almost as if he knew you. You know each other, don't you?" she asked.

After a pause, he replied, "Yes. Charvak was one of the best students I ever had!"

"He was your student? You taught him Vedanta?"

"Yes."

"Really? From the way he talks and behaves, it seems impossible that he was your student! Why didn't you tell me before? What happened?"

"I do not know what happened. The day his father passed away, he simply ended all contact with me. I tried reaching out but could not get to even speak to him. I read in the newspapers

155

that he became the Chairman of the Group. I have not seen him since. He never made any attempts to contact me. The manner in which he left broke my heart!"

It was rare for Swamiji to display emotions. She remained silent not knowing what to say. He was lost in his thoughts. After a while, he turned to her and said, "Asmi, be careful! For all his brilliance, Charvak had one flaw that I feared would undo him, and I fear it eventually did: he chose to loathe the world! People are not bad or evil. They are just ignorant. Pity them for their ignorance, but don't hate them; they are only doing what they think is right within the narrow confines of their comprehension. Hate is like a chain that will tie you to them. It will bind you to *Samsara* and destroy your chances of finding freedom. Asmi, be selfish, and for the sake of your own happiness, forgive them!"

"How is your meditation practice going?" Swamiji asked as they walked back to the library.

"I am not able to make much progress. I start meditating by focussing on external sounds and sensations. Then, I move inwards, and focus on observing my thoughts. When a thought emerges, I don't feed it or entertain it in any way, and quickly enough, it disappears. In this manner, I can sit steady for an hour keeping my mind almost free of thoughts. After my thoughts settle down, I begin *atma vichara*, the process of self-enquiry. I ask myself who thinks the thoughts, who asks the questions, who seeks the answers, but I get no reply, and nothing happens after I ask these questions. Every day I ask these questions, but I get no answers, and I feel a little disappointed."

"Keep practicing my child. Don't be disappointed. I am confident you will find what you are looking for!"

"But Swamiji, can't you tell me what to expect? What form will this answer be in? If you tell me I will, at least, be able to identify the answer when I come across it. I fear I will never find the answer, because I simply don't know what it looks like!"

"Don't worry! You will know when you see it. Keep asking yourself the question 'Who am I?' and persist in doing this. When you get bored, ask yourself 'Who is getting bored?' When you get tired, ask yourself 'Who is getting tired?' When you get angry, ask yourself 'Who is getting angry?' This path of self-enquiry will take you to the final answer, and you will realise that the seeker and the sought, the question and the answer, you and God, the *atman* and the *Brahman*, are all one and the same, and there is no duality! Your *atman*, the personal soul, and *Brahman*, the single unstained reality, are the same. Schrödinger called this insight of *atman* being the *Brahman* as the deepest of all human insights and the grandest of all thoughts!"

Asmi found these concepts of Vedanta fascinating, but she still did not completely believe in their validity. Vedanta had been helpful to her and had changed her in fundamental ways. She recognised these changes and acknowledged that they had been due to practising meditation and philosophy. But talking about being one with the *Brahman* and the universe, she wondered if all this was genuinely true or if it was just fantasy. "Swamiji, these are lofty ideas. How do we know that they are true? What proof do we have? Could they just be wishful thinking?" she said.

"I asked myself the same question many years ago. I wondered if *Brahman* existed and if these ideas had any solid foundation or if they were mere speculations. I kept wondering until that day when, in the temple on the banks of the Narmada, I saw truth for the first time. That experience erased all my doubts. Realising the truth first-hand is an experience that words can never do justice to. You must feel it yourself. That moment, when I saw the universe within me, when I realised that I was the brilliance of a thousand suns, I knew that I was on the right path. I decided to dedicate my life towards pursuing this path, and I

157

have never looked back. I know you have doubts, and it is only natural that you do. I urge you to continue in your efforts, and you too will see the truth!"

"Do you think I will? Do you think I have the strength to reach there?"

"Of course, my child! I am certain you will!"

Chapter 12: Renounce and Rejoice

THE FIRST BUSINESS VALLABH SATYASHAH started was the textile mill. After textile, he added manufacturing and chemicals to the list. Soon after, as the newly formed Satyashah Group diversified into multiple businesses, textile took a back seat. During Ravindra's tenure, textile remained in the Group's portfolio as a neglected, underperforming asset. In his last year, Ravindra decided to spin it off into clothing and apparel. The Satyashah Textile Company gave birth to the Satyashah Clothing and Retail Company. The clothing business did well with its lineup of products that included casual and formal wear. Their brands captured a decent share of the low to mid-range clothing market in the rural and semi-urban regions of the country. However, their many attempts to climb the ladder and launch upscale products that would appeal to high-spending urban consumers failed. The products, on their own, were good and compared favourably with the competition in all respects, but they failed to cut the ice with urban consumers. Analysts generally saw this as a marketing failure.

When Charvak took over, he focussed his attention on the heavyweight businesses. He won his first accolades when, three years later, the manufacturing business recorded its highest profit ever. He diversified the Group further by starting newer businesses in healthcare and hospitality. There were critics who wanted him to hold off expansion and focus on existing businesses, but these were silenced when the new ventures quickly became the Group's highest profit earners. He started chains of hospitals and hotels across the country leveraging the fact that both these businesses required common overlapping functions and depended on management of real estate. In the process, the Group ended up with a massive informal real estate business, which Charvak formally organised into the Satyashah Real Estate and Construction Company a few years later. Menaka Park was the first project undertaken by this company.

While all this was happening, the clothing business remained stagnant. It was just about profitable but was performing way below its potential. Multiple management reshuffles had done nothing to alter the fact that urban consumers simply could not relate to the brand. Frustrated by this stagnancy, Charvak appointed a new marketing team under Ritesh Sundaram to deal with this problem. Sundaram's team worked out an elaborate campaign to launch a new brand but got stuck on the choice of the brand ambassador. They had tried out the usual suspects including film stars and sportsmen before, but that had not worked. They wanted someone who was young but not too young, smart and fun but not immature, glamorous but not unapproachable, sophisticated but not snobbish, classy but not elitist. They wanted a brand ambassador who exuded confidence and charm. Sundaram presented Charvak with a list of people who his team thought might work, but Charvak rejected them all. Charvak told Sundaram, who was taken aback at the suggestion, that he himself will be the brand ambassador!

The new brand was named Mephysto. They hired international designers and used only the best raw materials. They exploited their massive distribution network to its fullest extent and ensured that Mephysto products were made available in every clothing store in all major cities. They leveraged the Group's real estate expertise to open dozens of stores across the country exclusively offering Mephysto products. Critics questioned his decision behind betting so heavily on Mephysto, but Charvak proved them wrong yet again. The entire operation was a resounding success. Two years later, the company sold off their rural brands to concentrate fully on Mephysto. The product lineup that had initially focussed on business casuals now included jeans, t-shirts, jackets, and footwear.

The marketing and advertising campaign for Mephysto had perhaps been the single most expensive campaign in the history of the Satyashah Group. Sundaram had been categorically instructed to leave no stone unturned. The risky decision to portray Charvak himself as the chief brand ambassador did wonders. Hundreds of hoardings bearing Charvak's photographs were put up. Many of these photographs were of real events that actually took place. There was a picture of him attending a board meeting wearing Mephysto branded clothes. There was another one where he was coming out of a private jet dressed in a Mephysto polo shirt. He even appeared in some TV advertisements. Mephysto sliced through the urban clothing market conquering it quickly and easily to become the country's most beloved clothing brand. This campaign also achieved another objective: it generated a massive burst of positive publicity for Charvak in newspapers, magazines, blogs, and social media. Huge attention in all forms of media, hoardings with his photographs across the country, and his spectacular business acumen made shareholders and the general public fall in love with him. Charvak became a superstar of immense popularity!

As Asmi entered the office, Charvak's face lit up. He had been submerged neck-deep in work for the past week; seeing her now made him put the week behind him.

"Today used to be Papa's birthday," he said.

"I hope he is happy wherever he is!" Asmi replied.

"It is also my uncle's birthday. He invited my mother and me for dinner. We refused."

"Why did you refuse? He is family after all. What happened that strained your ties so much?" she asked. The Satyashah family had kept their conflict under wraps and had never let the media get the details.

"When my grandfather passed away, he left the business to Papa and Manoj *kaka* in equal proportions. While Papa bore the entire responsibility of the business, Manoj *kaka* took his family and went to London to study management. The first few years were very difficult for Papa. I now understand how it would have been for him. My grandfather, when he started the businesses, took as partners and shareholders many friends and relatives from the extended family. He appointed them as managers of different units and gave them full authority to conduct business. When Papa took over, he had to deal with people much older than him in age and experience. These old-timers had known my grandfather personally; they resented Papa's authority and did not pay heed to his instructions. Lack of processes and standard practices meant that everyone ran amuck with business decisions. Papa worked hard and managed to reign in many of these intransigent managers. Some of them reluctantly acknowledged his authority. Others had to be fired. He tried to do this as far as possible without affecting personal ties, but many relations soured.

"Three years later, after Papa had finished doing the hard work of reorganising the business, Manoj *kaka* came back and demanded his position as an equal owner of the Satyashah Group. Papa agreed and put him in charge of Satyashah Chemicals so he could learn how business was conducted and get acquainted with people that mattered. However, Manoj *kaka* turned out to be a poor businessman, and the business struggled under his management. His subordinates were unhappy and financials suffered. While Papa was rewarded for his excellent work year after year through stock rewards linked to his performance,

162

Manoj *kaka* was chastised by shareholders and ended up severely resenting the fact that Papa, via his stock rewards, had amassed a much larger shareholding in the company than he had. Jealousy got the better of him. There were heated arguments between them, and they stopped talking to each other. Manoj *kaka* demanded larger responsibility in running the businesses, while Papa refused to favour him because he was his brother and told him that he must first prove himself. Most shareholders sided with Papa and Manoj *kaka* had no option but to eat the humble pie.

"When Papa passed away due to a heart attack, Manoj *kaka* saw an opportunity to usurp power. All our businesses are legally structured as individual companies. The Satyashah Group of Companies is a holding company that holds stocks in these individual companies. Manoj *kaka* was one of its largest shareholders after my mother, and most people assumed that he would succeed Papa as the Chairman of the Satyashah Group of Companies. However, my mother fought to have me appointed as the Chairman. Many shareholders did not want Manoj *kaka* since they did not trust his judgment, but they were sceptical about supporting me as I had no experience. We met and spoke with all major shareholders individually. We also managed to convince Charan Gupta, a close friend of my grandfather who has been there with the company since its formation and owns the largest chunk of shares outside the Satyashah family. A bitter boardroom battle followed. We won, and I was appointed the Chairman!"

"How did Manoj *kaka* take it?"

"He must have been furious, but he hid it well. He came to our house with Poonam *kaki*, Devika, and Prateek. They all congratulated me. Poonam *kaki* gave me gifts. Manoj *kaka* spoke to me for quite some time giving me general advice on running the business. But it was all fake! Have you heard of the massive strike that paralyzed our manufacturing business immediately after I was appointed chairman?"

"Yes, I have heard of it."

"Without giving any warning signs, the workers suddenly declared a strike. For a week, they did not even make any demands. When they finally made demands, they were so ridiculous that there was no point in even discussing them. The managers of the manufacturing plants resigned saying they could do nothing. There were voices on the board talking about shutting down or selling off manufacturing altogether. I was crushed and wouldn't have come out of it had it not been for Ramu *kaka*. He told me he would fix the problem if I gave him a chance. I was reluctant to give him authority. After all, he was only a driver's son, and I knew there were people who did not like the fact that Papa used to let him poke his nose in company affairs; but he was also someone I had known since childhood, and my father trusted in him completely. He assured me not to worry. Three days later, he came back with a grave face. He had used his channels to communicate with the union leaders and found out that the strike had not been spontaneous as it was made out to be, but it was a planned operation backed by someone important from the management. By joining the dots, we reached the conclusion that Manoj *kaka* had conspired and mobilised the strike with the objective of destabilizing my leadership in the hope that it would force me out of the office allowing him to step in, manage the situation, take credit for resolving it, and pin the blame on my inexperience. My mother, Ramu kaka, and I went to Manoj *kaka*'s house that night. Ramu *kaka* spoke to him. He told him to call off the strike first thing in the morning or face criminal charges. We had no direct proof of his role in organising the strike, and he knew that. He refused to accept his involvement and told us to go to hell. But he must have been involved, because the next morning, the union leaders agreed to hold talks for a compromise. Ramu *kaka* handled the negotiations masterfully. He did not budge an inch from his position. With external support removed, the union gave in, and the strike ended. My mother wanted to investigate and press charges against Manoj *kaka*, but Charan Gupta cautioned her against it saying it would not only destroy our family but also have repercussions for the business. He mediated between our families, and the chapter came to a conclusion. But ever since that incident, we treat them with absolute distrust. The last straw keeping our families together was severed that day. Later on, as years passed by, I tried my best to mend the relationship, but whenever I attempted any reconciliation, he took it as condescension. The damage is irreparable!"

Asmi saw a wave of sadness sweep over his face.

He proceeded, "Papa continues to be a source of strength for me. He is still my role model. Whenever I am in doubt, I think of him. Whenever I have to take a tough decision, I think what he would have done. He was always busy, and I wish I could have spent more time with him. My mother, despite her faults, is a terrific woman. She fought for me like a lioness would for her cub and always believed that I was destined for greatness. Her unshakeable belief in me gave me the courage to fight and triumph over the challenges I faced in life!"

Asmi moved forward. Touching his hand with her fingers, she said, "Charvak, you have achieved so much! I am sure you make your parents proud!"

Charvak smiled. He shook his head as if to shake off the sombre mood. He picked up the phone and told the attendant to get some tea.

He said, "Well, I am sorry I dumped all this on you. You tell me. How have you been?"

165

"Last week, I went to meet Swamiji. I asked him if he has ever met you. He told me that you were one of his best students, but you abruptly ended all contact and never spoke to him after that. It broke his heart! Why did you do that?" she asked pointedly.

Charvak froze at the unexpected question. "Asmi... I... I don't know!"

"How can you not know?"

The attendant came in and served them piping hot tea with a generous dose of ginger added to it. He kept the teacups on the table and left. Asmi continued looking sharply at Charvak with the question conspicuously present in her eyes. Painful memories of the night his father died came to his mind. That very evening before he died, Charvak had gone to see Swamiji. They had a nice walk in the garden. Seeing that Swamiji's watch had stopped working, he had taken it saying he will replace the batteries and return it to him the next day. Except, everything changed that night! The next day, he found himself in a completely new world. He could not return the watch, because that watch was from another world! He could not speak to Swamiji, because Swamiji lived in a world he could never go back to - a world that had simply ceased to exist!

Charvak, 24 years old, was asleep in his bed when Ramu *kaka* woke him and took him to the hospital. When they reached the hospital, Sumitra told him that his father died due to a heart attack in office. Charvak's whole world turned upside down. When they returned home the next day after performing the funeral rites, Sumitra sat him down.

"Charvak, we must stay strong, and we must stay together. Do you understand?" she said.

"Yes, Mamma!"

"These are difficult times. People will try to snatch from us what is rightfully ours, but we will fight, and we will win! Your father was a great man. His spirit will show us the way. He believed in you. I believe in you. You must carry forward his work. You will be the next Chairman of the Satyashah Group. You must take the torch from him and lead the way. Millions of people depend on you!"

"But I don't know how to!"

"Never say that again! We will figure out everything. Your father always knew that you were built for greatness! He wished that you would surpass his achievements and carry forward his legacy to greater heights! Promise me, my son, that you will fulfil your father's wishes! Do you promise?"

"Yes, mother, I promise!"

Sumitra had never approved of Charvak visiting Swamiji. For her, he was just a monk who preached useless philosophy. She had vehemently objected when Ravindra sent Charvak to Swamiji. "Our son needs to learn from you! He needs to understand business. He needs to understand how to deal with people. He needs to learn real things and not philosophy!" she had said. Ravindra patiently ignored her for two years and continued to encourage Charvak to meet Swamiji. But, with his passing away, the world order changed. The distribution of authority and influence changed. Sumitra was the architect of the new order, and this order had no place for Swamiji!

She told a bewildered Charvak sternly, "Papa wanted you to visit Swamiji, because he thought you would get a different perspective of things. But that was when you did not have all these responsibilities! Now, you have a billion-dollar empire to run! Philosophy is a thing for inactive or retired people, not for someone like you! For the sake of your father and for your love for me, do not ever visit Swamiji again!"

Sumitra worried for her son and feared that idle philosophical pursuits will come in the way of his success. She could not afford that. She had fought all her life for Ravindra. She had motivated him when he felt low. She had guided him when he had doubts. She would now do the same for Charvak. Success in the cutthroat world of business, she believed, required a measure of ruthlessness and selfishness. She knew that Charvak respected and admired Swamiji; she could not let the monk and his pointless philosophy that preached meditation, renunciation, and compassion interfere with her son's destiny!

Sipping on the hot tea, Charvak told Asmi his story. He said, "I was so overwhelmed with everything that I followed the path of least resistance. I heeded my mother's advice and did not meet Swamiji. I focussed on my work. Later, when I regained my confidence, I felt ashamed of the manner in which I had cut off all ties with him. But, by then, it was too late! I had already moved on to a new life. I never met Swamiji after that. I closed that chapter forever and did not venture there again."

"He tried contacting you!"

"I did not speak to him, because I was ashamed of myself. I had made a decision to give up philosophy, to give up his teachings, and I didn't know what to say to him after everything that happened. Please tell him, on my behalf, that I am truly sorry!"

"Why don't you tell him yourself? Come with me to the library, and speak to him directly!"

"I cannot face him! I have closed that chapter of my life. I have consciously forgotten not just my moments with Swamiji but everything that I was before Papa passed away! My childhood dreams and aspirations, the silly notions of my student days, the rebellious foolishness of my youth, all of it is locked away and buried deep inside of me. I have cloaked myself with an identity that suits my position and stature in society. Please understand, Asmi, that I cannot meet Swamiji, because I am afraid that, if I do, everything I buried will come back to life. A revenant self that I

168

locked away will return to claim its place, and it will push me into an internal conflict that will destroy me. I know surely that this is what will happen if I meet Swamiji, and that is why I cannot meet him!"

The desk phone rang. Rachana said over the phone, "Sir, there are some people in the reception room waiting to meet you for a long time. What should…"

"Set up appointments with them for tomorrow and send them away!" he said hurriedly.

"I should get going! You have work to do, and I don't want to hold you up," Asmi said.

"No, please stay for a little while longer! Asmi, do you really think philosophy can make a difference to us in our day-to-day life? They are all nice ideas. You hear them, you feel good for a while, and then you forget them! Can philosophy ever be practically useful?"

"Of course! Philosophy gives you a model to live your life. It gives you a direction and purpose."

"You have been practicing meditation for some time. Tell me, how has it helped you?"

"Meditation has helped me in many ways. It made me realise the transience of emotions. Instead of letting emotions drive me, I have learned to control them, and I am no more a slave to them. This has improved the clarity of my thoughts, and I can now think objectively without letting emotions hold my thoughts hostage. Meditation has helped me understand who I really am, and this knowledge has instilled in me a strong sense of confidence. Understanding that I am the *Brahman*, even though I have not realised it yet, is the greatest source of self-esteem and confidence I have ever known! By understanding myself better, knowing my strengths and weaknesses, dropping all pretenses, I have become a better friend to myself! I have forgotten what stress

169

means. I am rarely disturbed. I never feel bored or lonely. I am happy and content with my life!"

Charvak flinched as those words made him remember his discussions with Swamiji. He said, "I would have asked you how philosophy helped you find happiness, but I know what you will say. You will tell me to renounce my desires, to renounce my possessions, to renounce wealth and luxury, to renounce sex, to renounce a fine life! I don't agree with this insistence on renunciation. Why should I renounce these things? What will I achieve through this renunciation? Happiness? How can I achieve happiness by renouncing the very things that make me happy?"

Asmi smiled and said, "These things you speak of, they bring you pleasure, not happiness. Pleasure is momentary; it depends on an external stimulus and lasts only till the stimulus lasts. A new expensive car gives you pleasure, but what happens when, a year later, the novelty fades away? Possessions are fleeting illusions; they come and go. Ask an unhappy person what he needs to be happy, and he will give you a list. Ten years later, check with him again. Most of the things on that list would have been fulfilled, but would he be happy then? No, because he would have simply created a new list! Possessions can bring you pleasure, but remember that pleasure, sooner or later, will turn into pain! How will it turn into pain? What happens, Charvak, when the thing that brought you pleasure disappears? You find pleasure in vacationing on the beach, but what happens when you are back? You find pleasure in drinking the whole night, but what happens next morning? You find pleasure in blowing money on parties, but what happens when you have no money left? Nothing is permanent! Sooner or later, these things will desert you, and you will be left with the pain of longing for them. Your heart will crave for them. When one source of pleasure disappears, you will desperately seek a new one and will writhe in pain till you find it.

Thus, you will forever be bound in this endless cycle of pleasure and pain!

"A man who seeks happiness in momentary pleasures is always at the mercy of the universe. His happiness is dependent on circumstances; it is dependent on causality and factors outside his control. The more you get used to pleasure, the more dependent you become on it, and the more you start demanding from life. But life will not fulfil all your demands! When your demands are not met, you feel pain. You blame yourself, someone else, your luck, and circumstances for your failure. If your happiness depends on the fulfilment of your demands, it depends on circumstances that are not in your hands! You, thus, become a slave to your own desires!"

Charvak interrupted her and said, "So are you suggesting that I give up everything that I desire? That I give up my material possessions?"

"No, not at all! I am not asking you to give up your possessions! I am not asking you to give up your demands or desires! I am only asking you to give up your attachment to them! Do you see the difference?"

Charvak did not reply; he rigidly sat in his chair looking at her.

Asmi continued, "The Isha Upanishad is one of the shortest but sweetest of all Upanishads. Mahatma Gandhi had said that if all Upanishads and all other scriptures were suddenly reduced to ashes and only the first verse in the Isha Upanishad survived, Hinduism would still live on forever! This first verse that he spoke of is:

ॐ ईशा वास्यमिदँ सर्वं यत्किञ्च जगत्यां जगत् ।
तेन त्यक्तेन भुञ्जीथा मा गृधः कस्यस्विद्धनम् ॥

171

"This verse represents the essence of the Upanishads. It says that *Isha*, God, the *Brahman*, gives form to everything in the world. All things, living or non-living, material or abstract, in the past, present or future, real or imagined, are only manifestations of the *Brahman* and belong to God. Do not covet these things since they will never belong to you. You have come into this world empty-handed, and you will leave it empty-handed. You cannot own these things. You can only, temporarily, use them. Do not crave for them. Do not become a slave to your desires of possessing them. Renounce them, and break the chains that bind your happiness to them. When you have done so, you are free to take joy in the act of living. Renounce, and rejoice! Renounce the trivial and inconsequential things in life so you can embrace those that truly matter. Renunciation is not denying yourself the joy of life. It is denying the causes that prevent you from enjoying life. Happiness is not something to acquire by taking things from the external world. It is a state of being that exists inside of you. Renunciation is wiping away the layers of dust and letting your inner happiness shine forth."

Charvak could not sleep that night. The thoughts, questions, and doubts he had suppressed within himself for all these years revolted and took over. The time in the present blended with memories from the past to form an incoherent mosaic in his mind. The things Asmi said continued to ring in his head, but they were stitched together with Swamiji's voice from many years ago. He saw the bench under the giant banyan tree in his dreams. He saw Manoj *kaka*, bearing gifts in his hand, looking at him with rage in his eyes. He could not move. He felt suffocated and wanted to scream, but no sound left his throat. He saw the contractor's wife standing naked in front of him. She was laughing at him mocking him for his helplessness. Her eyes were full of contempt. He felt like vomiting. He wanted to cry, but no tears left his eyes. He saw Sundaram obsequiously waiting for his instructions. Next moment, Sundaram turned into a puppy wagging its tail. Charvak patted its head. The puppy smirked maliciously at him and tried to bite his hand. He wanted to run, but his legs would not move. He saw a huge crowd cheering for him. They were standing on chairs and hooting. They had come to see him perform tricks on the stage. He was a magnificent Bengal tiger and sat inside a cage made of pure gold. The door of the cage opened and somebody pushed him out. He felt weak with fear. His limbs shook, and he was terrified.

The trainer walked towards him and said, "Promise me, my son, that you will fulfil your father's wishes! Do you promise?"

Charvak felt the weight of the world crushing him. He could not take it anymore.

"Do you promise?" the trainer repeated.

"Do you promise?" the audience shrieked and howled at him with spiteful delight.

There was darkness in front of his eyes, and he lost consciousness.

Chapter 13: Loving the I in You and Me

MANOJ SATYASHAH – MEDIUM IN HEIGHT, fully bald, nearing sixty, and tired of his son's incompetence – sat in the living room in his pyjamas staring at the television. It was late at night, and a half empty glass of whiskey lay on the centre table. Poonam, his wife, sat next to him on the sofa with a bored expression on her face.

Turning off the television angrily, Manoj said, "This is the most ridiculous television channel ever created!"

Poonam nodded her head slightly to indicate agreement.

GalaxyTV was the first television channel launched by the newly formed Satyashah Media Company. The idea for the channel was floated by Manoj's son, Prateek, and Manoj had aggressively backed his application to the Board of Directors of the Satyashah Group of Companies. The board approved it with a few riders, and three years ago, a new company was formed with Prateek as its CEO. The new venture proved to be a disaster right from the beginning. GalaxyTV was severely plagued by the lack of good content. Although Prateek managed to strike some deals with production studios early on, many of them failed to deliver. Their in-house production studio guzzled money but produced only dull, unpopular content. The dismal financial performance he presented in the third annual report was the trigger that led shareholders and directors to demand Prateek's resignation. Before starting GalaxyTV, Prateek had assumed roles at several of the Satyashah companies, and his performance there had been far from stellar. Manoj knew his son's career was at stake and felt compelled to save GalaxyTV at all costs!

Manoj invested a lot of effort in drawing up a detailed plan that would inject fresh life into the company, but turning around a company took time, and time was what Manoj did not have. In a week, the board of the Satyashah Group of Companies was scheduled to decide upon the delicate question of renewing Prateek's appointment as the CEO. Judging on the basis of performance, Prateek had been a poor executive officer; however, he was the son of Manoj Satyashah, the grandson of Vallabh Satyashah, and replacing him was an emotional decision as much as it was a business one. Manoj had been lobbying hard to gather support for his son, but he had received only grudging murmurs of assurances so far.

Charan Gupta was 83 years old. He had been the first supervisor of the first mill that Vallabh Satyashah founded. Charan had loyally stuck with Vallabh through the ups and downs of business and had been a faithful friend, colleague, and partner. For a very long time, he had remained the second-in-command of the whole group. When Ravindra took over, Charan served as a mentor to him and helped him find his place at the helm. Charvak was the third generation of the Satyashah family that Charan was associated with. The wide gap in their age and experience had prevented the two of them from ever coming close. Although Charan resented Charvak's upstart position and Charvak resented Charan's outmoded views and disregard for his authority, they had managed to work around their differences maturely and amicably.

"Are you not going to finish it?" Poonam asked pointing at the whiskey glass.

"Charan Gupta is a cunning worm!" Manoj swore under his breath.

"Did he refuse to support Prateek?"

"Oh, no, that would have been too straightforward! He just did not let me bring up the topic!"

"What do you mean? Didn't you go to his house today to speak to him?"

"He knew I was coming. When I reached his house, he opened a large chest full of old articles and papers and started reminiscing about the old times. He pulled out company files from decades ago and told me stories of how he and my father fought against all odds to establish the Satyashah Group. He went on and on for almost an hour speaking with so much enthusiasm and excitement that I could not get myself to stop him. Finally, when I lost my patience and interrupted him, he got offended and chided me for not remembering my father! I realised he was avoiding the topic so I asked him point blank whether he would support the motion to renew Prateek's appointment. He pretended to be confused and said he knew nothing about Prateek's work. When I tried to explain, he muttered something about how he was old-school and simply did not understand how business was conducted these days. When I pressed him further, he said he will study the case before forming his opinion!"

"In short, he refused?"

"Yes, I don't think he will vote for us."

"Will you speak to Charvak?"

"Charvak?"

"Yes. And Sumitra! We will need their support if we are to secure another term for Prateek."

"Poonam, you know them! They would revel in making us miserable!"

"Manoj! Whatever has happened, they are still family!"

A week later, Devika met Charvak for dinner.

"You are here to solicit my support for Prateek, aren't you?" he asked her as soon as they settled down.

"Yes, I am!"

Charvak smiled. He liked her directness. They had always been very frank and outspoken with each other. He remembered how, during their teenage years, they used to tell each other their little secrets and make pacts of confidentiality. He was four years elder to her, and she had adored him then. He had taught her how to ride a bicycle and helped her do her homework. He had been involved in only one romantic relationship in his life, and he had ended that on her advice; that had been during his college years. Everything changed when they grew up and entered adulthood. Now, they met infrequently at social occasions. He did not remember the last time they had a heart-to-heart conversation.

"Charvak, We are family! Will you not support Prateek?" Devika said.

"The decision to support Prateek is not so simple and cannot be taken on the basis of family relations. Many board members are unhappy about the fact that the Satyashah family dominates all decision-making. By supporting Prateek, I run the risk of having allegations of nepotism levelled against me. People will accuse me of favouring family over merit and competence. These are serious accusations, and I do not wish to court them!"

"People will grumble. Let them! Give Prateek a chance!"

"Look, you have to understand that, as the Chairman of the Board, I am responsible for my decisions. Supporting Prateek means putting my judgment and reputation at stake. If I support him and he fails, my decision will backfire on me. Do you realise that you are asking me to stick out my neck for him?"

"I am asking you to give him a chance. When you became the Chairman, people doubted you too! Yet, you got your chance, so why should Prateek not get his? Like you, he is also a grandson of Vallabh Satyashah!"

Charvak looked at her aghast and felt anger rising inside him. With bitterness, he said, "After everything that has happened between our families, you still have the nerve to say this! Yes, people doubted my abilities, but you know who doubted them the most! It was your father! He accused me of naivety and immaturity in public! Now, when I doubt your brother's abilities, you suddenly recall that we are family!"

Devika kept down the fork. Tension simmered in the space between them.

"Charvak, let's put that episode behind us. Papa wanted to become the Chairman after Ravindra *kaka* passed away. He has always felt that he has been denied his rightful place in the business, and he saw an opportunity to claim it. He lost, and he accepted the defeat gracefully. He has moved on. We have all moved on."

"Wait!" Charvak said with a furrow, "What do you mean denied his place? What happened after grandfather passed away? My father slogged out day and night to stabilise the business, while Manoj *kaka* went off to London to study! Nobody denied him anything! He made his own choices!"

"He did not go of his own accord! He wanted to stay back and help, but he was sent away! Your parents pressurised him to go to London, and he only followed their wishes. When he came back, he found that Ravindra *kaka* had usurped the entire business. He returned to find that the Satyashah Group of Companies had become the Ravindra Satyashah Group of Companies, and he had no place in it!"

"That's not true! Papa gave him a company to run. Manoj *kaka* failed to deliver results!"

"Really? What company? Satyashah Chemicals? In the entire history of our Group, has that business ever been profitable? Your parents gave him that specific company, because they knew he would fail; they wanted him to fail! For years, they suppressed him. They kept him contained to Chemicals and refused to let him into other businesses saying he must first prove himself! Listen, I don't know what you believe, but the fact is that your parents consciously and deliberately thwarted his growth. In the meantime, Ravindra *kaka* kept accumulating additional stocks. This was all a planned ploy to acquire more power!"

Glaring at her furiously, he said, "Do you hear yourself? You are telling me that my parents intentionally did this to Manoj *kaka*? You think we are power hungry wolves?"

"Yes! That's what your mother is! Do you think you were qualified to lead a business empire when Ravindra *kaka* passed away? No, absolutely not! And yet, why did she push you so much? Why did she struggle so frantically to get you appointed as the Chairman if she weren't so desperately hungry for power?"

"Devika! Don't point fingers at my parents! What about the labour strike? It is your father who is desperately hungry for power! I never imagined Manoj *kaka* would stoop so low. He planned and supported the strike hoping to dislodge me and pull off a boardroom coup! That was a criminal offence, but we let it go. Do you know why? Because we are family!"

Devika's face had become ashen. Wiping the tears rolling down her cheeks, she said, "You and your mother! You are monsters! You seriously think we would do something like that? God damn you! How many times should we tell you that we had nothing to do with that strike?"

Devika picked up her bag and walked out leaving Charvak staring at the untouched plates on the table.

The next day Charvak spoke to Sumitra.

"Mother, is it true that you and Papa conspired to keep Manoj *kaka* away from power?" he said.

"Who gave you such an idea? Why would we do that?" Sumitra replied.

"Well, never mind!"

"What is it?"

"I was thinking about Prateek. The topic of his appointment will come up at the board meeting."

"Oh! I am sure you will do what is right!"

The plush boardroom was located on one of the upper floors of the corporate headquarters. Manoj Satyashah was duly anxious. In the past week, he had managed to get assurances of support from a few members, but most had remained evasive and guarded. When the topic came up for discussion, Manoj made a passionate appeal. He expected a vociferous debate to follow, but an ominous silence filled the room instead.

Charan Gupta broke the silence. Putting a calculated emphasis on every syllable, he said, "My fellow members, we wield a great responsibility! We are ultimately responsible for not just this organisation but also the millions of lives it touches every day! We must base our decisions on sound principles!" He had not said much, but Manoj felt as if he had spewed venom.

Bharat Singh, a senior board member, spoke next. He read out financial figures that described the Media Company as an absolute disaster. He also did not openly oppose Prateek's appointment but only stated objective facts about the case. The members discussed a couple of points amongst themselves, but nobody voiced any decisive opinions.

Charvak was amused with the charade. His instincts, honed over years of dealing with people, instantly told him everything he wanted to know. He sensed subtle indications of collusion when some of the members, when they glanced at Charan, held their glance a little too long. He had known for some time that, besides him and Manoj, a third power centre was emerging around Charan. He noticed Charan looking intently at him. He looked at Manoj and realised that he, too, was looking intently at him. He knew that the board would remain noncommittal until he voiced his decision. He was not particularly fond of Prateek and did not think he was capable of resuscitating GalaxyTV, but he did not want to offer Charan a chance at victory either. Interrupting the chatter, Charvak made a strong argument supporting the reappointment of Prateek. His emphatic statement put the matter to rest, and the board voted with him passing a resolution recommending that Prateek be reappointed as the CEO of Satyashah Media Company for another term.

After the meeting, as Manoj walked past Charvak, he slightly tilted his head and smiled as if to acknowledge the gesture. Devika called Charvak later. The ill aftertaste from their dinner lingered on, but she tried to diffuse the hostility, and he reciprocated. Prateek thanked him for the support and pledged that he would do his best.

Sumitra congratulated him saying, "You made the right decision. It is better to take the side of Manoj and Prateek than to prop up Charan."

"Manoj *kaka* and his family were very happy. Do you think our relations will ever mend?" Charvak asked.

"My son," Sumitra said, "Don't mix family relationships and business! Remember, today they are smiling and standing by your side, because you are strong, and they need you. But show them a moment of weakness, and they will not hesitate to topple you and snatch things from you when you are lying on the ground! Do not be complacent about them; you can take powerful blows by sworn enemies on the battlefield and remain unaffected, but it is the treachery of those closest to you that hurts the most!"

Asmi sat on her bed looking with concentration at a blank piece of paper. She loved doing this; she would pick up the pen and fill the paper with random sentences and fragments, with whatever came to her mind. She liked the tension it created: on one side was the gushing stream of words that she felt the urge to pour out on the paper; and then, on the other side, was the tender wish to protect the pristine and untouched blankness of the paper that represented to her infinite possibilities. She had always been good with words. For a long time, she had been aware of the strange power they had. She believed that words were not only a medium for expressing ideas, but they could also give birth to them. Thoughts that spring up in our minds are hazy and amorphous. They lack form and exist as vague notions, only as potentialities. Words give form to these notions, and transform them into ideas, which are solid and well defined. And that is why, as much as she loved words, she also hated them! Words turn amorphous thoughts into crystalline ideas, but these ideas are palpable and tangible. You cannot dissect a hazy notion, but once cast in words, an idea gets subjected to many brutalities; it no longer remains an intimate thought nestled safely within your imagination but is now open to interrogation by a monster called 'reason' who, without showing sympathy or appreciation for the beauty of the thought, will cut, stretch, fold, and squeeze it till it fits the hard, rigid rules of logic turning the innocent little thought into a cold, joyless artefact!

Her reverie was interrupted by the ringing phone. From the ringtone, she knew it was Agastya.

"Why don't you go out with your friends? What do you mean you don't feel like going? Are you just going to sit in your room doing nothing?" she said to him.

"Not nothing! I am going to think!"

"Think about what?"

"About you my darling!" he teased.

"No! I am serious. I am worried you are turning into a loner!"

Agastya had many friends on the campus. But, once in a while, he would retreat into his solitude where he would cut off all social contact other than the bare minimum. He used to say it fuelled his creativity.

She continued, "I understand your need for space, but isn't there a limit to the amount of time one should spend in loneliness?"

"Asmi, my dear, do not confuse solitude with loneliness!"

"All right! You don't want to go and hang out with your friends, I understand. Why don't you spend time working together with them? Don't you need to collaborate with other researchers or graduate students?"

"Yes, I do, but I see collaboration as a means of sharing information, not as a means of creation! I meet them, and we discuss results and work processes. We plan things together, but we don't do them together. I work best when I am alone. I am most productive when I am alone. Do you know, Asmi, the most creative and original things in the world have always come out of solitude? Albert Einstein did not develop relativity in collaboration! Leonardo did not paint Mona Lisa together with others!"

She gave up. She had just wanted to ensure he is not lonely, but she realised that she did not need to worry. She admired his passion. He would work days on end thinking of nothing but his equations, thinking only about his work without thinking of success and failure. He frequently gave her examples of Einstein.

"Agastya, do you think you will achieve what Einstein did?" she asked.

He laughed and said, "Of course, I will!"

She was startled by this brash confidence.

He elaborated, "Of course, I will achieve what Einstein did! Will I win the Nobel Prize? Maybe not. Will I be as famous as Einstein? Maybe not. But, you see, these are not the achievements that I wish to rival. What do you think was Einstein's greatest achievement? What did he work for? He did not work for the

Nobel or other awards. He did not work for the fame. He worked for the pure, unadulterated joy he felt when he derived his equations. His work was his reward. The joy he got from his work was the achievement that meant the most to him, and that is the one I want to match. I firmly believe that the joy I feel when I work is no lesser than what he would have felt. Yes, Asmi, in that regard, I have and will continue to achieve what Einstein did!"

Their love for each other was not frantic, impatient, or turbulent like the mountain stream; it was intimate, soulful, and powerful like the ocean. Untainted by the dirt and filth of the world, free from the Procrustean Bed of societal roles, unstained by jealousy and possessiveness, it was not a transaction based on expectations. There were no sacrifices or compromises. It was pure and untouched by divisive emotions, because between the two of them, they did not recognise the constructs of you and I!

He used to tell her, "Asmi, I love you as I love myself! I love you so much that no power on earth, not even yourself, can change that. If, from tomorrow, you never see me or speak to me again, I would continue to love you as I do today, because my love for you does not depend on your love for me. I love the 'you that I love' and not the 'you that loves me'! The 'you that I love' has become an inseparable part of my existence, and I can no longer differentiate between the act of loving you and the act of loving myself!"

They loved without distrust or guilt. They were not afraid of intimacy. She would tell him, "I love you so much, Agastya, that I have let you inside the deepest core of my being. My innermost hopes and fears, desires and repulsions, I have bared them all to you. By hiding nothing from you, I have learned more about myself. Before I met you, I was convinced that the world had no place for me. You proved, by simply being, that I was wrong. In you, I found someone who belonged to my world. Agastya, my world is what I perceive as reality. By belonging to my world, you belong to me. I know it in my heart that, eventually, through my love for you, I will learn to love the world!"

They loved, not empty identities, but the real essence of who they were. "Do you know, Asmi, that in loving each other, we actually love the same thing? When I love you, I love the real you, and not your social identity, your physical appearance, or any other hollow shell that goes by your name. The real self in me loves the real self in you. We can do this only because we know our true selves, because we don't bear false pretenses, and because we are intimately honest with ourselves and with each other. If I did not know myself, or you did not know yourself, how could we love each other? Then, our love would be hollow! But it is not hollow, because we know what we love: we both love the 'I' in 'you' and 'me'!

Chapter 14: The Tree That Grows to Heaven

AROUND THREE HUNDRED KILOMETRES FROM Mumbai, nestled outside a cosy village on the shore of the Arabian Sea, not very far from the Wadi, lay a beautiful plot of land on which Ravindra Satyashah had dreamed of building a weekend home for his family. He had hired an architect to draw up the plans, but his sudden demise meant the project was cancelled. The rectangular plot lay parallel in its length to the shore and ran north to south. Its northern end was elevated and formed a steep cliff facing the sea. From there, the hill gently sloped southwards, and the southern end was at the sea level. Ravindra had imagined a house built in steps. The top step would be on the cliff overlooking the sea, while the bottommost step would be a courtyard that opened onto the beach.

"Why don't you build it now?" Asmi asked Charvak. They were sitting on the rocks on the beach at the proposed site of this home looking at the waves rise and fall. It was a Sunday afternoon. Charvak had called her in the morning asking her if she would go with him to see this place. She had hesitated. They were good friends, but this was too personal; but he was persuasive and managed to convince her.

"What would I do building it? Really speaking, there's no family left. Who will stay in this house?" Charvak answered.

"Oh! You can get married and have children. Your mother, wife, and kids can come here on weekends," she said jokingly, but he looked away unable to stomach her humour.

A few days back, Sumitra had approached Charvak. He was sitting at the table reading something when she came and stood in front of him.

"You remember Saloni Choksi, right?" she said.

"The girl I could not stand for an hour?" he replied.

Sumitra ignored the jibe and continued, "I met her at Rinku's house the other day. She is now working at an orphanage. She plays with children and looks after them. She is doing good work!"

"I am glad to hear it!" he said carelessly.

Sumitra's expression did not change. She adjusted the chair and sat down. "She comes from a good family. She went to a foreign university to study!"

"Study what?"

"How does that matter? What matters is that she is well educated. Her father is a businessman. Her mother is well known in her circles. You have met them. Don't you think they are nice people?"

He did not respond to the question, which was obviously rhetorical.

She continued, "And don't you think Saloni is beautiful? She is sweet, charming, and…"

"Mother, she might be the most beautiful woman in the world, but I am not going to marry her!" he said impatiently.

Sumitra had anticipated this. Carefully maintaining just the right length of pause after his response, she replied, "Then whom do you want to marry? Asmi?"

Charvak stiffened. "What do you mean?" he mumbled.

"You know what I mean. You think of her all the time. You meet her all the time. You make people wait outside the office for hours when you are preoccupied with her. You go for dinner with her and…"

"Why do you know all this? Are you spying on me?"

Sumitra laughed and said, "Look at me! I am your mother. Yes, I keep a track of things in your life, but I do this only because I have your best interests at heart! I wonder why you are spending so much of your time and effort on a simpleton! What do you see in her? She is just an ordinary employee of the company you own. She has no social standing that befits you. She has no class, grace, or refinement that any woman in your life must have. She comes from a village. What has she studied? Some insignificant thing in some insignificant college?"

Sumitra paused to assess his reaction. Emboldened by seeing that there was none, she continued assuming a more serious tone, "And, Charvak, she is a divorcee! She deserted her husband and her family! That speaks of her selfishness and utter lack of values! I cannot accept that divorcee as a wife for my son! You are a role-model for millions of people; what will they say if you marry her?"

Startled by his mother's bitter polemic, Charvak struggled to organise his thoughts. He composed himself, and just as he was about to reply, Sumitra got up and walked off with indignation.

Charvak looked at Asmi as she sat on the rocks with her feet in the water. The gentle breeze softly ruffled her hair. The waves washed at her feet spraying droplets of water in the air as they broke on the rocks.

He was ten when he first came here with his father. They had sat at the same place, on the same rocks, looking at the same horizon.

Gazing at the endless expanse of water that lay before them, Ravindra had said, "We will build a cosy house here overlooking

188

the sea. This will be our secret place where we will retreat to find peace!"

"But Papa, there is nothing around here. What will we do?"

"We will enjoy the nothingness! When you grow up you will realise that, at times, you don't want to go somewhere to do things; you want to go somewhere to just get away from things!"

"Get away?" Charvak had said with consternation on his face, "What do you want to get away from, Papa?"

"We will come here to hide from the world; in this place, we will create our very own world!"

"Mamma says we should not run or hide! We should fight and we should win!"

"Asmi, constructing this house was Papa's dream! He did not speak about it often, but whenever he did, his eyes gave away how much it really meant to him!" Charvak said.

"Why did he never build it?" Asmi asked.

"I don't know! It was as if he was searching for something, and he would have built it once he found it. He passed away before that happened."

"What do you think your father was searching for?"

"I don't know!"

"What are you searching for, Charvak? What do you want in life?"

He turned to face her and said, with resignation in his voice, "I don't know!"

Charvak went to Sumitra afterwards.

"Mother, I will tell you what I see in Asmi. She makes me feel alive! Her presence awakens something within me. She reminds me of what I can be, of what I really am beneath the layers of masks I put on every day. I know you don't approve of her, but please understand that I am in love with her! I love her from the bottom of my heart! I think of her every day and every moment. In the past few months, the only time I remember smiling was when I was with her. I see in her a woman who can pierce through my masks and reach the real me. I have never felt like that with anyone before!"

Sumitra rolled her eyes and, putting on a disinterested look, said, "I understand you are in love, but what is love? It's just a passing thing! You will love her now, but you will not love her tomorrow. And all this gibberish you speak of, your masks and the real you, where is that coming from? Love is blind, and you are struggling to justify your feelings for her, but do not pretend to believe this rubbish! What do you think she wants from you? I tell you she is nothing but another gold digger! You are the most eligible bachelor in the whole country. You are a billionaire; hundreds of women will marry you in the blink of an eye for all the wealth you have. She might have said a couple of smart things that provoked your thoughts. She might have said sweet nothings to you that made you feel good, but that does not mean she loves you. Look at the stakes for her. By enticing you, she wants to marry you; that is her game plan. Don't be naive and fall for it. She is only after your money!"

Charvak raised his eyebrows perplexed at her remarks. "Mother, I think you have completely misunderstood the situation! I never said she loves me. I only said I love her. She has never done anything to entice me; you are jumping way ahead! She may not even agree to marry me if I ask her! Where is the question of her being a gold digger?"

It was Sumitra's turn to be confused. "What do you mean she does not love you?"

"She has never said anything or given any indication that she has any feelings of love towards me. And I have never told her how I feel about her!"

"If she doesn't love you, then what in the name of the devil does she want from you?"

"That's the funny part: she wants nothing! She is the first person I have met in years who wants nothing from me!"

It was low tide. The waves had receded from the beach and no longer reached the rocks.

"You cannot not know! What drives you?" Asmi asked.

Charvak replied, "For all these years, I thought I knew, but I was wrong. I have devoted my life to the Satyashah Group of Companies, but I now question what this Group really means! I have been fighting for the progress of the Group and the growth of our businesses. I have put my heart and soul into achieving sustainability, improving efficiency, entering new markets, and other godforsaken business jargon. I have been evaluating my success and failure by the means of financial figures in our annual reports. I was blindly doing all of this until I met you. It was you, Asmi, who opened my eyes; and sometimes I wish you hadn't, because now I feel lost like a rudderless ship!"

"When you entered the business, what did you dream of then?"

"I dreamed of money; all my ambitions revolved around money! When I realised that I already had more than enough to buy all the things I wanted, I started using money as a symbol of status. I paraded my wealth to attract attention. It felt nice when people ogled with awe at the trappings of my wealth. Then, I realised it was not money but fame that I was after. I became famous, as famous as I wanted to be, before I realised the futility of it: by chasing fame, I was seeking approval of people whom I did not even care about! When fame stopped exciting me, I started chasing power. I wanted to wield power over the wretched flies that I despised. I feel ashamed of some of the antics I performed in my pursuit of power; but now that I have power, I feel all of this was meaningless! While I was busy chasing money, fame, and power, I lost myself somewhere along the way!"

"What do you think you wanted from money, fame, and power?"

"I did not know it then, but after meeting you, I realised that I was looking for freedom! I do not really care about money, and I have enough to meet all my needs. The moment I became the Chairman of the Group, I was already famous. By acquiring power, I wanted to liberate myself from the world. I have never particularly liked people. They are nasty and cunning. They feel smug in their slimy existence and always want to pull you down into their dirty little worlds. I wanted to be so powerful that I could stop being bothered by them altogether!"

Asmi smiled at him and said softly, "Do you know the story of the tree that wanted to rise high above the world, rise so high that it would reach the heaven? The tree detested the rotten world. It decided one day to rise above the filthy earth. It grew strong branches and rose in height. It became taller than all other trees in the forest. It became taller than the hills. But then, it realised that, in order to sustain its strong branches, it had grown its roots deep into the vile earth. The more it struggled to grow into height and light, the more vigorously its roots struggled earthward, downward, into the dark and the evil. Have you heard of the philosopher Friedrich Nietzsche? He has written that the tree that grows to heaven must send its roots to hell! Charvak, I hope that you have not become that tree!"

They had driven from Mumbai in his unnecessarily long, silver Rolls Royce. It was a winter day; the warm sun felt good on his skin. The rhythmic sound of the waves breaking on the shore produced an unreal calm in his mind. He ran his eyes over her delicate body and felt a shiver shoot up his spine. Her hair was messed up and a few strands were loosely flying in the wind. She looked beautiful, astonishingly beautiful! He wanted to hold her in his arms and kiss her on her lips. He shrugged and turned his mind to other thoughts. She was right: he had already become that tree! He had accumulated power thinking it would fetch him freedom. He realised now that, in some twisted way, power had made him dependent on the very people he wanted to wield it on!

He said, "All my life, I have only known that I should work for money, fame, and power. I don't know anything else. I have started feeling weary and tired of all this. What should I do?"

"Quit!" she said nonchalantly.

"Quit what?"

"The Satyashah Group!"

He looked at her in bewildered amazement. "Are you out of your mind? You are asking me to leave the Satyashah Group!"

"Yes! The Satyashah Group has become a golden cage for you! What other option do you have if you don't like doing it anymore?"

"Asmi, that is not an option! Don't you understand? My entire adulthood has been spent working for it. I have done nothing else. I know nothing else. I am Charvak Satyashah! I am the son of Ravindra Satyashah and the grandson of Vallabh Satyashah! I am the Chairman of the largest conglomerate in India. The entire country knows me. I am rich, and I am famous. People burn with envy at what I have. Do not devalue what I have even if I say I'm tired of it!"

"If you put a high value on freedom, you must put a lower value on everything else! What is the use of your wealth if you cannot enjoy it? What is the use of power if you are tired of maintaining it?"

He shook his head in disbelief and said, "You are insane! You don't know the value of what I have! People will give up anything to be in my place!"

"No!" she said in a fiery voice, "They will not give up their life for it, and neither should you!"

He felt offended at her, because she had so easily dismissed his wealth and prestige, something that still gave meaning to his identity; but in his heart, he knew she was right. They would have to leave back for Mumbai in a while.

"Thank you for coming with me today. There's something I wish to tell you," he said in a serene voice. "My life has changed irrevocably after I met you. I had forgotten my self, buried it inside my soul, and spent years constructing barriers to prevent it from ever coming out. I had succeeded in doing that until you made those barriers melt away. There's a conflict going on inside me that I cannot understand: the things that I wanted in life so far are now meaningless to me, and the things I want in life now..." He paused unable to continue.

"What do you want now?" she asked.

"Asmi... I want you! I have never wanted anything so much before. I love you, Asmi! I love you so much that I have no words to describe it. I feel my life means nothing without you. You are my purpose; you are my reason and my meaning. I look at you, and I see the world in your eyes; I touch you, and I feel my heart stop beating. I have never loved before, and I know I will never love again. I love you!"

Asmi was looking in the direction of the sun that was now sinking beyond the horizon. She closed her eyes for a brief moment and turned towards him.

"Charvak, I am overwhelmed! Thank you for sharing your feelings with me!"

She said nothing after that; he kept on waiting with bated breath hanging on to hope.

Finally, she spoke in a whisper, "I am sorry! I have nothing more to say!"

On the way back, in the unnecessarily long, silver Rolls Royce, they sat quietly facing each other. Through all the time they had spent together, there had not been a single moment when they had run out of things to say. They sat quietly, not because they had nothing to say, but because the silence spoke louder than words could have.

After a while, he said, "I know you do not love me. You probably have no feelings for me other than just friendship. But I still want to ask you this: Asmi, will you marry me?"

Asmi looked up sharply at him. He was fidgeting nervously staring at the floor mat. She felt pity for him. Telling her he loved her was a declaration; asking her to marry him was a plea!

She said, "You are a great friend to me, a friend whom I value most dearly in my life, but I do not love you. Charvak, I am sorry! I cannot marry you!"

His eyes became moist. He felt life had brought him to an impassable chasm, and she was the only one who could help him cross it. She had awakened a spirit inside him that had been asleep for years; she had provoked it, and he could not fight it alone. Without her, he was lost. Without her, the struggle with the spirit, his own self buried and forgotten within, would destroy him!

"Asmi, I will give you everything. I know and understand your needs. I will provide you an environment that fosters your quest for freedom. Please, I beg of you, accept my love and marry me!"

"I am sorry, Charvak! I cannot!"

In a fit of desperation, he asked, "Why not? Don't you believe I love you?"

She replied without mincing her words, "You say 'I love you' but you do not understand the meaning of 'I'! Where is the 'I' in you Charvak? I don't see it! You are doing things not because you want to but because you are supposed to! You have lost your originality and become a hollow shell blindly following expectations and demands, and…"

"I am not a hollow shell, Asmi! The hollow 'I' would not have loved you and would have married Saloni Choksi instead! The real 'I' loves you! You mean the whole world to me. Please tell me what I should give up, and I will give it up this instant for you!"

"See, you still don't get it! I don't want you to give up anything for me; that will defeat the purpose! The question is: what will you give up for yourself?"

When they reached back, he said in an exhausted voice, "Asmi, I feel compelled to ask you one last time. I will not ask you again. I will not bother you again. Will you marry me? If you say yes, I will turn the world upside down to make you happy. If you say no, I never want to see or talk to you again! Will you marry me?"

"No!" she said and got out of the car.

Chapter 15: The Law of Karma

ASMI TENDERED HER RESIGNATION NEXT morning. Sundaram was perplexed since she gave no reason for leaving the job. She was one of his best employees, and he was sorry to see her go. She tried calling Charvak to inform him of her decision to leave, but he did not answer her calls. She went up to his office where Rachana told her that he did not want to see her. Her notice period was waived off, and she turned in her identity and access card that same evening. She walked out of the building calmly and did not look back one last time.

She went to the Sahyadri office the next day. She told the Joshis that she had left her job and wanted to spend more time working with them. They were overjoyed to hear that. They sat her down and discussed their plans for the next few months. The admission season was around the corner. Last year, with Asmi's help, they had accommodated a few dozen students in various colleges and hostels in the city.

Mrs Joshi said, "Asmi, we started Sahyadri after our retirement to keep us occupied and do a bit of good while we were at it. It has been eight wonderful years running this organisation, but we are getting old and tired. This year we expect hundreds of students to show up at our doorstep. As you can see, we have a plan, but we need you to turn it into reality. Will you work fulltime with Sahyadri? The money will be lesser than what you will get paid elsewhere, but you might derive more satisfaction from this!"

"Yes, I would love to!" Asmi replied.

At fifty-six, Yogesh Naik had been the principal of the District Primary and Secondary School in the Wadi for eighteen long years. He remembered Asmi as one of the best students of her batch. He had been a classmate of her father in the same school during their childhood. He had been disappointed when he came to know that her father had refused to let Asmi pursue engineering in the city. Kamble, the owner of the local general store, had visited him carrying sweets to celebrate his daughter's admission into the Government College of Commerce in Mumbai. He mentioned Asmi and her invaluable contribution.

"Asmi? What does she do in the city?" Naik asked Kamble.

"Principal sir, have you not heard? She has helped so many children from the Wadi and the neighbouring villages get education in the city. She is a god-sent angel!"

"Oh! I did not know. Do you happen to have her phone number?"

He called Asmi one afternoon, "Asmi, do you remember me? I am Principal Naik calling from the Wadi."

Asmi replied, "Of course, I remember you, sir! It's a pleasure speaking to you. How are you?"

"I am doing well. I wanted to discuss something with you. Once the Secondary School exams get over, many students from our school come to me asking for help in pursuing further education, but I don't know what to tell them. Can you help them if I direct them to you?"

"Most certainly!"

Naik smiled to himself. He had seen many students over the years struggle to find decent college education. He used to feel guilty at times about his inability to help them. But now, through Asmi, he had an opportunity to change that!

Asmi went to the Sahyadri office in the mornings. In preparation for the admissions season, the first task she chased was creating a team of volunteers who would work with them. With a team in place, the work became a lot easier. She learned to delegate and keep track of activities. She spent her day running around meeting officials in various educational institutes across the city. She successfully pitched Sahyadri to numerous donor and funding agencies and raised working capital. She wrote articles for newspapers and magazines. Most importantly, with the help of Principal Naik and some other contacts of the Joshis, she started spreading word about Sahyadri in villages and towns across the region.

Swamiji was happy to know she had joined Sahyadri and encouraged her work.

She told him, "Swamiji, I like the work I am doing. By helping these students, I feel I am working for a worthy cause, but I do not feel like sacrificing my life for it. I want to help people, but I do not want to make it the purpose of my life. I am getting sucked into this altruistic environment where everyone around me talks about serving the society, but I cannot figure out why I am doing this; I have not made my peace with the world! When I hear the word 'society', I cringe, because I remember the dragon. I remember Fernandes and the crack in the door. The society I am trying to help is the same society that has caused me pain and suffering; the world I am trying to change is the same world I have never belonged to. Why, then, am I doing this?"

Swamiji smiled and said, "You are not doing it for them, Asmi; you are doing it for yourself!"

"I don't understand! How am I doing this for myself? What do I stand to gain by it?"

"My child, you will understand someday that your own interests are best served by also serving the interests of others. As long as you live in a society, whether you despise the society or not, you cannot deny the fact that you are a part of it. I am not asking you to put someone else's interest above yours. I am not saying that you should sacrifice your life to help others. Life is a struggle to come to terms with our brief existence in an absurd world! If you can help a fellow traveller along the journey, why not do it? Remember, by helping them, you are helping yourself!"

Asmi shrugged. She was not completely convinced by his answer. They were sitting on the bench under the giant banyan when she asked, "Swamiji, what is Karma?"

"What do you think it is?"

"It is something like a divine accounting system. Every action we perform has consequences. Your karma is the sum total of the consequences of all your actions. Good actions bring good karma, and bad actions bring bad karma. Good karma brings happiness, and bad karma brings suffering."

"No, Asmi, there is no divine accounting system, but yes, there is cause and effect! What you described is the concept of karma in its most simplified form. That is how karma manifests itself, but that is not what it is."

"Then what is it?"

"In Vedanta philosophy, in all Eastern religions, karma is intricately tied to liberation. What do you think happens when you help others? You start empathizing with them. Empathy and compassion make you see the world through their eyes. By experiencing their feelings, by sharing their joys and sorrows, in a way, you start becoming them! Compassion creates a subconscious movement where you begin to realise the non-duality between you and them. By beginning to identify yourself with them, you start identifying yourself with the world! The illusion of the ego is caused by wrongly identifying your self with social roles and material possessions. Removing this illusion is the first step towards realising the truth. Good karma, being compassionate, helping others, and empathizing with them helps you take this step!"

"So, the concept of karma essentially says what you told me: by helping others, I am helping myself?"

"Yes! Compassion will help you discover yourself in others. Asmi, you are on the right path. Your work with Sahyadri will help you in your quest for freedom. However, I must caution you: do not get so carried away in helping others that you forget yourself. Be selfish, and keep your quest at the centre of your life; everything else is secondary!"

"Will I ever find what I am looking for?"

"Yes, my child, you will! Do not doubt it!"

"The kind of freedom I want, is it real Swamiji? I asked you once whether you have met a living person who has attained *Moksha*; you said you had met one of the *Saptarishis*. How did you meet him?"

"It's a long story!"

"Come on, we have time! Please tell me!"

Decades ago, Narayan Thosar excitedly stood in front of a pile of neatly-folded, freshly-dyed saffron robes. At the age of 26, he was one of the youngest members of the Saraswati Mission to be ordained as a *swami*. That morning, Acharya Swami Suryananda Saraswati, the founder and head of the Saraswati Mission, had formally pronounced Narayan Thosar as Swami Narayanananda Saraswati in a traditional ordination ceremony. Narayan had worked and studied hard for the last four years since joining the Mission. He had thoroughly read all the major scriptures and passed tests designed to evaluate his knowledge, sincerity, and dedication to the study and practice of Vedanta. The *acharya* had been impressed with Narayan. The ordination ceremony marked his induction as a *swami*, a master, a monk who has devoted his life to the pursuit of spiritual realisation.

The *acharya* asked him after the ceremony, "Do you know, Narayan, why a *swami's* robes are saffron in colour?"

"Yes, I do!"

In Hindu tradition, when a person dies, he is cremated. A *swami*, however, is buried and not cremated. It is believed that in the act of becoming a *swami*, the person has already undergone a spiritual death of the ego. He has burned his false identity in the fire of self-knowledge, and hence, there's no need to cremate his body. Saffron represents that fire!

Saraswati Mission had over a hundred *ashrams* in India and an equal number of them spread across Europe and North America. Narayan rose rapidly in the hierarchy of the organisation. He travelled across the country delivering lectures and conducting workshops to spread the teachings of Vedanta. His excellent oratory and modern vocabulary made him quite popular. His lectures were recorded and audiocassettes were made available in *ashrams* and offices of the Mission. He spent five years setting up and running *ashrams* in Germany, England, Canada, and USA. Narayan, though popular, got embroiled in conflicts over matters of principle with other *swamis* of the Mission. While giving discourses, he liked to draw on stories from different sources. He used Buddhist tales abundantly to drive home his points; this irked many members of the Mission. During a scintillating lecture he gave in New York, he weaved together in his talk Zen stories and the poetry of Rumi.

Swami Radhananda, who was much senior to Narayan, came up to him the next day and said, "Your talk was very good, but why do you mention stories from other religions? Hinduism has enough tales to tell!"

"I tell stories only to illustrate the points I am trying to make. I don't worry about what religion they come from."

202

Swami Radhananda shook his head and said, "Narayan, the Mission has a purpose. We are here to spread the word of Hinduism, not of other religions!"

"I thought we were here to spread the word of knowledge!" replied Narayan.

As the years passed by, Narayan became increasingly disillusioned by life in the Mission. His fellow *swamis*, although very knowledgeable in the scriptures, could not satisfy many of his doubts. What frustrated him was the fact that they never questioned the scriptures and they took them as they were served to them, word for word, and never let him question them either. Whenever he went to the senior *swamis* with a genuine question, they would try to answer it superficially by giving references. But Narayan did not want references; he had already read all of them! He wanted answers. On pressing them further, they would retreat to a moral high ground and say, "You cannot interrogate the texts! That is blasphemous. Yes, it is important to ask questions, but you must learn to believe! These scriptures represent the word of God! Who are we to question them?"

Unable to reconcile his curiosity with the morally binding nature of Mission life, Narayan went to the *acharya* and poured out his frustrations. "Acharya, I want to realise the truth, but I don't see how I can do it living with the Mission. We renounce the chains of materialism only to adopt chains of authoritative religious life, but those are still chains!"

Narayan admired and respected the *acharya* who was nearing ninety. It was because of him that he had joined the Saraswati Mission. The *acharya* replied, "You are right when you say that you cannot realise the truth by staying with the Mission. To do that, you need solitude. It is very difficult to live in a community and drop your identity completely. When you are alone, there's no need for an identity to differentiate 'you' from 'them'. If you

203

are really serious about seeking liberation, leave the Mission. The Mission cannot help you; you must do it on your own!"

Narayan stepped out the next day with nothing but a bottle of water, a pair of garments, and the blessings of the *acharya*. He wandered directionless for a few weeks till he came across a group of six Jain *sadhus* walking along the road. They were bareheaded and wore minimal white clothes. Whether freezing cold or scorching hot, they never wore footwear. They walked from place to place, barefoot, and never used any other mode of transport. They never stayed at one place for more than a week to avoid developing any attachment to the place or people living there. They stayed in monasteries, temples, houses of Jain followers, or any other shelter they could find. When they walked, which is what they did for most part of the day, they chanted hymns and passages from Jain scriptures. They welcomed him to stay with them.

One of the *sadhus* told him, "There is no God. There is no creator or destroyer. There is no heaven or hell. There is no divine judge. There is only the law of cause and effect! The world is full of people perpetually looking to shift blame away from themselves. Narayan, the purest thing you can do in your life is to own responsibility for every action you take however big or small it may be. Every step you take, every morsel of food you eat, every deed you perform, every word you speak, every thought you think, whether you do it through your physical body or in the realm of your imagination, do it consciously and mindfully, and own responsibility for it. When you understand that your every action leaves a mark on the world and a mark on your soul, you will realise the meaning of life!"

Narayan spent a year wandering with the *sadhus* and learned a lot from them. The Saraswati Mission had given him knowledge; the *sadhus* taught him how to put it to practice. On the banks of the Godavari, on a rainy day, he parted ways with them. He bid them farewell, and they wished him luck!

Narayan started walking north. In a small village on the banks of the Narmada, he attained his first experience of *Nirvikalpa Samadhi*. Armed with the confirmation that he was on the right path, he resolved to go to the Himalayas to continue his search. He travelled through Bihar into Bhutan and Nepal where he spent time at some Buddhist monasteries. It was at these monasteries that he first heard of the *Saptarishis* being spoken of as real people; until then, he had only heard legends about them. The *Saptarishis* were thought to be a group of wandering *rishis*, sages who lived in the most isolated stretches of the Himalayas. Some said they were immortal and had lived for thousands of years; others said they did not need food and could survive on sunlight. Some said they were monks who taught their wisdom to Gautam Buddha; others said they were heavenly beings that revealed knowledge of the Vedas to the first men who inhabited the earth.

A Tibetan Buddhist master told him, "The *Saptarishis* are enlightened souls. They belong to no religion or caste. They live in isolation from the world, perhaps in solitude even from one another. They are not a group or a sect. They are individuals who have attained the ultimate liberation."

"Are they immortal?" Narayan asked.

The master smiled and said, "Narayan, you yourself are a *swami*; you should know that a person who has attained enlightenment has already transcended the boundaries of life and death. He is not alive or dead; he simply exists in the moment."

Narayan's search was not for the *Saptarishis*. His search was for the final liberation that would free him from human bondage. For that, he had to get away from the world of people, relationships, and material possessions. After leaving the Mission, he had gradually weaned himself off these things. He now adopted a life of complete renunciation. He left the Buddhist monastery and started walking. He spent months wandering through desolate regions of cold and barren land nestled in the womb of the great mountains. He climbed hills and crossed valleys. When he came to villages, someone invariably offered him food. When he was away from human habitation, he survived on whatever he could scavenge off the land. A madness took over him. He did not notice when he fell sick and recovered. He lost weight and shrivelled in size. He walked through forests and deserts oblivious to any care in the world. The utter solitude slowly started dissolving the ego within him. He often forgot himself when walking through stark stretches of sand and snow with no living being in sight. He walked as if he was the wind and the sand. While meditating for long hours, he often went into deep *samadhi*, a state of heightened consciousness, where he lost all sense of identity. He wandered like this for almost two years, remaining in *samadhi* for days on end, walking under the scorching sun and the freezing snow wearing only a tattered woollen blanket on his shoulders. Sensations like hunger, thirst, fatigue, and cold meant nothing to him. Days rolled by, but the passage of time meant nothing to him. He, himself, meant nothing to him. It was almost as if he had ceased to exist. He was nothing and everything!

Narayan had not spoken a word to anyone in months. He was walking one evening when he heard some noise behind him. He turned to see that he was staring in the face of a giant Himalayan bear. She was a mother-bear and behind her were two little cubs. She growled menacingly at him, but he strangely felt nothing. He looked at the bear with a smile on his face. He felt no fear, because nothing could happen to him. He was a withered tangled mess of muscles and bones, but he was also the bear! He was the bear, the cubs, the sand, the sky, and the mountains! He was the whole universe! That is when he spoke to the bear. He did not speak in a human language; he spoke in the language of compassion. He loved the bear as much as he loved himself. He was the bear as much as he was himself. His eyes were full of infinite compassion for her and her cubs. The bear calmed down. She came up to him and sniffed his feet. He touched her forehead. She slowly withdrew and walked away with her cubs.

It was a warm summer afternoon. Narayan climbed up a hill and, on reaching the top, saw a man sitting beneath a tree with a wicker basket in his hand. The man saw Narayan and beckoned him to come closer. He was wearing a loose white garment and had grey hair and a flowing beard. He offered Narayan some wild figs from his basket. Narayan was famished and gladly devoured them. When he finished eating, he looked up at the man. He had a kind and friendly expression on his face. He looked around seventy, but his face was that of a child. Narayan was mesmerised by his childlike beauty and could not take his eyes off him.

"Who are you?" Narayan asked him.

"I am!" the man replied.

Narayan immediately understood that he was standing in front of a man who had realised the truth: a sage, a *rishi*, who was an embodiment of truth itself! Narayan folded his hands in a *namaskar* and bowed before him. They sat together in silence for a while looking at the blue sky and the snow-capped peaks on the horizon. Just the mere presence of the *rishi* next to him invoked in Narayan a feeling of pure bliss!

"What do you want?" the *rishi* finally spoke.

"I want liberation. I have searched for it all my life. I have spent years studying the scriptures. I know the answer, and I understand what it means. I am so close to the truth, but yet so far from it, because although I understand it, I fail to realise it. I want to realise freedom and liberation in its true form. I want *Moksha*!"

"Let me ask you a question! What is *Moksha*?" The *rishi's* eyes twinkled as he spoke.

"*Moksha* is freedom from all bondage!" Narayan replied.

"What is bondage?"

"Bondage is when your mind longs for something, when it desires something. *Maya,* the web of desires, is everywhere. Chains of causality tightly hold this web together. Even one small desire will push me into this web, and then I will be chained to the whole world! A single desire, however small, will make me a slave of causality. It will make me a slave of my own mind. Bondage arises out of desire!"

"And what is liberation?"

"Liberation is when there is no bondage, when there are no desires to bind me to the web of *Maya.* Understanding this, I have given up all desires. One by one, I have renounced everything!"

The *rishi* looked at Narayan affectionately. The smile had not left his face. "Let me ask you again! What do you want?"

"I want…" Narayan started to speak but stopped suddenly realising the contradiction.

The *rishi* smiled a bit wider and said, "Do you see? You still want something. In seeking liberation, you desire to be free of desire. You want to not want. Your pursuit of liberation has become an end in itself. The seeking has become an obstacle to finding that which you seek. Stop seeking, and you will find!"

Narayan was overwhelmed by the intense wisdom that exuded from the *rishi* and wanted to stay by his side forever. "Will you accept me as your disciple?" he said.

"Who should accept you as a disciple?" the *rishi* asked.

"You should accept me as a disciple!"

"But who am I? I am you! I am the universe! Go back, my friend, go back to where you came from!"

"I cannot go back to the world of people. I do not belong there!"

"Do not look down upon them! See yourself in them! You are as much them as you are yourself. Treat them with compassion. You owe them a debt which you must repay!"

"What debt?"

"Did you grow up all by yourself without their help? Did your mother not give you birth and feed you? Did you not drink from the wisdom of the scriptures in your pursuit of liberation? Who wrote these scriptures? Who preserved them over thousands of years so you could read them? The society that you have renounced did all this for you! Without people, without civilization, without society having taught you these things, you would have been only an animal! The moment you are born, you enter into an unwritten contract with the society. The society does many things for you. Until you repay this debt that you owe, you remain bound and obligated to the society. Only when you have repaid it in full, can you truly be free - this is the law of *karma!*"

"How do I repay it?"

"Go back to society and do your bit to make it better! Treat all people, however small and pitiful, however consumed by greed, with love and compassion."

"How will I know when this debt has been repaid?"

"You will know it in your heart!"

Narayan's spiritual journey had taken him away from society for five years. When he returned, he went to the university. Some of his former classmates were now members of the faculty, and they still remembered the brilliant talks he used to give at the *katta*. The dean offered him the post of the librarian. Many of Narayan's followers from the days of the Mission flocked to see him again. Swamiji, as most people referred to him now, had worked for 17 years in the library. He had transformed an aging, dilapidated library into one of the most prestigious libraries in the country. He had worked tirelessly to disseminate knowledge. He did not give mass public lectures on philosophy like he used to while working with the Mission, but he counselled people in private giving them personal attention and showing them the path towards a better life. He had served the society well, and he had repaid his debt!

Chapter 16: The Golden Shoulds

SAHYADRI HELPED MORE THAN TWO hundred students that summer; they worked tirelessly and were happy with the results. With the Joshis providing their guidance and support, Asmi engineered and managed everything. Help poured in from unexpected quarters. Some former colleagues of the Joshis donated money, while others came to office and assisted with counselling the students. Many volunteers offered their services and were instrumental in getting things done. Two vital helping hands were Principal Naik and Kamble who took upon themselves the responsibility of spreading the word in villages. Principal Naik, having been the principal of a school for years, had rapport with many rural schools in the district. The two of them made hundreds of phone calls and personally visited dozens of villages telling teachers, parents, and students about Sahyadri.

When the admissions season came to a close, they organised a small celebration. Everyone involved in the effort was invited. After the party, once the volunteers left, only Asmi, the Joshis, Principal Naik, and Kamble remained in the office. Mr Joshi prepared some hot tea. Kamble and Principal Naik were having beer.

"Asmi, you did a wonderful job!" Principal Naik said.

"No, sir, we all did a wonderful job!" she replied smilingly.

He continued, "We helped many students, but I don't know if what we are doing is the right thing. We are helping students from rural areas to come to the city for education. Some can do that by themselves, and some are able to do that with our assistance; but still, for many others, leaving their home and coming to the city is not an option!"

"Then what should we do?" Kamble asked.

"The nearest college from the Wadi is 40 kilometres away. That is where you studied, isn't it?" Principal Naik asked Asmi.

"Yes. I used to travel by bus every day. It was extremely inconvenient and tiring. The buses were frequently late, and I would lose hours in transit. Besides, the quality of education was really poor!" Asmi answered.

Principal Naik nodded. "I have taught in our little school for decades. I have a dream that there will be a college for higher education in our very own Wadi. Asmi, we have all seen your dedication and energy. If someone can do justice to my dream, it is you! Why don't you start a college in the Wadi?"

The thought had crossed her mind before, but she had never seriously considered it. Helping students find hostels and colleges was one thing; starting a new college was something entirely different! "It's a great idea, sir, but I don't know if I can take on such a project. We will need a lot of funds. We will need land for the buildings. We will have to recruit good teaching and non-teaching staff. And there will be an enormous amount of red tape to deal with!"

Mrs Joshi spoke, "Asmi, I am sure starting a new college will be a massive project, but if you decide to do it, rest assured that you have our complete support!"

Kamble had been sitting quietly in a corner having beer. He rapped the table hard with his knuckles and said in a tipsy voice, "Nothing is difficult! We will get money. I will go from door-to-door asking for money, and the whole Wadi will contribute!"

"But Kamble, starting a college will require a lot more money than you can raise by going door-to-door in the Wadi!" Mr Joshi interjected.

Kamble's enthusiasm was unabated by Joshi's remark. He said, "Joshi *saheb*, the people of the Wadi may not be able to contribute a lot through their wallets and purses, but I give you my word that they will contribute more than you can imagine through their hearts!"

Charvak woke up with a start. He had a hangover headache and a rancid aftertaste in his mouth. There was a leftover bottle of vodka lying on the table. It was almost noon. He looked at Rachana's naked body sprawled on the bed beside him. He got up, went to the bathroom, and vomited. The repugnant smell of alcohol, vomit, and sex had filled the room, and he was disgusted by it. When he climbed out of his unnecessarily long, silver Rolls Royce that day when they came back from the beach, the last time he saw Asmi, he knew he faced a clear choice. He had lived a certain way all through his adult life until Asmi awakened in him another self that wanted to live in a different way. To go back to the old or to embrace the new was the question! He had fought hard all his life for the old; he could not abandon it now. Whatever it was, however it was, it was something he had constructed. It was not what he truly wanted, but he had lived with it until now, and he could live with it for the rest of his days. The new was difficult and littered with uncertainty; he didn't know if he was strong enough for it. He made a decision to go back to the old.

He thought going back to the old would be easy; he would only have to do what he had been doing all his life. Thinking so, Charvak buried himself in his work and undertook a spate of aggressive acquisitions. In a matter of months, the Satyashah Group of Companies and its subsidiaries acquired businesses worth billions. The media hailed him as one of the most dynamic business leaders in the world, and shareholders were overjoyed to see their stock holdings climb in value. Some people amongst the

213

management, however, raised eyebrows; they questioned the necessity of those big-ticket acquisitions and if they would be sustainable in the long run. They sensed that something had changed. Charvak had always been aggressive in his dealings, but his aggression used to be carefully calculated and backed by judgment and tact. In recent months, however, Charvak had lost his masterful touch and had been aggressive without consideration. This had put the entire Group in a high-tension situation.

Charvak was aware of what was happening to him and why it was happening. In trying to get back to the old, he was emulating the same actions he used to perform before, but he could not get himself to feel the same way he felt then! The day-to-day challenges in business that used to stimulate him before did not excite him anymore. The pursuit of success and power, which used to give meaning to his life, no longer evoked an emotional response in him. Something inside of him was irreparably broken.

In emulating the old, he went back to his debauchery and indulged in indiscriminate sex. These things provided symptomatic relief but they did not solve the problem. He was afraid, because for the first time in his life, he was dealing with a situation that was hopelessly out of his control.

Sumitra told him, "My son, what happens is only for the good! Your love for Asmi may have been genuine, but she did not love you back. And if you ask me, I think that was for the best; she was not the right girl for you! Listen, if you don't like Saloni, we will find someone else, but you must marry and get yourself a partner! Only a woman can heal the wounds on your heart left by another woman!"

Charvak smiled weakly at his mother. Shaking his head, he said, "You don't understand! I loved Asmi, and she did not love me back. It crushed me, but I gracefully accepted it, and I have moved on. I am over her now. I have made my peace. The wounds on my heart have healed, and I don't need another woman for that!"

"If you are over her, why are you behaving as if the world has ended?"

"Mother, something has changed in me! All this while, I lived my life without questioning it, but Asmi taught me to introspect and examine. Now, I am unable to go back to being ignorant! I have started asking questions about what I do, why I do it, what do I want to get out of it, how long will I do it etc., and the answers I get are disturbing! They are… unacceptable!"

"What answers do you get?" Sumitra asked. She looked very worried.

"That I don't want to accumulate more wealth, fame, and power! That I don't want to run the Satyashah Group of Companies! I almost feel as if I don't want to be Charvak Satyashah anymore!"

Sumitra's mouth fell open. She felt weak in her knees. Old memories came to her mind. "This cannot happen again," she thought. She had survived it once; she could not survive it again! She said in a petrified voice, "You are talking nonsense! Successfully fulfilling your responsibilities in life is the true religion! Questioning your responsibilities is just another way of avoiding them, and that is a sin! Expel these thoughts from your head; otherwise, they will ruin you! My son, promise me that you will never say something like that again! Please! Do you promise?"

Charvak did not promise and remained sitting motionless. Sumitra felt dizzy and collapsed in her chair. When she came back to her senses, she saw him still sitting there in front of her. She got up and hugged him.

She said, "I love you, my son! Don't worry! You are showing classic symptoms of a broken heart. Give it time and you will go back to being yourself!"

215

"My dear mother, how should I make you understand that my problem is not that of mending a broken heart? Why do you refuse to accept that I might not want to continue running the business anymore?"

Sumitra's face hardened. There was fire in her eyes. "I refuse to accept it! I refuse to accept that my son is a coward! I refuse to accept that he wants to run away from his duties!"

Charvak shrugged said in a resigned voice, "Okay! You tell me then! What should I do?"

Sumitra sat up straight and spoke agitatedly, "What should you do? I'll tell you what you should do! Stop running away from your duties! You should put your heart and soul into your work, because doing your work to the best of your abilities is your duty! You should earn money, because earning money for yourself and your family, no matter how rich or poor you are, is your duty! You should strive for success, because success will do justice to your capabilities, and putting your capabilities to good use is your duty! You are the Chairman of the Satyashah Group, the largest business house in the country, and steering and leading the Group is your privilege and your duty! Perform your duties to the best of your potential; that is what you should do, and that is what life is all about!"

Charvak remembered Asmi telling him about a golden-scaled dragon; on each of his thousand scales was written a Should!

Sumitra continued, "It is the duty of every man to marry and start a family. God created us this way, and you are being irresponsible when you say you don't want to marry! Trust me, seeing your children grow up is the ultimate form of satisfaction you can get from life. You should get married and start a family; that is your duty!"

He could hear the dragon swirl around him; he could feel the icy touch of his scales creeping along his skin.

216

"Your grandfather started this business empire from scratch. Your father gave his life to it. I, your mother, have fought to make the world recognise your merit and make you the Chairman. Don't you remember our fight? We fought, and we won! Two generations before you have toiled to create what you own today. Your father left you an unparalleled legacy; taking care of it, nurturing it, and growing it is your duty!"

He felt suffocated and could not move. He remembered Raja jumping through the hoop.

"Millions of people, directly or indirectly, depend on you and the Satyashah companies. By managing the business, you are providing for their livelihood! Don't you see that? You are a pillar of the society. You are a support of the nation. Continuing to be a responsible member of the society is your duty! Remove these stupid ideas from your head! Shrug off the lethargy and despondency! Stand up and stand tall like a Satyashah! I want you to go back to being the Charvak you were!"

Chapter 17: The Other Gita

RAVINDRA SATYASHAH, FORTY-SEVEN YEARS old, opened the door of the car and sat in the front seat next to the driver. He was utterly exhausted after a long day of meetings. In the morning, he met with local politicians who wanted him to give a directive to the Satyashah manufacturing units to hire workers from their community. The afternoon was spent in a meeting with finance executives of various subsidiaries to plan a small financial reorganisation that had been pending for a long time. For lunch, in between the two meetings, a team of lawyers gave him a summary of pending litigations and a list of action-items that needed his attention. He had planned to relax that evening, but an important issue came up for which he had urgently called a meeting that went on for hours.

Getting into the car, he said, "Ramu, let's go!" to Ramesh Kadam, his driver whom he treated like a friend.

"Where to?" Ramu asked.

"Anywhere. Just away from here!" Pointing to the cassette player in the car, Ravindra asked, "What are you listening to?"

"Oh, I am sorry! It's nothing!" Ramu said and reached to turn it off.

"No, I want to listen to it! What is it?"

"It's a lecture given by Swami Narayanananda Saraswati. He is a *swami* of the Saraswati Mission. Someone gave me this cassette. It's really nothing; let me turn it off!"

"No, Ramu, let it play!"

A deep, powerful voice coming out of the speakers was narrating a story: "King Janaka of the Kingdom of Mithila was a very wise man. He was a great ruler whose fame had spread far and wide. He was a great scholar whose thirst for knowledge was unquenchable. He had won innumerable battles and read countless scriptures. He had all the riches in the world. He had wonderful wives as queens. He had brave sons and beautiful daughters. Janaka had everything that a man could possibly want; yet he was not happy! Plagued by his woes, he summoned all the wise men in the country. They came to his court as royal guests. He accommodated them in comfortable quarters and fed them sumptuous food. They brought with them knowledge of various traditions and beliefs, but all their combined knowledge could not satisfy Janaka, and he remained restless. One day, a young boy named Ashtavakra came to his court. His body was severely deformed in eight places. When the king asked him what he wanted, he told Janaka that he had come to solve his problem. The courtiers laughed at him. Many great men had come before him, and they had all failed. Ignoring his courtiers, Janaka treated him courteously and permitted him to speak. As soon as Ashtavakra stood up to speak, a deafening silence engulfed the court!"

The voice on the cassette continued, "All of us here know the Bhagavad Gita, but how many of us have heard of the Ashtavakra Gita? The Bhagavad Gita is a dialogue between Krishna and Arjuna on the battlefield of the Mahabharata. Likewise, the dialogue between Ashtavakra and Janaka is called the Ashtavakra Gita. While Krishna's Bhagavad Gita is very popular and widely known, the Ashtavakra Gita is obscure and known only to a few. The Bhagavad Gita is a great book. However, it is syncretic in nature and offers multiple paths to the truth. It is ambiguous at times and leaves room for a commentator to impose his own thoughts onto its teachings. The Gita of Ashtavakra, on the other

219

hand, is pure and distilled wisdom. It is terse, direct, and unambiguous. The Bhagavad Gita takes a soft approach to expound concepts and accommodates different points of view making it easier for a layman to accept it. The Ashtavakra Gita, because it is condensed and succinct, needs greater insight to understand and assimilate.

"Janaka asked many questions and was satisfied by Ashtavakra's answers. The countless scriptures Janaka had read started making sense, and the pieces of the jigsaw puzzle in his mind suddenly fell together. Ashtavakra helped Janaka when no one else could. Janaka's restlessness went away, and he finally found peace and happiness. My friends, Janaka was no ordinary man. He had a kingdom to govern and look after. There were hundreds of things that needed his attention every day. Thousands of people depended on him. He had to fulfil many duties and responsibilities. Ashtavakra taught him how, in spite of all these dependencies, one could still be free! Only freedom brings ultimate happiness. My brothers and sisters, if King Janaka could find solace in the wisdom of Ashtavakra, so can people like you and me!"

Ravindra had been listening to the story intently. When it got over, he said, "Ramu, I want to meet this man!"

"I will find out about him."

A few days later, Ramu came to Ravindra and said, "Swamiji had left the Mission to go on a spiritual pilgrimage. He came back recently after many years. I can take you to see him."

It was late evening. Swamiji was about to leave when the night-watchman told him someone wanted to meet him. Wondering to himself who would have come so late, he told the watchman to send the visitor to his office. Moments later, he was surprised to see the tall figure of Ravindra Satyashah walk in.

Making a courteous bow, Ravindra said, "Namaste, Swamiji! My name is Ravindra Satyashah, and I have come here to seek your help."

"I am humbled by your visit. How can I be of assistance?" Swamiji replied.

"I heard your discourse on the Ashtavakra Gita on an audiocassette and was overwhelmed by it. Swamiji, I have the same problems as Janaka. I have a business empire to run. I have a thousand duties to discharge. I have everything I want, but I am not happy. I tried reading the Ashtavakra Gita, but I could not comprehend it."

"Yes, directly reading the Ashtavakra Gita is not recommended. You must first read other books to develop an understanding of the concepts and terminology. This will arm you with the correct background to understand Ashtavakra. I can give you a reading list that will help you..."

"No, Swamiji! I have not come here for myself. I have come here for someone else: my son. I am too old to change my ways, but he is still of an impressionable age. You can see for yourself that he is intelligent and perceptive. One day, he will inherit all that I have including my problems. When that time comes, I want him to be better equipped to deal with them than I am. Swamiji, I kindly request you to accept him as your *shishya*. I want him to be great and successful, but more than that, I want him to be happy!"

The Sahyadri office looked like a war room ever since Asmi took the decision to establish the first college in the Wadi. Founding a new educational institute, especially a government recognised college, was no easy task. They first made a checklist of the critical requirements for obtaining the requisite licenses to start a college. Then, they created a detailed plan on how to go about fulfilling these requirements. The Joshis, considering their experience and recognition in the field of education, took the responsibility of drafting the application that had to be submitted to the government. Principal Naik was given the charge of navigating the red tape. Asmi started the process of finding investors and raising funds. Kamble, ever enthusiastic, proclaimed himself as the man on the ground and was assigned the job of mobilizing the people in the Wadi and identifying a piece of land for the college. Asmi was the glue that held these disparate people together and coordinated all activities between them.

Although she dedicated a large part of her time and energy for the college, she did not deprioritise her quest for self-realisation. She diligently kept aside thirty minutes every morning for meditation. Sometimes in the evenings, she met Swamiji to discuss her progress.

She asked him once, "Swamiji, I have hit a plateau, and I am unable to move forward. I can keep my mind still for considerable stretches of time. I do not feed the thoughts that arise, do not entertain them, and they quickly dissolve away. Like you told me, I follow the method of self-enquiry. I ask myself 'Who am I?' and I understand that I am the *Brahman*, but I still do not realise it! When I open my eyes, it is all the same. What should I do now?"

Swamiji said, "You have done very well so far. Now, you have reached the most difficult part of your journey. I must warn you that this is where most seekers give up. You must be patient and maintain your persistence! Tell me, Asmi, which possession of yours are you most attached to?"

"Well, I don't know!"

"It is your name! Asmi is a name that you possess. Are you ready to renounce it?"

She looked confused and did not reply.

He continued, "Your name is a device society has created. To realise your true self, you must renounce all false identities and break free from all societal roles. You must realise that you are not Asmi! Asmi might be a daughter, a student, a friend, or an employee; you are none of these. You are free. You are your self!"

"How do I learn to differentiate between Asmi and me?"

"All your life, the world has told you that you are Asmi; you must unlearn that. You can do that only if you retreat into solitude to a place where you are not constantly reminded of Asmi."

"What place is that?"

"What reminds you of Asmi? You are reminded of your name when people use it. You are reminded of people when you see other people. Familiarity reminds you of people and places. Familiar activities, familiar places, familiar sounds, all of these remind you of Asmi. While you are in society, in the midst of people, you will not be able to forget Asmi. To do that, you must retreat to a place where you are absolutely and utterly alone, a place you have never been before so you have no past memories associated with it. There, you must go and meditate!"

"For how long should I go?"

"For one week!"

Asmi contemplated for a moment. She had the stamina to meditate for at most a few hours at a time. "Swamiji, I am not ready for it. I cannot meditate for a full week!"

"Of course, you are not ready for it! A week of sincere meditation is an extremely difficult feat to perform. Before you attempt it, you will need to train for it. From today, before you sleep, try meditating for an hour. Gradually increase this duration till you can meditate for the whole night. You can also meditate during the day, but it is more difficult, because there are more distractions. Train in this manner for a few months, and you will be ready!"

Asmi was excited to undertake this exercise, but she still doubted what would come out of it. She said, "I have asked you this question before, but I feel like asking it again. What will happen when I attain *Moksha*? How will my behaviour change? Will I still laugh and cry? Will I still experience emotions? Swamiji, how does it feel to be liberated?"

It was a Sunday evening in the monsoon month of July, and the university campus was almost empty. They were sitting in the canteen under a covered shelter. It was raining heavily outside. Considering the low turnout in the canteen, most staff had left. There was only a young boy who made for them delicious masala tea with ginger in it.

Swamiji shifted in his chair as he prepared a cogent answer to her question. Speaking in a calm, profound voice, in a manner as if he were reciting Sanskrit verses, he said:

"My child, when you attain *Moksha*, you realise that you do not consist of bones, muscles, and tissues. You are not your body! You are pure awareness!

You do not belong to any caste, religion, or community. You are not at any stage. You are formless and unattached!

You have burnt the dark web of ignorance with the fire of understanding. You have severed the chains that bound you to your ego. Recognizing that you are God, that you are the *Brahman*, you are forever happy!

You have always been free and happy, but you did not know that, because you believed in an illusion. The illusion has been dispelled, and now you can see!

You understand that what is apparent is not real, and what is real cannot be known by our senses, but only through our mind.

You realise that everything, all of existence, originates from you and will one day dissolve back into you!

Righteousness and unrighteousness, rights and duties, joy and sorrow are no longer of any concern to you!

Equal in pleasure and pain, in life and death, in gain and loss, in victory and defeat, in hope and disappointment, you are complete and happy!

For you, bondage and liberation no longer exist, and you recognise them as mere fantasies. Neither possession nor renunciation means anything to you. You are beyond that!

You understand that desires are creations of your mind, but your mind never belonged to you and is only an instrument of causality. By recognizing bondage in the guise of desire and by being unattached to it, you remain sublimely happy!

Realising that you have control only over your actions but not over their results, you put your best in performing those actions without being invested in their outcome!

You enjoy life to your heart's content without being attached to the things you have and without yearning for the things you do not have!

Reaping the benefits of wealth and comfort without depending on them for your happiness, you remain free!

Relishing the company of family and friends without longing for them and without being hurt by their shortcomings, you remain free!

Performing your actions to the best of your efforts while remaining unaffected by praise or blame, you remain free!

You are no longer dependent on anything and no longer entangled in the web of *Maya*!

You live like a worldly person, but unlike the worldly person, you are free from the bondage caused by desire and causality!

You feel no fear, neither of life nor death!

You feel no anger, neither of people nor circumstances!

You grieve for no one, neither living nor dead!

You feel compassion towards the world, because you see that the world is you, and you are the world!

You see yourself in all beings and see them in you, and you love them as you love yourself!

You move through the world undisturbed, untouched, untainted, and unaffected by it!

You no longer have any use for books, scriptures, or teachers!

You need no meditation to practise stillness of thought, because by seeing yourself in everything, you always remain intensely aware of your consciousness!

You realise that the man seeking liberation can never find peace, and a man who is liberated never seeks anything!

For you, who are no longer a slave to things that must be done, there are no 'musts'!

Recognizing that the feeling 'something needs to be done' is bondage, you remain free of it!

You are no longer chained to duties or responsibilities! By remaining free of things you have done and things that you are yet to do, you are happy!

You have no attachment in your heart for wealth, fame, power, objects, people, ideas, and most importantly, for your ego!

Happy you stand, happy you sit, happy you eat, happy you sleep, happy you come and go!

For you, there is no past, present or future, no life or death, no space or time!

For you, there is no good or bad, no right or wrong, no moral or immoral!

For you, there is no joy or sorrow, no pleasure or pain, no gain or loss!

For you, there is no 'done' or 'to be done', no 'want' or 'should', no rights or duties!

For you, there is no god or devil, no angel or demon, no heaven or hell!

For you, there is no cause or effect, no action or inaction, no reward or punishment!

For you, there is only everlasting freedom and happiness! You are *sat-chit-ananda!*"

Chapter 18: I am That

CHARAN GUPTA SAT IN MANOJ Satyashah's living room having orange juice.

"Manoj, my dear, how are you? It's been a while since we spoke, hasn't it?" he said.

Manoj was surprised when Charan called that morning and came over to see him, but he knew the reason behind the visit. There was a rising wave of discontent within the shareholders and the upper management against Charvak's unsteady leadership. In the last few months, many top, long-serving executives had left the Group; their loyalty that had held fast for so many years had easily caved in now. The company fundamentals were strong and the figures on the balance sheet were largely unaffected. The stock prices, however, had been steadily dropping week after week. Market analysts who only months ago had been aggressively recommending people to buy Satyashah stocks had changed their recommendations to hold, and last week they downgraded them to sell. Reputed news agencies were silent on the issue, but second and third tier ones carried rumours about Charvak resigning. The reports were vague to the tune of 'An undisclosed source commented that...', 'We have inside information that...', 'Someone close to the Satyashah family mentioned that...', 'The absence of Charvak Satyashah at the meeting suggests that...'

Charan kept the empty glass on the table. He looked at Manoj and said simply, without preamble, "Manoj, Charvak has to go!"

Manoj smiled at his directness but did not reply. He let the silence hang in the air putting the onus on Charan to elaborate further.

Charan said, "Listen Manoj, you know very well what is going on here. Charvak is young and immature. He is not fit to lead the Group. Yes, yes, I know you will point out that the Group performed well under him so far, but let me ask you a question: how do you know that the Group performed well because of Charvak and not because of the management team under him? I tell you, it was the team the whole time! Take the case of Clothing and Retail. The marketing team did a spectacular job. The production team worked overtime. Our procurements were already in place because of our previous range of products. What did Charvak do? He posed for advertisements with sleazy models! The team did all the great work, while Charvak got all the credit. And now, the team is disintegrating because of Charvak's ineptitude! Our best people are remorselessly leaving us!"

Manoj did not defend Charvak, but he did not support Charan either. He had been slow at learning the art of business politics, but he had learned enough to understand that he held the cards in his hand this time. Charan made his intention clear: he was going straight for the jugular and would move a motion to remove Charvak as the chairman at the next meeting of the board without even waiting for his term to expire. But Manoj knew that Charan could not pull this off on his own. Most members would reserve their judgment until they got an idea of which way the wind was blowing. It was in Manoj's hand now to decide which way he wanted the wind to blow!

Charan continued, "Look Manoj, I know you were disappointed with me for not supporting Prateek. I am sorry I did not understand the situation correctly. At that moment, I genuinely thought that Prateek might not be able to cope with the situation. I admit I was wrong, and his performance since then has been excellent."

"Well, then, could you be wrong this time too with regards to Charvak?"

Charan ignored his question and continued, "I was your father's right hand man. I have seen the Satyashah Group of Companies grow from an obscure mill into a global business empire. I am an octogenarian, and I have no interest in position or money. When I believed Prateek needed to be replaced, I spoke out my mind. Now, I am convinced Charvak needs to go. Look at his behaviour! He is engrossed in his nocturnal activities. He is more interested in the anatomy of women than the balance sheet of the company!"

Charan lowered his voice, leaned forward, and spoke almost in a whisper, "The Satyashah Group needs a more mature and experienced Chairman. Someone like you, Manoj!"

The dream of the first college in the Wadi started becoming increasingly real every passing day. Swamiji put Asmi in touch with the vice chancellor of the university whose help proved immensely valuable in understanding the complex mesh of licenses, approvals, permissions, certificates, and agreements required to make a formal proposal to start a new college. Principal Naik helped Asmi compile these documents. Once they were in place, the Joshis put together a proposal and submitted it to the Ministry of Education. Approval from the ministry would give them a green signal to move ahead full steam. However, for their proposal to be accepted, they first needed to acquire the land on which the college would be built. Realising that availability of funds would be crucial to this process, Asmi focussed her attention on raising money.

She spent six months soliciting donations. She met hundreds of people and managed to raise a substantial amount of money from individuals and organisations. All these meetings required an exceptional degree of patience on her part. Whenever people rejected her request, Asmi thanked them politely and moved on; some of these people later called her back. She resolutely worked according to the plan and refused to get disappointed. Her determination and patience bore fruits. One day, the Corporate Social Responsibility cell of a large software company awarded them a giant donation that covered up their entire deficit in a single stroke. They would need to raise more money later, but they had enough to buy land and begin construction.

Kamble became their man on the ground, like he had said he would. He identified several plots of land that were available for sale and pushed Principal Naik to negotiate with the owners. Asmi made trips to the Wadi to finalise the location of the new college and settled on a 4-acre plot that was large enough for their needs. It was some distance away from the crowded market areas but close enough to walk to from the centre of the Wadi. It lay at the base of the winding path going up the hill that ended at the quiet temple at the top. Buying land was the final sign that the college would indeed become a reality.

New bureaucratic hurdles kept coming in their way. Additional documents and permissions were necessary and obtaining them was a nightmare, because each new document meant additional trips to government offices. Mr Joshi was anxious and tensed, but Asmi reassured him saying that they should do their best, and everything will sort itself out. She worked patiently, without worrying or doubting, and never stopped smiling!

Mr Joshi later complimented her saying, "Asmi, an ordinary person would have long given up due to the irritation and stress. You worked through it with so much ease and grace that I am simply amazed! God bless you!"

Aai had gone to the market to buy household items when she saw a big poster outside Kamble's general store. On it was a photo of two young girls carrying books in their hands. There were slogans encouraging parents to educate their children. There was a request for donations for 'The First College in Our Very Own Wadi'. On the top of the poster, written in large letters, was the name of the college: 'Pandit Abbasaheb College of Science and Arts'; at the bottom, written in bold, was the name of her daughter! Aai was shocked to see the poster. Until then, she had no idea what Asmi had been up to. There were tears in her eyes. Kamble saw her and waved to her.

"*Tai*, did you like the poster?" he said.

"Yes, it is nice!" Aai replied hiding her surprise.

"I was very happy when Asmi decided to name the college after her grandfather. Abba was a father figure to me. Did you know that Abba had helped me buy this shop where I have made my livelihood for thirty years? Everyone remembers how, even in those times, he insisted on sending his sisters to college! His neighbours said he was wasting his money, but he was adamant. Despite his financial difficulties, he ensured that they completed their education. I think it is apt to name the college after a man who was amongst the first in the Wadi to recognise the value of education. Don't you think so?"

"Absolutely!" she said fighting her tears.

"I am going to tell the whole Wadi to contribute to this cause. Please help me spread the word!" he said and then added, "*Tai*, this college will bring great honour to your family and to the whole Wadi!"

Kamble called on hundreds of people personally and requested their contributions saying, "*Saheb*, when your son grows up, where will he study? Will you send him away to the city, or will you send him to some pathetic college in some nearby town where his intelligence will rot? No, those are not the only

233

options! Lend us a helping hand, and play a part in setting up the first college in our town. Help us in any way you can. A small contribution from you will go a long way in creating history!"

He put up posters and distributed pamphlets. He urged Principal Naik to enlist the help of the teachers in his school. At the annual parent-teacher meeting, Principal Naik made an emotional appeal to all parents to contribute keeping the future of their children in mind.

During the festival season of Diwali, Kamble announced that he would donate all profit his store makes during that month towards the college funds. Many students that Sahyadri had helped in the past joined the effort; they went door-to-door and village-to-village spreading the word about the college and encouraging parents and children to avoid spending on firecrackers, sweets, and gifts that Diwali and contribute that money to their cause instead.

Their campaign galvanised the whole district, and people came out in support with open arms. The college had not even been constructed, but Asmi had already started receiving applications for teaching and non-teaching roles. Local politicians, sensing the pulse of the people, paid her visits and extended their cooperation.

Neha called her one evening. She was excited and blabbered about how everyone was speaking only about Asmi and the college.

"Neha, calm down! Tell me, how are Aai and Baba?" Asmi asked.

"They are good!" Neha replied.

"Did they say anything about the college?"

"Aai cried when she saw the posters. Baba did not say anything. Why don't you call them?"

"Call them and say what? I don't know what I can speak to them!"

"Asmi, little sister, it is time you came home!"

A year after they started working on the college project and after countless trips to various government offices, the seal of approval was finally stamped on their application. With this, the last hurdle in their path disappeared. They hired an architect to design the college buildings. The construction would be done in phases. The various programs the college offered would also be rolled out in phases. They had worked hard throughout the year. Before they shifted gears and moved to the next step, Asmi declared for all of them a small vacation.

She had not forgotten her quest amidst all the excitement. All through these months, she had been training rigorously for the weeklong meditation exercise she wanted to undertake. She could now meditate continuously for hours on end. She spoke to Swamiji about her experiences, and he carefully guided her along.

He told her, "The mind wanders; that is what it does. Don't judge yourself harshly if you cannot keep your mind still. If it gets distracted, gently get it back on track without feeling disappointed. Focus on your breathing, and persist in your efforts."

He chastised her whenever she skipped meditation saying, "Remember, your mind works every day, so you must meditate every day too! If you do not have one hour, meditate only for five minutes. The difference between not meditating and meditating for those five minutes is the difference between bondage and liberation!"

He told her to keep the broader picture in sight saying, "Meditation is only the means and not the end. Stillness of thought is not your final goal. The benefits of meditation must percolate into your daily life. The deep mindful state you reach when meditating, you must learn to carry it with you at all times!"

There was a small, quaint village in the southern part of Konkan. As she sat in the bus that would take her there, Asmi wondered how dramatically her life had changed courses. Every step she had taken after leaving the Wadi had been so different from anything she had previously experienced. Working at Fernandes Media, her love for Agastya, her work at the Satyashah Group, her turmoil with Charvak, and now her adventure with Sahyadri - she could never have planned all this. And then, of course, her spiritual journey with Swamiji! Of all the people she had met, she paid her highest form of reverence to Swamiji, who had been not only her teacher and guide but her *guru* in the true sense of the term! She wondered where life would lead her next. For months, she had practised intense meditation and had rigorously prepared for this week. Swamiji was confident that she was ready to take this step. The bus trudged along the dusty roads taking her closer and closer to it.

As she climbed out of the bus, she saw an elderly man waiting for her. He was a disciple of Swamiji from the time when he was still associated with the Saraswati Mission. He welcomed her and led her to a battered van parked nearby. The village was a thirty-minute drive from the bus stop. The man lived in an old house next to the beach. A short walk away was an outhouse where arrangements had been made for Asmi to stay completely undisturbed. Her food would be kept on a platform outside the outhouse, and she was to keep the utensils back at the same place after finishing her meals. After giving her some minor instructions, the man wished her luck and left!

Before leaving, Swamiji had told her, "My child, being alone, even for a moment, is difficult for most people. Being alone, truly alone, for a full week is a momentous task. Your goal is to find your true self by dissociating yourself from your ego and layers of false identities. When you dismantle your ego, you are destroying something that you have constructed and nurtured throughout your life. You are destroying the power your mind wields over you. Your mind will resist this. It will fight back, and it won't be easy. Exorcising demons that have lived inside you for so long will be exceedingly painful. You will cry. You will doubt. You will feel like abandoning your effort at every step of the way. But, you will succeed! Remember, your real struggle in life is only with yourself!"

Asmi had a clean bath, changed into loose comfortable clothes, and ate a simple but delicious dinner. There was a stash of food items at hand if she felt hungry at odd times consisting of a basket of fresh fruits, a jar of biscuits, a packet of cereals, and a bottle of milk in the refrigerator. She turned off her mobile phone and kept it in her bag. She turned off all the lights, closed the curtains, and prepared for a nightlong meditation session. It was pitch-dark, and she could barely see her own hands.

"Swamiji, my knees hurt if I sit on the floor cross-legged for a long time. Is it necessary to sit cross-legged?" she had asked before leaving.

"The posture in which you meditate is not important. You can sit cross-legged on the floor as is recommended, but you can also lie down or sit in a chair with a comfortable backrest. It is inevitable that there will be pain and soreness in your body when you meditate continuously for days, and there is no need to make it worse by sticking to one position. Change your position as often as you want; just take care that it doesn't become a distraction!"

"How long can I sleep?"

"Sleep no more than eight hours a day and no less than six hours a day. Adequate, good quality sleep is of primary importance, but do not get tempted to put yourself to sleep just because you are bored of meditation. Do not sleep in patches. When you sleep, sleep for eight hours straight, and then do not sleep again until the next day."

237

"Should I meditate during the day or the night?"

"I advise you to meditate through the night; the darkness helps in staying focussed. Sleep at sunrise, wake up in the afternoon, and meditate for the rest of the time. And one more thing: feed yourself well. Do not meditate on an empty stomach. If you feel hungry, take a quick break and eat something. Hunger plays on your mind!"

Asmi sat upright on the bed in a cross-legged posture, propped her back for support against the headboard, and closed her eyes. Taking deep breaths, she chanted the magical Om three times. Her mind gently settled down like a feather lightly floating towards the earth. She joined her palms together in the form of a *namaskar* and recited the Gayatri Mantra: "I pray to you, the infinite energy that keeps the Sun burning, the fundamental vibrations that sustain all life; I pray to you to reveal to me the understanding of the universe and the understanding of my self!"

She slipped into a deeply aware state of consciousness. Thoughts arose in her mind and gently dissolved back into it.

She asked herself, "*Koham?* Who am I?"

Her mind replied, "I am the *Brahman!*"

She asked, "Who is answering?", and she knew it was her mind that was feigning the answer. She knew the real answer would come, if and when it came, from her heart and not from her mind, and she would feel it and not just know it. She remained sitting cross-legged on the bed throughout the night, in a state of deep awareness, until she could see the sunlight filtering through the drawn curtains.

Swamiji had said, "You are battling your mind, and your mind will do everything it can to distract you. It will play tricks and make you doubt what you are doing. You lose as soon as you let the seed of doubt enter you; do not let that happen!"

On the third night, the boredom got unbearable. Asmi cried with tears rolling down her cheeks. She was so bored, so incredibly bored, that she felt like killing herself just to get rid of the boredom! Her legs hurt as if she were pierced with a thousand needles. She changed her position often, but that did not help. Nothing seemed to be working. Hours of meditation had brought her nowhere. She worried if she would survive the week. She was tempted to turn on her mobile phone just for fifteen minutes or to take a quick walk outside, but she did not allow herself the satisfaction of even thinking about these luxuries.

On the fifth night, Asmi had dinner and prepared herself for meditation. She had stopped crying and become better at managing her boredom. She did not know if any good would come out of all this, but she did not fuel the doubt. She remained focussed on her actions, which were within her control, and did not worry about the results, which were outside her control. She could no longer sit straight in a cross-legged position so she sat on the bed with her back against the headboard and kept her legs stretched. She relaxed and closed her eyes. Like every other night, she chanted Om thrice, recited the Gayatri Mantra, and began another long night of penance.

A little while later, although she had a full dinner, she started feeling hungry. Remembering Swamiji's advice of not meditating on an empty stomach, she got up and had two bananas and a glass of milk. Months of rigorous training had made her quite proficient at keeping her mind still and devoid of thoughts, but on that night, weird thoughts started coming to her. They were not the usual thoughts arising out of momentary distractions; they were visions of deep carnal desires. She felt Agastya's arms around her body. With one hand on her waist and the other in her hair, he pulled her towards him and kissed her passionately on her mouth. With tremendous effort, she disrupted the chain of thoughts and fought to regain control of her mind. She calmed herself by concentrating on her breathing. Gradually, the visions ebbed away.

After a while, she started feeling unusually restless. The restlessness began disguised as ordinary boredom but quickly grew in intensity. She shifted positions and tried harder to concentrate, but it did not go away. She felt like jumping out of the bed that instant and leaving the village that moment. She didn't care where she went; she just wanted to get up and leave.

After prevailing over the restlessness with great difficulty, she suddenly felt piercing anger; it was not ordinary anger but raging anger of a ferocity she had never experienced before. Violent thoughts came to her mind; she felt like throwing things and breaking the glass windows. She was so angry that she felt she would not hesitate to kill someone who came before her! The intensity of her emotions overwhelmed her. She did not open her eyes and kept them tightly shut knowing that if she opened them, she would cave in, and it would all be over. She was walking a thin line between continuing the fight and accepting defeat. She repeated Om thrice. Her voice was shaky, and her breath was short, but it helped calm her mind and gave her renewed confidence. The anger subsided, and her breathing normalised. Asmi permitted herself a little smile that showed on the corners of her lips; she had passed the test and staved off the distractions her mind had hurled at her.

She remained in a state of deep awareness for some time, but nothing happened. She asked herself, "*Koham?* Who am I?" and there was no answer. She felt disappointed. She asked again, there was still no answer, and she felt a little more disappointed. Before she could realise what was happening, the disappointment curdled into sadness, and she was swept away into a fit of unimaginable depression. She felt like weeping, but there were no tears in her eyes. She felt like giving up, not because she could not stand it, but because she was suddenly convinced that everything including her quest and her life was meaningless. She was about to open her eyes and wind up her experiment, but something held her back; she continued to meditate, and after a while, her depression disappeared as abruptly as it came.

Asmi breathed more easily. She realised that the depression had just been another trick her mind had played on her to make her abandon her quest. When it could not defeat her by casting boredom, hunger, restlessness, and anger at her, it tried to make her give up by convincing her of its meaninglessness. She recovered and collected herself. "The worst is over," she thought. For the first time since she came to this place, she felt like she would be successful in her quest. She felt a ray of hope that shone brighter and brighter every passing moment. As her hope rose higher and higher, her desire for liberation became stronger and stronger.

Swamiji had told her, "You may get rid of all your desires, but you will still fail if you do not break free from the final one: the desire for liberation! The desire for liberation is still a desire, and every desire binds you to the web of *Maya*. You will not find freedom by seeking it; you will find it only by destroying obstacles within yourself that prevent you from realising it! Stop seeking, and you will find!"

Remembering this, Asmi kept her rising hope and desire at bay. She continued her self-enquiry and asked herself, "*Koham*? Who am I?" but there was still no answer. Her feeling of hope, like other emotions, gradually dissolved away into the recesses of her mind.

Suddenly, a chill shot up through her spine, and she felt very afraid. It was not the fear of someone or something; it was the primordial and visceral fear for survival. She felt she was going to die that night and was fully convinced of it. She desperately wanted to call Agastya and Swamiji and tell them she was dying. She wanted to talk to Aai and Baba one last time. The muscles of her legs tensed in preparation for getting up, and her eyelids fluttered.

Her entire existence was screaming at her to get up and open her eyes, but a tiny little voice in her heart told her to stay. In frightful desperation, she frantically repeated, *"Koham? Koham? Koham?"*

There was no reply.

She asked again, *"Koham?"*, and something stirred deep inside her. She could feel it awakening.

She asked again, *"Koham? Who am I?"*

She heard a faint whisper that said, *"Soham! I am that!"*

She recognised it as the same voice that had, a long time ago, whispered to her at the small temple at the top of the hill in the Wadi.

The voice did not stop. It kept chanting, *"Soham! Soham! Soham!..."*

The chant came from her heart. It came from her bones. It came from her spine. It got louder! It came from every cell in her body. It came from within her. Louder! It came from outside her. It came from the floor and the ceiling. It came from the walls and the furniture. Louder! It came from the coconut trees. It came from the beach. Louder! The crescendo reached mammoth proportions. The voice roared from the earth. It roared from the sea. It roared from the sky. Still louder! As if the whole universe spoke in one voice, her entire existence reverberated with the chant, *"Soham! Soham! Soham!..."*

The bubble of Asmi's identity burst! She broke free and rose to become one with the universe. She was no more just Asmi! She was God! She was the *Brahman*! She was the universe! Through the pitch-black darkness of the night, she became the brilliance of a thousand splendid suns! She had read the poetic Sanskrit verses innumerable times. She had read them in the Upanishads. She had read them in the Gita. She had read them in the Vedas. She had known the words. She had understood what they meant. Now, for the first time, she realised! She saw!

She asked, "*Koham?* Who am I?"

The voice thundered, "*Soham!* I am that!

I am that, which is the origin of all things!

I am the consciousness of all beings!

I am the beginning, the middle, and the end!

I am the creator, the maintainer, and the destroyer!

I am the knowledge of the self!

I am the logic of arguments!

I am the might of the kings!

I am the victory of the victorious!

I am the silence of secrets!

I am the wisdom of the sages!

I am the sweetness of sugar!

I am the wetness of water!

I am the light of the day!

I am the dark of the night!

I am existence!

I am time!

I am space!

I am energy!

I am the universe!

I am you!

The brilliant light in its most blessed form, the infinite energy that keeps the Sun burning, the fundamental vibrations that sustain the universe, I am that!"

Chapter 19: The Final Cause

CHARVAK SATYASHAH WAS NOT DRIFTING with the wind. He did not lack energy. He lacked neither ability nor intelligence. What he lacked was direction. He ploughed ahead aggressively, his engines thrashing furiously, but like a deserted ship, he did not know where to go! The old was familiar but no longer acceptable. The new was alluring but beyond his reach. He could not change his way of life or stop being the person he had been for so long. He carried on moving in a spiral creating meaningless ripples on the water. The spiral was becoming smaller and smaller every day causing the ship to tilt inwards further and further leading to an inevitable disaster!

It had been a year since he last saw Asmi. The Satyashah Group of Companies still operated much the same way it did before, but there were subtle changes; he wondered whether they were real, or he was simply imagining them. The clerk, who always left files on his desk in carefully arranged stacks, had, for the first time, kept them carelessly causing the stack to collapse and create a mess on the table. The attendant, who always got his afternoon tea made to perfection, had added a little extra sugar. Sundaram, who always stood before him slightly hunched, had straightened up, and his voice, although still courteous and polite, had lost some of its obsequiousness. His subordinates, always on time for meetings, had started showing up a little late. Small decisions around the office were being taken without informing him. The Mephysto posters featuring him that he used to see on his way to work every day had been replaced by other advertisements.

On the eve of Vallabh Satyashah's eighty-seventh birth anniversary, continuing the annual tradition, Sumitra invited Manoj and his family for lunch. Food was served and, just as they were about to start, Sumitra said, "Manoj, I hear there's some dissent amongst shareholders regarding Charvak. Is that true?"

Manoj looked up at her; they never discussed business matters at the dining table! He replied, "I don't know. There might be some discontent over the falling share prices and the latest quarterly results, but I would not worry about it."

"What about the board? Did anyone from the board speak to you?"

"Ah, yes! Charan Gupta met me some days back. He mentioned that shareholders were not happy with the performance this year."

"What did he say they were not happy about? The Company's performance or Charvak's performance?"

"I guess both!" Manoj replied cautiously.

"I see! So what is Charan going to do about it?"

"Well, how will I know what he will do?"

"You don't? All right! I will tell you what he is going to do. At the next board meeting, he is going to move a motion for removing Charvak as the Chairman. We have to defeat it!"

"Yes, of course!"

Sumitra kept staring at Manoj. The food on her plate was untouched. She said in a clear, deliberate voice, "Manoj, will you support us and help us defeat that motion?"

"I don't actually know what you are talking about. I have not heard of any such motion!"

Looking directly into his face, she said, "Manoj, I asked you a simple question. If a motion to remove Charvak comes up for discussion at the meeting, will you support us? Can we count on you as family?"

Manoj moved uneasily in his chair. "Sumitra, yes, we are family! Charvak is like my own son! But... but the position of the Chairman is a lot of responsibility. I feel Charvak is not interested in running the business anymore. I mean... see for yourself... he..."

Sumitra banged her fist on the table. Glaring at Manoj, she said, "Do not dare to tell me what my son is interested or not interested in! I did not ask you questions about your son when he was getting skinned. We supported you unconditionally! I am now asking you to do the same for us! Don't beat around the bush. Tell me! Will you or will you not support us at the meeting?"

Manoj straightened up in his chair. "Do not intimidate me! Shall we talk about this like mature adults?"

Sumitra shook her head. "No! Give me my answer! Yes or No?"

Manoj did not reply.

"Manoj, either give me an answer, or get out of here and never come back!"

Manoj slowly got up from his chair and walked through the door. His family followed him.

Sumitra turned towards Charvak who had been sitting silently toying with the food in his plate and said, "Don't worry, my son! We will fight, and we will win! Let the wolves howl! Let the vultures gather! I will show them what we are made of! All I ask of you is one thing: promise me that you will wake up from your slumber! Do you promise?"

"Yes," he replied weakly without looking up.

Sumitra summoned Ramesh Kadam later that day and said, "Ramu, I have some very important work for you. Do you remember the files we had kept away after the labour strike? I want those files immediately!"

"Yes, madam!" he said but lingered on.

"Is something wrong?"

"Madam, are you sure you want them?"

Sumitra smiled at him and said affectionately, "Ramu, you have been with our family ever since you were born! The work I am giving you is extremely important for all of us. Please do it for me!"

It was early morning on a Sunday. There was no one in the office building except for the security staff. Charvak walked through the empty building, through its empty workspaces and corridors, looking at the empty desks. On working days, the building pulsated with energy and activity; today, it looked lifeless. He reached the top floor, entered his office, opened the blinds to let in the light, and looked at the city that lay sprawled beneath him.

He asked himself, "What do you want, Charvak? You are one of the richest people in the world. You are famous. You are powerful. You run a business empire that touches the lives of millions of people. Is that not enough for you to find happiness in? What else can anyone want?"

His musings were interrupted by a knock on the door. He opened it to see Ramu *kaka* standing outside. He came in and said, "*Chote saheb,* I wanted to speak to you. I heard what happened yesterday with Manoj *saheb* at lunch. What is happening is not right! A fight within the family will destroy everything! Please can't you do something about it?"

"Ramu *kaka*, please sit down. You know the situation. They have brought the battle to our doorstep. We must fight!"

"I apologise for taking liberty in saying this: if I may ask, what are you fighting for?"

248

Charvak raised his eyebrows at the question but, letting it pass, he said, "My grandfather and my father have put in their lives for this company. They have built it with their sweat and blood. I must fight for the wellbeing of the Satyashah Group. I will not forgive myself if I give in to my weakness and let them down!"

Ramu *kaka* shook his head. There were tears in his eyes.

Charvak got up and put his hand on his shoulder. "What's wrong?" he asked.

"Your father was a great man! He would not have wanted you to do this to yourself!"

Charvak withdrew his hand. "Enough! You are overstepping your boundaries! You do not know what my father would have wanted me to do!"

Ramu *kaka* spoke with difficulty. Gasping for breath, he said, "*Chote saheb*, I am so sorry… for not telling you before but… Ravindra *saheb* did not die of a heart attack! He committed suicide!"

When Asmi told Swamiji of her experience, he closed his eyes and smiled; and that smile became a permanent feature of his face. From that day, Swamiji withdrew into himself. He became frugal with his speech and started avoiding people.

He told her, "You have attained *Nirvikalpa Samadhi* and seen truth yourself. The road ahead to *Moksha* is long and difficult, but you have already overcome the biggest hurdle on the path – your own scepticism!"

They were sitting under the giant banyan. She told him about her plans for the upcoming days. "The construction of the college building has begun. Agastya's flight will arrive tomorrow; he will be here for the whole semester. Oh, and Principal Naik called yesterday. He has invited me to be the Chief Guest for the Independence Day ceremony next Wednesday in the Wadi. Will you please join me for the ceremony?"

He did not answer; he was looking at the ground in front of him lost in his thoughts.

"Swamiji? Are you all right?"

Taking his time, he replied, "I was thinking about a monastery in Kashmir where I once stayed for a few months. It is located in an extremely remote area. The nearest human inhabitation is a small village a three-day trek away. The monastery is perched on the top of a tall, flat mountain. On one side of the mountain is a narrow pathway that leads to its entrance. The other sides are right-angled cliffs; they look like someone took a knife and cleanly cut the mountain as if it were a piece of cake. The region is surrounded by tall, majestic, snowcapped peaks. There is a stream of pristine water that flows at the base of the monastery. It is the most beautiful place I have ever seen!"

"The way you describe it, I am sure it is!"

"That monastery was my last base before I set out to look for the *Saptarishis*. When I left the monastery, I decided to return to it when I took *Sannyasa*!"

Asmi's heart skipped a beat. She knew what *Sannyasa* meant: it was the final stage of a person's spiritual life where he renounced the last vestiges of *Samsara* and retired from society to seek liberation in solitude and renunciation.

There was a peaceful glow radiating from his face. "Asmi, my time has come. You attaining *Samadhi* was the only thing I was waiting for. I have lived my life as fully as I hoped to. I have played my role as a part of the society for all these years. I am content and at peace. I want nothing more from life, and I owe nothing more to life. I must go. I will take *Sannyasa* and live my remaining days at that monastery!"

"Does this mean I will never see you again?"

"Yes, I am afraid so! I was waiting for you to stand on your own two feet on the path of Vedanta; you have now done that.

You don't need me anymore. You don't need anyone anymore. I have given you everything I had, taught you everything I know, and guided you as far as I could. Now, it is time to say goodbye!"

She nodded her head in understanding. "When will you leave, Swamiji?"

"In a few days, at dawn on Sunday!"

Charan Gupta idly finished his breakfast. He had woken up early and performed his Saturday ritual of visiting the temple. He was in a good mood and felt accomplished for successfully weaving the web around Charvak. Vallabh had been a dear friend to him, but even in those days, he had resented the fact that although both of them worked equally hard, Vallabh got most of the credit while he remained in the background. After three generations, the time had come to end the hegemony of the Satyashah family once and for all. He had no interest in becoming the Chairman; he was far too old for that. He didn't really care who became the Chairman as long as it was not a Satyashah. His previous attempts to divide the Satyashahs had failed, but he had now finally succeeded in driving a wedge between the two families. Manoj had taken the bait and agreed to support the motion to oust Charvak. Once Charvak and Sumitra were out of the picture, he could easily dispose off Manoj. The doorbell rang, and the maid opened the door.

Charan was surprised, but he hid it well and said heartily, "Ah, Sumitra! What a pleasure! Please come in. Ramesh? Is that you? I am getting old and my eyesight sometimes deceives me. Ramesh, would you like to wait in the drivers' room downstairs?"

"Ramesh is family. He will stay here!" Sumitra replied curtly.

Charan beckoned them to the sofa in the living room. Moving laboriously as if to emphasise his old age, he pulled out a large chest of old articles and said, "Vallabh was like an elder brother to me! He was..."

"I am very well aware of the story of how Vallabh and you started the company. I am not here to talk about the past; shall we speak about the present?" Sumitra rudely interrupted him.

Charan shook his head. "You young people are all about business. You don't value relationships. Sumitra, my dear, I have been associated with three generations of the Satyashah family. Vallabh and I have washed the floor of the mill with our own hands. Look at these pictures…"

He bent forward to pick up an old photo album from the chest. Before he could reach it, however, Sumitra got up and forcefully slammed the chest shut. It closed with a loud metallic clang.

"I am sorry, but I am not here to indulge your reveries!" she remarked.

Charan Gupta was shocked and stared at Sumitra with an open mouth. No one had ever behaved with him with such arrogance!

He said briskly, "What do you want?"

"Do you remember the labour strike that Manoj organised just after Charvak became the Chairman?"

"Of course! I am not that old to forget such things! What about it?"

"Are you sure it was the one Manoj organised? Or was it the one you organised?"

Charan's eyes widened. He shifted back in his chair. After a brief pause, he replied, "I don't know what you are talking about!"

Sumitra's lips curved into a smile. Speaking with contempt and enunciating every word clearly, she said, "You are such a rotten bastard! We have met every single union leader still alive who was involved in that strike. We have details of how the money was transferred, handwritten notes, and even voice recordings that your over-smart union workers happily gave us. You were not thorough in covering your tracks, were you? Is that

252

why you so strongly dissuaded us at that time from investigating the strike further? Charan Gupta, you are finished! Our lawyers have a criminal case ready against you. Frankly, I don't expect you to live long enough to see the trial. Nevertheless, the media will take care of shredding whatever reputation you have to pieces!"

Charan's mouth went dry, and his limbs started shivering. In a shaky voice, he said, "Sumitra, what do you want me to do?"

"Weren't you planning to move a motion at the next meeting to remove Charvak from his position?"

"Yes. I am sorry, but I genuinely think that…"

"Do I look as if I give a damn about what you think? There will be no motion of that kind. If anyone, you or otherwise, moves a motion that has anything to do with Charvak or the position of the chairman, you will face trial in court for criminal offences!"

"But Sumitra, please try to understand! The wheels have already been set in motion and cannot be stopped. I am not alone in this. Even if I don't, someone else will move that motion. I cannot stop them!"

"Oh yes, you can! You better stop them!"

"Sumitra! Manoj will not stop. He has made up his mind!"

"Don't worry about Manoj! He is a puppy on my leash. I will handle him. You get to work. On Monday morning, a press conference has been arranged for you, here, at your residence. Make a strong, unambiguous statement of support for Charvak. Will you do that?"

"Yes."

"I didn't think you could write the statement yourself, so I wrote one for you. Here it is. Memorise this and parrot it out on Monday, word for word! Do we understand each other clearly or is there something you have not understood? Should I repeat myself?"

Charan said meekly, "I understand. I will give this statement to the press on Monday, word for word."

Charvak sat brooding in the living room. His mother would be back anytime bearing news of how Charan Gupta reacted. There was a lot of work to be done. Once Charan was handled, they would have to meet and convince each board member individually. They would need to boost Charvak's image in the media. He would have to sort out the mess of acquisitions he had made in the last few months. But Charvak was not thinking of these things; he was thinking only of the yellow sheet of paper lying in front of him.

In his office last Sunday, a weeping Ramu *kaka* had told him what happened on the night his father died. "*Chote saheb,* I dropped Ravindra *saheb* home in the evening. He looked perfectly normal. He had dinner with Sumitra madam and you. Then, he drove himself to office. Around 11 pm, he called Sumitra madam and told her to get me and come to office immediately. When we entered his office, we saw him slumped in his chair. I thought he was asleep. *Chote saheb,* I swear to you, I have never seen him so happy; the expression on his face was that of pure bliss. Sumitra madam tried to wake him up, and she screamed!"

"How do you know it was a suicide?" Charvak asked.

"There was a note on the table. I do not know what was written on it. Sumitra madam read it and tore it to pieces. She said to me, 'Ramu, no one should ever know that my husband killed himself! No one! Ever! If anyone finds out, including my son, it will destroy the Satyashah family. Promise me that you won't breathe a word to anyone! Do you promise?' I promised her and gave her my word. She arranged for the whole incident to be passed off as a heart attack."

Ramu *kaka* continued, "There is another thing. Previously in the evening, when I dropped Ravindra *saheb* home, he gave me an envelope with your name on it and told me to give it to you the next day. I had no idea what was to happen so I kept it in my bag.

I would have given it to you had it not been for the promise Sumitra madam forced out of me. From the day I was born, I have been nothing but a loyal and faithful servant to the Satyashah family. *Chote saheb,* I was faced with a difficult decision whether to disobey an instruction of Ravindra *saheb,* a dead man, or break my promise to Sumitra madam, who was now the person I owed my loyalty to. I decided I could not break my promise. I never said a word to you. I have kept that envelope hidden under the cushion of my bed for all these years. I cannot do that anymore!"

Saying so, Ramu *kaka* put a sealed envelope on the table and walked out of the office. Charvak picked it up and held it in his hands for a long time. He slowly opened it and took out a yellow sheet of paper. Written in a handwriting he recognised, the letter read:

My dear son,

I beg your forgiveness in the thing I am about to do. I write this note to let you know my reasons behind it, give you a final piece of advice, and say goodbye!

Throughout my adult life, I have thought only of the Company. I spent every waking moment working for the Company and made it the purpose of my life. When I realised that I was not happy, I worked still harder and set my goals still further thinking that achieving them will make me happy. I achieved the goals but happiness still eluded me. I am exhausted doing this, and I don't know what else to do. I am unhappy, and I no longer want to live the life I have, but I am unable to change. My identity has become larger than myself, and I cannot let it go. I cannot give up being Ravindra Satyashah simply because I have no alternative. The only alternative I have to not being myself is to not be at all!

Sometimes, I wish I were not the Chairman of the Satyashah Group. Maybe, if the stakes were smaller, I might have attempted to give it all up and move on to another life. I realise that I am caught in a vicious trap that life sets for all of us: the higher the stakes, the more attached we are to them, the more invested we are in them, the more they demand from us, the more they suck out our life from us, and the more unhappy we become; but yet, because the stakes are so high, we cannot walk away!

But it is not impossible to walk away! Over two thousand five hundred years ago, there lived a king and a queen who had a boy named Siddhartha. They raised the prince amidst all comforts and luxuries and shielded him from all human suffering. Siddhartha got married and had children. He had everything he wanted, but he was still not happy. So what did the young prince do? He renounced his unhappy life and the kingdom along with all its riches and comforts. Siddhartha set out to find answers and became Gautam Buddha! When you were born, I wanted to name you Siddhartha, which means one who has attained the ultimate knowledge. But your mother refused and named you Charvak, which means one who enjoys the fruits of riches and luxuries!

Siddhartha – I wish to call you that now – the final cause of human life is happiness. I love you, my son, more than anything else in the world, and my ultimate wish for you is that you find happiness in life. I had no guide, but you have one! Swami Narayanananda Saraswati is a wise man. Stay by his side and seek his counsel; he will show you the right way. Be a responsible man and fulfil your duties, but always remember that everything is secondary to your happiness! I hope for you the strength to carry the burden of the Satyashah Group on your shoulders and also the courage to put it down and walk away if it becomes too much. I hope for you the courage that I never had: the courage to say no, embrace change, and start a new life!

Do not worry about me! I have made a conscious decision to do what I am about to do. It is a far far better thing that I do than I have ever done before; it is a far far better rest I go to than I have ever known before! Goodbye, my son!

Two days after reading the letter, Charvak confronted Sumitra.

"Mother, why did you not name me Siddhartha?" he said.

"Your father and I considered that name for you, but we decided to name you Charvak instead! Do you not like your name?"

"Why did you not tell me that Papa committed suicide?"

Sumitra looked up startled at the question. "Charvak, your father was a great man, but he had his weaknesses. He could not deal with the pressures of running a business empire. You have always looked up to him. I wanted to protect you from the knowledge that he was not as strong as you thought. Nevertheless, the fact that he gave up does not take anything away from what he achieved!"

"Why did you lie to me for all these years?"

Sumitra's iron countenance cracked and tears welled up in her eyes. "I did not want you to inherit his weakness. I thought I could protect you from acquiring it if I shielded you from its knowledge. Look at me and tell me if we would have fought the world and won if you knew about your father's suicide? I love you, my son! I might have made mistakes, but whatever I did, I did it for your best!"

Sumitra apologised profusely for keeping him in the dark; after that, she told him point blank that what is done is done, they cannot change it, and they must look forward!

Charvak heard the door open. Sumitra came in and sat down in front of him.

With a triumphant smile, she said, "I had a nice chat with Charan. He will speak at the press conference on Monday. With their leader having defected, the rest of the pack will scatter!"

Charvak looked at Sumitra but said nothing. He had barely spoken to her since he found out about the suicide.

Annoyed at his lifelessness and apathy, Sumitra said angrily, "You have been sulking for months. Enough of it! This is your last chance. If you do not want to end up as a miserable failure, you must snap out of your sickness and torpidity. I don't want to see any more of it. I want to see you in action. Do you understand? And there's another thing. I have invited Rinku and Saloni to our house tomorrow for lunch. Be on your best behaviour! I don't want to hear a no from you!"

Saying so, she got up and left. Looking at her figure disappear up the stairs, for the first time in months, he smiled!

Next morning, when Charvak did not turn up for breakfast, Sumitra went to his room. She did not find him there; instead, she found a handwritten note propped up against the pillow!

Chapter 20: No Longer

SWAMIJI HAD INSISTED THERE BE no fanfare or social gathering to mark his taking *Sannyasa*. Only the people closest to him had been informed; they visited Swamiji during his last week of stay in the city. He greeted them joyfully and gave his blessings. There weren't many arrangements to be made. The library was in good order and would continue to run smoothly till a new librarian was appointed. Swamiji had few belongings. He had no property or assets. He had a single bank account. On Saturday evening, Swamiji called Asmi to his office and gave her a cheque transferring whatever money he had to her. She tried to refuse, but he insisted. It was a substantial figure amounting to seventeen years of his salary as the librarian. The memory of how Abba had given her all his money when she left the Wadi surfaced to her mind.

Asmi and Agastya stayed over at the library on Saturday. On Sunday morning, Asmi woke up early and made three cups of tea. Swamiji's little bag consisting of a bottle of water and a spare pair of loose, white garments was ready. He needed nothing else. He would walk barefoot to the Elysian monastery in the Himalayas and spend the rest of his days there. He picked up his bag and told them to accompany him to the garden. He sat down on the bench below the patriarchal banyan while Asmi and Agastya stood by. The sun was still below the horizon, but the sky had turned red awaiting its impending arrival.

Asmi sensed a movement at a distance and turned to see the figure of a man dressed in a plain white *kurta* walking towards

259

them. When he reached them, she recognised him and smiled. He sat down next to Swamiji and took out an old, golden-coloured wristwatch from his pocket.

Handing it over, he said, "I am sorry it took so long!"

Swamiji smilingly took the watch and strapped it to his wrist. Both of them stood up. Asmi and Agastya did a *namaskar* to Swamiji, and he wished them a happy life ahead. A small, fiery sliver of the sun could be seen peeping from beyond the horizon. The *guru* and the *shishya* started walking.

Sumitra picked up the note with trembling hands. It read:

Mother, you made me promise you years ago that I will live up to my father's wishes. You made me promise you some days back that I will wake up from my deep slumber. I am now wide awake. The clouds of confusion have drifted away, and I can see clearly that I no longer wish to continue living the way I have lived till now. I no longer wish to be a part of the circus. I am sorry that I have disappointed you. I love you and thank you for everything you have done for me. I must leave now. I must go and fulfil my first promise to live up to my father's ultimate wish that I find happiness in life! I may never see you again. Farewell, mother!

Charvak Satyashah had vanished. He had left notes and sent emails to people that mattered. He had conducted detailed discussions with his lawyers and drafted papers to transfer his stake in the Satyashah companies to his mother. All his remaining wealth was bequeathed to a newly founded Ravindra Satyashah Foundation. Ramu *kaka* had been appointed to oversee these transfers.

The Independence Day ceremony was held early in the morning. Asmi, Agastya, and the Joshis drove to the Wadi in Mr Joshi's car. By the time they arrived, the students had assembled on the school ground in neatly filed rows. The school staff stood alongside the students. Some parents and enthusiastic bystanders had gathered on one side. Asmi hoisted the Indian Tricolour Flag. Everyone sang the National Anthem while saluting the flag. The students performed a small drama that included songs and dance. At the end of the ceremony, Principal Naik invited Asmi to address the students.

As she took the microphone in her hands, her eyes welled up with tears. Looking at the children standing at attention in their clean, ironed uniforms reminded her of the days when she had stood in their place. Not much had changed since then: the school building, the ground, and even the principal were the same; and so was the hope and determination that gleamed in the eyes of the students.

She took a deep breath and unfolded the paper on which she had written a short speech. She had planned to speak about the importance of education, but looking at them, she folded the paper and kept it back. She spoke to them, instead, of life and happiness. She told them to never stop playing, to never stop dreaming, to never let go of the child within them. She spoke to them of curiosity. She told them to never stop wondering about the world, to never stop asking questions and seeking answers. She spoke to them of courage and determination. She told them to never stop fighting for what they believed in, to never give up, to never fear. She spoke to them of faith. She told them to believe in themselves and their capabilities. She spoke to them of love and joy. She spoke to them, finally, of the lightness of life. She told them not to take life too seriously. She told them to never worry too much, to never stop having fun, to never stop loving, to never stop living!

261

After the ceremony, their team convened in Principal Naik's office along with volunteers, sympathisers, and some local officials. Asmi presented a plan on how they would proceed with the work for the college. Everyone unanimously voiced their support. The construction activities had begun, and the work for the foundation of the main building was almost complete. A small site office had been built. Staff recruitments were to begin soon. The college was scheduled to start accepting admissions from the following academic year.

Asmi felt nostalgic as she walked with Agastya from the school to the house her great-grandfather had built more than eighty years ago. Aai was sitting on the steps waiting for them. As soon as she saw them, she rushed forward and hugged Asmi tightly. They entered the house, and Neha flitted across the large living room and pounced on Asmi. As they exchanged hugs and kisses, Asmi saw Baba climb down the stairs. He looked at her unsure of what to do. Without waiting for an invitation, she walked to him and embraced him. He closed his eyes and lovingly patted her head. They had a delicious meal. Aai had prepared her favourite *bharli bhendi* along with the sweet *shrikhand*. Asmi told them about the events in her life. Aai smilingly nodded at everything she said. Neha enthusiastically asked questions. Baba remained silent through the whole time and said nothing. Aai coaxed Agastya to take more *shrikhand* and asked him about his life and work. Their conversation continued into the afternoon. When it was teatime, Aai made tea for everyone.

The first person to come was Kamble, who brought along his entire family. Immediately after, Neha's husband arrived with his parents and little Saurabh. Asmi hugged her nephew, but he did not recognise her. Soon, people started pouring in: Asmi's school friends, Shweta and her mother, Baba's bank colleagues, Aai's circle of friends, parents of students that Asmi had helped.

Hundreds of people thronged their house that evening. When the living room could no longer hold them, they spilled over into the courtyard, and then onto the street outside. Some came to say hello and meet her; some came to express their support and gratitude. There were parents who brought along their children to seek her blessings. All these people came bearing admiration in their eyes and warmth in their hearts; they came to welcome their estranged daughter back to the Wadi!

When the crowd finally dispersed, they had a quiet dinner. Aai convinced them to stay over for the night. After dinner, when they got up from the table, Baba walked over to her.

"*Beta*, I am glad you came today!" he said.

"Yes, Baba! I am happy to see all of you!"

He did not reply and kept looking at her with a strange expression on his face. He struggled to say something, but words deserted him. "Asmi... I..." he choked and broke down into tears. Through a bout of sobbing, he reached into his pocket and pulled out a cheque.

He thrust it into her hands and said, "Asmi, I am truly sorry I did not encourage your education. I regret it every single day. I wrongly believed that spending money on educating a daughter was wasting it. This cheque is my small contribution towards your cause."

Asmi looked at the cheque. It was a substantial amount; she wondered if he could afford it. "Baba, there's no need for this!" she said.

"Please take it for my sake! Asmi, when you were born, I was disappointed, because I wanted a son. I thought only a son would bring honour to our family. I could not have been farther from the truth! By establishing a college named after Abba, you have made our family's name immortal! You have made the entire Wadi proud, and I am confident that, one day, you will make the whole country proud! Asmi, today you have made your aging

263

parents proud; I told everyone who had gathered with pride that I am Asmi's father! I am sorry for being unfair to you. I am sorry for everything. Please forgive me!"

That night, Asmi and Agastya walked through the lanes of the Wadi to the construction site of the college, which lay at the base of the winding path going up the hill. There was no one at the site. They went inside the small one-room office and sat down on a dusty bench. Two yellow lamps hung from the ceiling. Architectural design plans and record books were scattered across the place. In one corner was a makeshift storage area where equipment lay piled on top of one another. In the other corner stood an old steel cupboard. The wall next to the cupboard had a large full-sized portrait of Abba. Standing upright, dressed in a black sleeveless jacket on a white *dhoti* and *kurta* with a black traditional cap on his head, he looked handsome and elegant in the picture. In his right hand was a walking stick he carried with him everywhere. In his left hand, close to his chest, he held a book. On the cover of the book was an illustration that showed a muscular man carrying a globe on his shoulders, his knees buckling and arms trembling under the heavy weight.

Pointing towards the man in the illustration, Asmi said, "That man who is carrying the weight of the world on his shoulders, he doesn't hate the world, does he?"

"No, he does not hate the world!" Agastya replied putting his arms around her shoulders.

"Even if the world bears down on him and calls him heartless and selfish? Even if it blackmails him into guilt when he does not follow their protocols? Even if it mercilessly tries to break him down?"

"Even then he does not hate the world!"

"Why?"

"You tell me why!"

264

Asmi leaned in closer to him and put her head on his chest. She could hear his heart beating. She said softly, "After that night in the quaint village, I began seeing myself in the people around me. The boundaries of my ego started dissolving. I realised how negative emotions like anger and jealousy have their roots in the illusion of the ego. When there is no ego, there is no 'I' and 'them', there is no anger, and there is no hatred!"

He smiled.

She continued, "Agastya, I no longer hate them or avoid them. No longer do I think of them with contempt. I realised that compassion is far more than just being nice to people; it is about loving them as you love yourself, and treating them as you treat yourself. More than anything else, it is about identifying with them as you identify with yourself! When I started doing that, so many things happened on their own. I stopped judging people. I stopped getting angry at them. I realised that they were not in control of their actions but were mere slaves of causality. They were not evil or vindictive but were only ignorant. The moment I removed the thorny barriers of anger and judgment from my heart, the warm and joyful emotions of love and compassion surged forth!

"Agastya, Swamiji and you were right when you said that I should forgive them, not for their sake, but for my own! I now realise the selfish virtue of compassion and forgiveness. Compassion has made me stronger! When I stood in front of powerful politicians and ministry officials for getting licenses and permissions, I felt no nervousness. I did not feel even a shred of anxiety. I spoke to them calmly and confidently. They sensed in me the compassion and solidarity I felt for them, and they reciprocated. I formed instant connections and bonds with them like Swamiji did with people who came to meet him. I was always socially awkward when dealing with people before. Somewhere in my mind, I used to be afraid of them. The ease and confidence with which I now deal with people astounds me. I no longer hate them and make feeble attempts to protect myself from them. I no longer inherently distrust them. I embrace them and become them! Their misguided actions borne out of ignorance no longer hurt me!

"I know the man in that book who carries the world on his shoulders does not hate the world. He does not hate the society, because he loves himself! His dream is to realise the infinite potential latent inside of him. The society, with the help of the golden-scaled dragon, creates obstacles in his path. People ridicule him, because he does not follow their conventions. They fear him, because he is different from them. But he does not fight them! He forgives them and forges ahead on his own path towards his own happiness. He does not hate them, because he knows that they know not!"

Asmi looked up at Agastya. His face wore a light smile as he looked affectionately into her eyes. He pulled her closer and kissed her forehead. Asmi closed her eyes and gently drifted into sleep to the rhythm of his beating heart.

THE END

About the Author

Viraj Kulkarni is an entrepreneur involved in various businesses in technology consulting, real estate, and hospitality. He has a master's degree in Computer Science from the University of California, Berkeley. He lives in Pune, India and has been actively studying Vedanta and practising meditation for the past 5 years.

You can contact him at kulkarni.viraj@gmail.com or follow him at his website www.virajkulkarni.org.

Made in the USA
Coppell, TX
28 November 2020

42294090R10163